The HIGH LIFE

Anise Starre

SIMON &
SCHUSTER

London · New York · Amsterdam/Antwerp · Sydney/Melbourne · Toronto · New Delhi

First published in Great Britain by Simon & Schuster UK Ltd, 2026

1 3 5 7 9 10 8 6 4 2

Simon & Schuster UK Ltd, 7th Floor,
199 Bishopsgate, London, EC2M 3TY

Simon & Schuster Australia, Sydney
Simon & Schuster India, New Delhi

www.simonandschuster.co.uk
www.simonandschuster.com.au
www.simonandschuster.co.in

The authorised representative in the EEA is Simon & Schuster Netherlands BV, Herculesplein 96, 3584 AA Utrecht, Netherlands. info@simonandschuster.nl

A CIP catalogue record for this book is available from the British Library

Paperback ISBN: 978-1-3985-4420-8
eBook ISBN: 978-1-3985-4421-5
Audio ISBN: 978-1-3985-4440-6

Typeset in Bembo by M Rules
Printed and Bound in the UK using 100% Renewable Electricity at CPI Group (UK) Ltd

Praise for Anise Starre

'Fun, fresh and always sexy – Anise Starre knows romance'
Hannah Grace

'Anise has a magnetic, tender and butterfly-inducing way of writing'
Soraya Bouazzaoui

'I adore getting swept up in Anise Starre's swoony stories'
Lizzie Huxley-Jones

'I loved this witty, captivating story of two hearts finding each other and two people finding themselves'
Frances Mensah Williams

'A fresh take on the fake dating trope, this sexy novel had me hooked from page one'
Camilla Isley

'*The High Life* is a delightful spin on arranged marriage . . . sweet, sexy, and filled to the brim with delicious tension'
Etta Easton

'A gratifying combination of steamy and swoony . . . This romance is the escape we've all been looking for'
Allie Samberts

'*The High Life* has it all! Laugh-out-loud shenanigans. Swoonworthy declarations. Moments so hot you'll have to fan yourself'
Jamie Wesley

Anise Starre is a born and bred Londoner who now travels the world with her husband. She loves writing sweet, fluffy romances featuring Black women being loved on and adored, with a hint of steam and spice to get the heart going. Anise is the author of *One Week in Paradise*, *One Last Job*, *One More Shot* and *Just a Taste*. Her fifth novel is *The High Life*.

You can follow Anise on Instagram @authoranisestarre and TikTok @anisestarre. Her website is anisestarre.com.

Also by Anise Starre

One Week in Paradise

One Last Job

One More Shot

Just a Taste

For Tyra,

You can read this one xoxo

CHAPTER ONE

Imani

Something is wrong.

I should be working on re-upping my tan and swimming with the turtles and dolphins off the coast of Curieuse Island in the Seychelles right now. Instead I'm sitting in a charged silence, listening to the rain pelt my father's car as we hurtle down the motorway. Even Nathan, my father's driver, hasn't dared to play any music.

I risk a sideways glance at my father. His fingers are tapping incessantly against his thigh and I can only describe the expression on his face as one of pure unease.

Yes. Something is definitely wrong. Because Malcolm Davies, business tycoon and owner of Peregrine Airways, doesn't do unease. He doesn't do anxiety, or vulnerability, or fear. There's a reason he's unrivalled in the aviation industry, conducting deals, acquisitions and strategic manoeuvres with all the finesse of a grandmaster playing chess. I've sat in boardrooms and watched him negotiate multimillion-pound contracts without so much as breaking a sweat. But right now? Right now, my father looks like he'd rather be anywhere but here. This doesn't bode well for me.

'Dad?' My voice is swallowed by the sound of the rain on the roof, but he hears me all the same. His gaze flickers towards me and, for a moment, his expression softens slightly. But then I blink and his deep brown eyes are cool and guarded once more. He leans forward and presses the button to activate the divider between Nathan and us.

I sit up a little straighter.

Nathan has been in my father's employ since I was a teen and has proved his loyalty and discretion a thousand times over. If there's something my father doesn't want Nathan to hear, it must be big.

'Sorry to cut your trip to Bali short,' he starts, once it's just the two of us.

'It was the Seychelles,' I say with a wry grin. 'Bali was last month.' I can't blame him for not being able to keep track of my comings and goings – I can barely keep track myself. I have a permanently packed suitcase on standby and I'm on my third passport in as many years. Being the only daughter of Malcolm Davies has many, many perks, but the ability to fly to any country on a whim is definitely my favourite. 'And it's fine. I've rebooked onto a flight later this evening.'

My father clears his throat, and there is it again. That unfamiliar look of unease flashing across his face. It doesn't suit him at all. 'I'm going to need you to put a pin in the Seychelles for now.'

A squawk of surprise gets stuck in my throat and he shoots me a surprisingly sympathetic look.

'It's just for now. Just until we've . . .' He trails off and resumes tapping his fingers against his thigh. 'Just until we've ironed out a few kinks.'

'Ironed out a few kinks in *what*?' A knot starts to form in my stomach. My father and I have an unspoken agreement, one that's been in place since I was old enough to talk. I play the role of dutiful heiress to the Peregrine Airways fortune and the Davies legacy, and I don't do anything to put that in jeopardy.

Unlike others my age in the social circles we orbit, I've never been involved in a scandal. Never been plastered across Instagram socialite gossip pages with nasty rumours attached to my name. Never done *anything* that could be used to lower the value of our stock. And, in return, my bank account remains limitless and I have free rein to do whatever I like to do. Namely, travelling to countries with sprawling golden beaches and delicious fruity cocktails on tap. So why does it sound like my father is planning on reneging on that agreement?

He sighs and runs a tired hand over his face. 'You've heard of Vouvalis Resorts?'

The name rings a bell in more ways than one, but I know what my father is asking. You'd be hard pressed to find someone who hasn't heard of Vouvalis Resorts – a luxury hotel and resort brand founded by Georgios Vouvalis ten years ago, which has rapidly flown up the ranks and become a fast favourite among the upper echelon of society – me included. If there's a Vouvalis hotel or resort in a country I'm visiting, I don't think twice about booking a room.

'Georgios and I connected at an event a few months back,' my father continues. 'I won't bore you with the specifics, but it seems we have a lot in common when it comes to the future of our respective companies.'

I nod. To call Georgios' rapid expansion of Vouvalis Resorts impressive would be an understatement. He's the current darling of the hospitality industry and barely a week seems to go by without him securing another high-profile interview or feature with *Forbes*, *Fortune* or *Bloomberg*. Everyone wants a piece of him, and apparently my father is no exception.

'Peregrine Airways has dominated the skies for the last thirty years but the sky doesn't have to be the limit.' He shifts in his seat and fixes me with a slightly desperate look. 'Georgios and I have been discussing the benefits of a merger.'

'You're joking.' I may be his only daughter, but I've always known that Peregrine Airways is my father's first child. He built this company from the ground up and transformed it into the titan of aviation it is today. The idea of him doing anything that would relinquish any of his control or jeopardise the success of the company is laughable. Pure insanity. 'You've *got* to be joking.'

He ignores my splutter of disbelief and continues. 'This

is what I meant by needing to iron out the kinks. Georgios and I obviously have a vested interest in retaining ownership and control of our respective companies, but it's undeniable that we could help each other here. I've been toying with the idea of breaking into the hospitality industry for a while now and, it just so happens, Georgios has had similar thoughts about aviation.'

I'd be lying if I said I didn't understand the appeal. Georgios already has a stronghold on the luxury hospitality industry and combining forces with him would give my father a ten-year head start that his competitors could only dream of. I imagine the opposite is the same for Georgios: being able to claim a stake in the skies without having to do any of the hard work to get there.

'Why are you telling me this?' I ask with a frown. My father has never once brought me in on a business decision before he makes the final call. I may be his daughter, but I know better than anyone else that I have no sway with him. When it comes to money matters, Malcolm Davies does what Malcolm Davies wants, and usually it's the right decision. But this just doesn't feel right. There's something else. Something he's not telling me.

'It's been a difficult few years for both the aviation and hospitality industries,' he continues, as if I haven't asked him anything. 'The pandemic did a number across the board, and we're only just recovering.'

The car crawls to a slow halt and my father starts to look slightly panicked. 'And our shareholders and investors are still a little reluctant to make large decisions like this. They think a move like this is still too risky in the current climate. Georgios also has a bit of a . . .' He clicks his tongue. 'A *reputation*. He's ruthless in a way I've never been and some may say joining forces with him is too much of a risk.'

'So don't do it,' I say bluntly. I've read enough profiles of Georgios in *Forbes* and *Fortune* to know exactly what he means by *ruthless*. The man started out in the construction industry over twenty years ago, and rumours of sidelined partners and maliciously undercutting his competition have followed him his entire career. It doesn't surprise me at all that the shareholders don't think they can trust him.

'But we think we've found a way around that,' my father says, deftly ignoring my interruption. 'A way for everyone to trust that Georgios isn't going to run the company into the ground at the first opportunity.'

'The fact that that's even a possibility should be turning you off the whole idea,' I mutter.

Once again he ignores my interruption, but I'm pretty sure I see his lip twitch.

'Georgios has a son. Well, he has three, but this only concerns Asher.'

And there's that second bell.

Asher Vouvalis.

Everything I know about Asher Vouvalis could fit on a Post-it note – and there'd still be room left to write on it. I know that he's the third Vouvalis boy, that we attended the same university ten years ago, and – well, that's about it. Vouvalis Resorts was still in its infancy a decade ago and Asher and I didn't really exist in the same social circles at university. I can vaguely picture him in the periphery of my memories, but it's nothing concrete. The only thing I *do* remember is that he was a friend of a friend's friend, and I think I wordlessly passed a bottle of wine to him at a party years ago.

Maybe.

Aside from that one potential interaction, Asher and I have never said so much as one word to each other and, over the last ten years, he's faded into relative obscurity. Nothing like his brothers Andreas and Theodore, who have dominated business broadsheets and Instagram gossip pages with deal after deal, and scandal after scandal, for as long as I can remember.

'What about him?' I ask cautiously, the knot in my stomach growing tenfold.

My father meets my eye and holds my gaze for the first time since I stepped into his car. 'Georgios and I have been discussing a union of sorts.'

'A union?'

'A marriage,' my father clarifies, with only a hint of a wince. 'Between you and his son. Asher.'

'A marriage,' I repeat slowly, blinking in disbelief at my father. 'Between me and Asher Vouvalis?'

I think he interprets the stunned look on my face as something else entirely – something positive – because he relaxes ever so slightly into his seat. 'Yes, exactly. If the relationship between our two families goes beyond just business, the shareholders and investors will be more likely to jump aboard the idea.'

'You want to *marry* me off to Asher Vouvalis so you can get a deal over the line?' I can't tell whether it's rage or pain that's making my voice crack like this. 'This is . . . This is—'

'This is just *business*, Imani. And it won't be forever,' he says. 'A year or two. Three, tops. Just enough time for us to get the merger through and make sure everything is settled and sorted.'

'Oh, just a year?' I ask sarcastically. 'Well, that's fine then, isn't it? Force me to marry a complete stranger for a couple of years and then I can divorce him and get on with my life. A perfectly normal ask.'

'Imani,' my father says. 'Please be reasonable.' He reaches across the seat and tries to place a placating hand on my thigh.

'Reasonable? *Reasonable?*' I jerk away like his touch is acid. 'I'm your daughter. Not a business deal. Not an asset. Not a means to an end. Your *daughter. You* be reasonable.'

His expression shifts, a mix of regret and frustration clouding his features. 'I knew you would need some time to adjust to the idea—'

A hysterical laugh bubbles out of my throat and I shake my head. 'There's no adjusting, Dad. I can't believe you would even *suggest*—'

'It's not a suggestion, Imani.' His gaze hardens, the veneer of fatherly concern slipping away as quickly as it came. 'Things are different than they used to be. Air travel across the board is lower than it's ever been.' There's a touch of frantic desperation to his tone, and alarm bells start to ring in my mind. 'If we want to survive, we need to adapt. Make sacrifices.'

'And what's the sacrifice here supposed to be?' I scoff. 'Because all I see is you prioritising profits over your own daughter's happiness.'

'Enough, Imani. *Enough.*' His voice echoes around the car. 'Your happiness has been my one vice for as long as I can remember. I can't force you down that aisle, Imani—'

Damn right, he can't.

'But understand this. The life you know now? The trips, the clothes, the life of luxury *my* hard work has afforded you? That will all cease to exist if you refuse to cooperate.'

It feels like he's got a hold of my neck.

He's bluffing. Surely, he's got to be bluffing.

'Mum won't allow it. She won't let you—' I start, but my father shakes his head.

'Your mother is already in agreement. We've discussed this at length.'

Something splits inside me. I don't believe it. I *won't* believe it. I've grown up listening to Gwendoline Davies recount, always with a soft, shy smile, the story of how she and my father met at a mutual friend's wedding. How he couldn't take his eyes off her as she glided down the aisle ahead of the bride. How he spent the entire ceremony committing every inch of her to memory, barely even listening to the priest or the happy couple as they shared their vows. How he strongarmed one of the groomsmen into swapping seats with him so he could sit beside her at dinner. How, when she first turned to look at him, her brows furrowed in confusion when she realised he wasn't who she was expecting to be sitting beside, my father knew he was already in love. How they spent the night wrapped in each other's arms, dancing the night away under the moonlight.

Surely my parents want that for me? The kind of love that sweeps you off your feet, leaves you breathless and promises you the world?

'You know, not everyone has it as easy as you do, Imani,' my father continues, a pained expression flitting across his face. 'You don't know what I've had to sacrifice to get us here. I'm just asking that you do your part for once.'

Not everyone has it as easy as you do.

Easy.

What part of this is easy? I know from the outside looking in that the life I lead is an enviable one filled with privilege and luxury, but that doesn't mean it's been easy. That I haven't felt the crushing weight of it all from the moment I could walk.

I've been doing my part my whole life. Doesn't he realise that? For every action I take, there's a voice in the back of my mind reminding me of the expectations, the legacy, the burden of being Imani Davies. And now he's threatening to take it all away. He's acting like I'm a toddler throwing a tantrum over being told no more snacks before dinner and like he hasn't turned my life upside down in an instant.

'So,' my father leans back and laces his fingers together, 'what do you say?'

'I . . .' My voice comes out as a croak. 'Daddy, I *can't*.'

The look he gives me is beyond disappointment. 'I see.'

'No, I just . . .' I swallow and count back from five, giving myself some time to think. I can't do this. I *won't* do this. But the tiny slither of happiness I've managed to carve out from life is on the line and I'm not willing to give that up either.

A spark of hope alights in my chest. I can't say no, but *he* can. My father can still change his mind; I just need him to think that it's *his* idea.

'I'm willing to do my part,' I say slowly. The words feel like poison on my tongue, but I force them out all the same. 'And do what's best for us. For the business. But not like this. Not with Asher Vouvalis.'

He huffs out an impatient sigh. 'And what's so wrong with the Vouvalis boy?'

When it comes down to it, the lie comes easily – easier than anything else I've said today. 'We've already dated,' I blurt out. 'Back at university.'

My father's brows shoot into his slowly receding hairline. 'Excuse me?'

'We dated,' I grit out, pushing through the lie. 'And it didn't end well. It was a mess, Dad. And I can't go through that again.'

His expression shifts from confusion to contemplation. 'I had no idea.'

'I didn't see the need to burden you with it,' I lie smoothly.

'But now you're talking about marriage, and I . . .' I sniff delicately and force a tearful hiccup. 'I just can't do it. Not with him.'

Not with anyone. Not like this. Call me a hopeless romantic, but I don't think wanting to fall in love is too much to ask for.

I reach forward and squeeze my father's hands. 'Please, Daddy.'

For a moment, I think I've got him. The expression on his face is full of genuine fatherly concern and hope sparks in my chest.

But then he snatches his hands away from mine and places one on the door. 'It's been nearly ten years,' he says gruffly, refusing to make eye contact.

Any wisp of hope is snuffed out immediately.

'Whatever issues the two of you had, I'm sure you're both mature enough to put it past you.'

My mouth falls open, a retort already on the tip of my tongue, but then he pushes open the door and I get my first glimpse of where we've been heading today. We're parked outside a sleek and elegant-looking building and I immediately recognise the gold 'V' above the large double doors in front of us.

I grip the leather seats in my father's car and shake my head. 'No. Absolutely not.'

'Come on,' he sighs without even looking at me, before stepping out of the car and brushing the imaginary creases out of his suit. He waits a few seconds then, apparently realising I have no intention of moving, crouches down slightly and inclines his head towards me. 'I wasn't joking, Imani. You can have one last trip, as a courtesy, but that's it.' He snaps his fingers and stares at me expectantly. 'Are you coming or not?'

The urge to glue myself to this seat for the rest of eternity is overwhelming, but I need to play this right. One false move and everything could shatter around me. Right now there's still a chance, as slim as it may be, that I can get out of this with my life intact. So I grit my teeth and force a smile, the one I've perfected over the years, and step out of the car.

'Of course,' I say coolly. 'Lead the way.'

I watch the way his shoulders relax ever so slightly as he guides me up the stone steps into the towering Vouvalis building, and I realise something.

He thinks he's won.

That this is the end, and I'm going to go forward with this ridiculous proposal with a dutiful smile on my face.

I bite back a satisfied grin. He's in for a huge surprise.

CHAPTER TWO

Asher

My future wife steps into the room looking like she wants to set the whole building ablaze.

I can't say that I blame her. I watch as she pointedly leaves two seats between her and her father and rigidly angles her body away from him when they sit down. There's no doubt in my mind that she's just received exactly the same news I have.

You're going to marry the Davies girl. Get us into the aviation industry. Do something right for once.

I wonder if her father was as blunt as mine. If he gave her any room to argue back, or if he simply uttered his command and expected her to agree.

I shoot her what I hope is a sympathetic smile from across the table. I'm not used to having anyone to commiserate with when it comes to my father's schemes and, as ridiculous as this one is, I'm glad I'm not alone.

She doesn't return the smile. She doesn't even look at me. Her jaw is set, her chin lifted, and there's a steely determination flashing in her eyes. Imani Davies looks like she's preparing to go to war.

My father clears his throat suddenly and my attention snaps right back to him. Everyone's does.

'It's so good to see you again, Malcolm,' my father says with a wide grin. I think he's trying to seem friendly and approachable but, just like always, it feels off. Forced. 'And you, Ms Imani. I've heard so much about you.'

Imani offers my father a stiff . . . Well, I wouldn't call it a smile. More like a grimace. Her jaw is still tightly clenched as she bares her teeth at the two of us. 'I'm sure you have.'

My father blinks at the obvious hostility radiating off her.

Malcolm shifts beside her. 'Yes, it's a pleasure, Georgios.' He inclines his head in my direction. 'Asher.'

'It's a—' I start.

'Shall we get down to business?' My father cuts my greeting off without so much as a cursory glance in my direction. 'I've got a call in twenty with our publicist and I'd really like to go to her with some good news.'

If Malcolm is thrown off by my father's abruptness, he doesn't let it show. His face is a mask of neutrality as he leans back into his seat and steeples his fingers together. 'Then let's begin.'

'Yes,' Imani says icily, speaking up before my father can launch into whatever spiel he has planned. 'Let's begin. I'm sure you've noticed the tension in the room?'

I blink. The tension in the room is palpable, yes, but I'd assumed it was between Imani and her father. But she's currently staring daggers at me, like I'm her worst enemy and just being in the same room with me is enough to tip her over the edge.

I shift uncomfortably in my seat and quickly flit through my memories, trying to remember if I've ever had an interaction with Imani Davies to warrant this kind of ire. I know we studied at university at the same time, but we weren't even remotely close. Not for lack of trying on my behalf. The Vouvalis' have had money all our lives, but it's only in the last decade or so that we've been propelled into the upper echelon of society, and I was still definitely on the outer rim back at university. Still am, if I'm being honest.

It's been nearly a decade since I last thought of her, but suddenly a vague memory of Imani grinning at me over the rim of a wine glass slams into the forefront of my mind. It was during our first year at university and, up until that moment, I'd never interacted with her. I don't remember what brought me to that party that night – I have to assume Teddy had dragged me out with him, because I'd never been much for the social scene even back then – but I went. And she was there. Our first interaction of the night was entirely uneventful. She wordlessly passed me a bottle of wine not long after I arrived, probably not even registering who she was passing it to. But I can fully recollect our second interaction.

The party was winding down and there were just a

handful of us left. I was wondering if Teddy – who had disappeared into some dark corner with the host – would even notice if I left without him. Almost certainly not. Just as I'd made the decision to leave, a burst of laughter cut across the room. The kind of beautiful sound that makes you turn your head without thinking. Imani was perched on the kitchen island, surrounded by a small handful of friends, swinging her legs and idly twirling the stem of an empty wine glass. She reflexively glanced up as I slipped past her and I was treated to a soft smile.

'Heading out?' she asked and I had to fight the urge to point at my chest to check she was actually talking to me.

I cleared my throat. 'Yeah. Got an early start tomorrow.'

She nodded once, then reached for a bottle of water poking out of an already open twenty-four-pack beside her. 'Since our gracious host is currently AWOL . . .'

I felt my cheeks heat on Teddy's behalf.

'. . . I guess this is up to me. Here. Take this. You'll feel less awful tomorrow.'

Our fingers brushed as I reach for the bottle. It was only the briefest of touches, but it was enough to send a strange flutter shooting through my stomach.

'Thanks,' I murmured.

'Night. Get home safely,' she said with a small smile. It was absolutely the kind of smile a person might give to a stranger in the street, but somehow it felt like it was just for me. She turned back to her friends immediately and the moment – if you can even call it that – was over as quickly as it had begun.

I'm more than a little embarrassed to admit that I may have harboured a tiny crush on Imani after that. *Maybe.*

We never spoke again but on the odd occasion we passed each other on campus, we'd share a polite smile. I'd like to say that she remembered me from the party and there was a hint of recognition in her eyes, but that would be wishful thinking.

It's strange, remembering her like that – the soft, small smile whenever we accidentally crossed paths – when the version of her sitting in front of me right now might as well be a different person entirely. I haven't thought about or seen her since we graduated, so I have no idea why she's currently staring at me like she'd very much like to sink a knife into my chest right now.

Beside her, Malcolm grits his teeth and shoots his daughter a sideways glance. 'Imani—'

'If we're going to be talking about marriage,' Imani continues frostily, 'I think it's only right we get this all out in the open. Clear the air, so to speak.'

Now it's my father's turn to shoot me a sideways glance. His dark eyes narrow and I don't miss the way his fist clenches slightly under the table. The unspoken message is clear. *What the fuck have you messed up now?*

Funnily enough, this time I'm not even sure.

Imani shifts in her seat so she's facing me head on. 'Do you want to tell them, or should I?'

'I . . .' I glance over at my father. His eyes have narrowed into thin slits and a dangerous vein is bulging on the side of his neck. 'I don't know what you're talking about?'

I don't intend for it to come out as a weak question, but it does anyway.

Imani rolls her eyes. 'Typical.'

Typical?

I lean forward and press a hand down onto the table. 'I'm sorry. Did I—'

'Your son and I dated during our university days,' Imani says, sending the entire room into a stunned silence. Well, me and my father at least. Malcolm just looks pissed. 'Needless to say, things didn't end well.'

I should be focusing on the absurdity of her claim – that I've apparently dated and broken the heart of a woman without even realising it – but something else catches my attention.

She's talking to my father, but she's not looking at him.

Her gaze is fixed firmly on *me*.

And she doesn't look like she's five seconds away from throttling me anymore. Her chestnut eyes are wide and imploring and I get the distinct sense that she's trying to tell me something.

I steal a quick glance at my father, whose expression has morphed into a potent mix of disbelief and simmering anger.

'I'm not surprised you didn't mention it,' Imani continues, still staring at me with wide, desperate eyes. I feel like I'm missing something important here, that would click everything into place. 'The last time we spoke, I told you I didn't want to have anything to do with you ever again. But,' she pauses and spreads her arms with dramatic flair, 'it seems things are out of our hands now.'

'We've already discussed this,' Malcolm says through gritted teeth. He shoots my father an apologetic grimace. 'The two of them dated some ten years ago now.'

From across the table, Imani winces.

'Ten years ago?' my father splutters, staring at me in disbelief. He's quiet for a few moments, but then he shakes his head and lets out a rough chuckle. 'They were practically children back then.'

Imani narrows her eyes and seems to brace herself for what comes next.

'Ten years is a long time,' my father continues. 'Whatever childish or idiotic thing my son said or did back then, I'm sure you two can move past it as two, mature adults.'

Malcolm sighs in relief. 'My sentiments exactly.'

'He broke my heart,' Imani says swiftly. 'Crushed it into tiny pieces. That's just not something you get over.'

Everyone turns to look at me. My father looks like he's about to explode and even Malcolm looks displeased, an inkling of fatherly rage simmering below the surface.

Either Imani Davies is a seriously unwell young woman or she's doing this for a reason. I'm praying it's the latter. She's got a game plan and I get the sense that she's not going to let up anytime soon. Not without a fight. She's staring at me with that desperate look again. I have no idea what game she's playing but, for now anyway, I can't deny that I'm not curious to see where this is heading. I clear my throat and fix my features into a sheepish expression. 'It was a mutual heartbreak.'

Imani's façade slips for a brief second and I get to enjoy

the look of surprise that flits across her face before she pulls her mask back up and twists her lips into a scowl. 'Of *course* you would say that. You were the one who—'

'Enough.' Malcolm puts a hand in the air and shakes his head. 'We're not here to hash out a decade-long grudge.'

My father nods enthusiastically. 'Quite right.'

'But maybe we *should* slow things down, Georgios.'

My father deflates. 'Excuse me?'

'The merger will still go ahead,' Malcolm says quickly. 'But it's clear these two need some time to reacclimatise to one another. It'll do us no good on the publicity front if we announce the engagement and these two are constantly at each other's throats.'

'What are you suggesting?' my father asks with a frown.

'We'll start off with floating the idea of them as a couple in a relationship.'

Imani opens her mouth but Malcolm cuts her off with a piercing glare and she sinks into her seat like a chastised child.

'See how the shareholders and investors take the idea of our families joining together in this way,' Malcolm continues. 'Remember, we need them to see that this is beyond business. That our companies and families are capable of existing and thriving side-by-side.'

'This is ridiculous,' Imani mutters.

Both my father and Malcolm ignore her.

'Fine,' my father says gruffly. 'We'll delay officially announcing anything concrete until these two can learn how to put on a united front.'

'And that starts *today*,' Malcolm says firmly. He pushes himself up from the table and gestures to the door. 'Georgios, why don't you and I discuss some more pressing matters in another room? We'll leave the two of them to catch up and begin to mend broken bridges.'

My father hesitates for a second and then nods. I can see the irritation flashing across his face at being ordered around in his own building. But he swallows down the anger and stands up. 'Follow me.'

The two storm out of the room without so much as a second glance at me or Imani. It isn't until the door slams firmly shut and the sound of their footsteps fades away into nothing that Imani heaves out a deep sigh and slumps against the table.

'I am *so* sorry!' she groans, her head in her hands. 'Genuinely, I'm so sorry. I know that was insane and . . . Fucking *hell*!' She slams a hand down on the table and glares at the door. 'Why do they have to be so stubborn?'

I blink at her. Every single thing about her demeanour has changed. The rigidity to her posture is gone and the cold expression on her face has melted into a warm, if not a little sheepish, smile.

'I'm just really, really *sorry*,' she says again before she drops her chin into the palm of her hand and shoots me an inquisitive look. 'You held your own though. I have to admit, I didn't think you'd catch on.'

'It *was* strange,' I say slowly, feeling myself relax with each passing second in her presence. 'But I figured you had to be going somewhere with it.' I mimic her action and drop my own chin into my hand and raise a brow. 'Or you were just certifiably insane.'

She laughs the kind of laugh that takes over her whole body. It starts deep in her chest and rises up in waves, making her shoulders shake with each chuckle. She throws her head back, eyes crinkling at the corners. It's oddly captivating, watching her let go like this. I've spent the last twenty minutes watching her sit rigidly with a scowl on her face, refusing to let even the slightest hint of emotion slip through, but now she's transformed into someone completely different before my eyes. It's like watching a storm give way to a calm, sunny day.

'I guess I could be certifiably insane,' she says between laughs, her smile infectious. 'But if I'm insane, then what are you for going along with it?'

'A very intrigued hostage?' I offer, unable to stop my lips from twitching up at the corners. 'Am I going to get any kind of explanation, by the way?'

Her laughter subsides into a soft grin. 'It's definitely not a *sane* explanation,' she says, almost apologetically.

'Try me.'

She hesitates for a beat or two and then lets out a soft sigh. 'My father isn't the kind of person who backtracks on something, not when he's already decided it's going to happen. When I was younger, he put me in ballet classes because the daughter of some potential investor was also in the same class. I hated it. I couldn't make sense of any of the steps and none of the other girls in the class really liked me. I wouldn't call it *bullying*, but . . .' She gives me a wry smile, her expression wistful. 'Anyway, I begged him to let me quit. I said I'd do anything else. Tap, or piano, or horse riding. Anything but ballet. But he wouldn't budge, even though I was obviously miserable.'

'So what did you do?' I ask, feeling an unexpected wave of sympathy towards this little girl I never even knew. 'How did you get out of the classes?'

Imani snorts. 'I didn't. I was seven.'

'He let you stop once he got the investment, right?'

Another snort, this one accompanied with a roll of the eyes. 'Pretty sure he gave up on that plan about two months into me taking the classes. But he'd decided that ballet was beneficial for the *perception* of the Davies name. It looked good for him to have a daughter who spent two days a week rubbing shoulders with the children of politicians, celebrities and wealthy businessmen. Even if they didn't even like me.' She shrugs and then points to her hair. Her dark brown curls are pulled into a tight bun. 'I hated ballet, but some things stick. The hairstyle *and* the lesson it taught me. I don't know if it's a pride thing or what, but once my father has decided something, there's no amount of begging I can do that'll change his mind. I learned that from a very young age.'

She chews the inside of her cheek for a few seconds, and I can practically see the cogs turning in her mind. 'My father is the kind of person who only listens to himself. He's got financial advisors and people he'll confide in, but they're pretty much echo chambers these days. They just tell him exactly what he's already planning on doing.' Her lips split into a wry grin. 'And don't get me wrong – he is usually right.'

'But not now?'

Her smile drops immediately. 'Definitely not.'

'So, what was that back there?' I ask with a frown. It's good to know that Imani *isn't* certifiably insane, but I still can't figure out what her game plan is here.

'I'm never going to change his mind by just asking him. Not even I, his only daughter, have that privilege.' She says it with a shrug, but it's impossible to miss the hint of bitterness lacing her words. There's a lifetime of hidden pain there. 'But if he thinks it's *his* idea . . .' She trails off and the pieces of the puzzle start to come together in my mind.

'Then he'll call it off,' I finish for her.

Imani leans back into her seat and gives me a nod, obviously pleased I've finally caught up. 'Exactly. As soon as he realises this isn't going to get him the positive press and good standing with the investors he thinks it will, he'll call the whole thing off. Anything that puts the Peregrine Airways name in jeopardy is a hard no in my father's mind. And that includes me.'

There's that hint of bitterness again, and I get it. I truly do. I'm no stranger to growing up with the knowledge that you'll always be in second place – or fourth, in my case – when it comes to the family business. But I've made my peace with it. Imani clearly hasn't.

She also hasn't thought this plan through.

I shake my head. '*Your* father might change his mind after a few bad headlines, but mine won't.'

Scandal has been following Georgios Vouvalis since before I was even born. A little more would be nothing to him – not if it will ultimately get him what he wants. And right now, that's Peregrine Airways.

Imani shakes her head. 'It doesn't matter if yours won't change his mind. We just need mine to. Trust me, Daddy will never sign anything if he think it'll hurt the business. Not even your father could get him to change his mind once he's decided.'

I want to tell her that she's underestimating just how persuasive my father can be once he's set his sights on something, but her eyes are wide and imploring and the thought of dashing all her hopes right now makes something unpleasant settle in the pit of my stomach.

She'll get it eventually.

There's no need for me to push it along. No reason for me to give her an actual reason to resent or hate me. My father will make sure that happens soon enough when he forces me to put a ring on her finger.

'So,' Imani says with a tentative grin. 'Are you in?'

'In?'

She nods enthusiastically. 'With my plan? We'll need to work out some kinks, and figure out a believable backstory of course, but I think we could pull this off.'

There's absolutely no chance in hell that we'll be able to pull *anything* off, but her smile is widening and her energy is infectious. For a moment, I allow myself the delusion that I'm not constantly under my father's thumb and that I have any kind of say in my life at all.

'Unless,' Imani says suddenly, 'you had your own plan to get out of it? Sorry, just realising I came in here hot, and I never even asked what your plan was.'

My plan?

Is it pathetic that I never even had one? Yes. No doubt about it.

What does it say about me that I was ready to say *yes* to marrying her, just to keep him happy? My father says jump, and I don't even ask how high. I just do it. That's how it's always been.

A silence stretches between us long enough to make Imani frown. 'Or, I mean – surely you weren't just going to say yes? You weren't about to accept that your father's been planning on marrying you off to some random girl just to get a deal over the line?'

Another beat of silence.

I can practically feel the disappointment rolling off Imani in waves.

Not sure why that bothers me, but it does and before I know it, I'm forcing out a laugh. 'Of course not.'

Imani visibly relaxes. 'Oh, thank *God*. Because, you know, *that* would be certifiably insane.'

'Right.' I continue to laugh even though my cheeks are hurting with the force of it all. 'He only told me about five minutes before you came into the room. I was still processing the madness of it all.' The lie rolls off my tongue easily and it's clear Imani doesn't doubt me. I should feel more guilty for that, but I don't. Over the years I've got used to lying and keeping things hidden and squashed down.

'So, yes,' I say, still forcing the same easy grin. 'I'm in.'

She makes a delighted sound and claps her hands together. '*Thank you.* Trust me, Asher, this is going to work.'

I wish I could believe it.

CHAPTER THREE

Imani

'So, you're engaged now?'

'Hello to you, too,' I say over the rim of my glass as I w[illegible] my best friend slide into our booth. She's twenty minutes late which, to be honest, is actually pretty good for her.

Sloane gives me a sheepish grin, tossing her long, black wavy curls over her shoulder as she settles in front of me. I know for a fact that she only woke up an hour ago, but she looks immaculate. Such is the life of a top model. Always got to be ready. Sloane, unfortunately, is no stranger to weirdos trying to snap a sneaky, off-guard photo of her to plaster all over social media.

As Malcolm Davies' daughter, I get my fair share of public interest and headlines, but for Sloane it's on another level. Top model, daughter of A-list actors Kiran and Margot Chavan, and granddaughter to British Indo-Caribbean theatre icon, Veera Chavan, Sloane has had the glare of the camera flash in her eye from the moment she was born.

Luckily, she's gorgeous and I can count the number of 'bad photos' I've seen of her on one hand and still have a finger or two left over. But still, it must get annoying always having to be primped and preened the way she does. Not that I've ever heard her complain. She leans into the chaos and makes it part of her persona – the two-time nepo baby everyone *wants* to hate but can't because, well, just look at the material.

'Sorry,' she drawls. 'Late night last night, and I wasn't expecting to hear from you for a while. Shouldn't you be somewhere over the Mediterranean Sea by now?'

'I should be three hours away from paradise right about now,' I whimper dramatically as a waiter approaches and wordlessly fills up Sloane's glass before disappearing back into the shadows. 'But I'm officially grounded.'

Sloane arches a thick, perfectly fluffed brow and snorts. 'Grounded? Are you sixteen?'

'Unfortunately, I mean in the literal sense. No flights for me for the foreseeable future. He's done everything but cut up my passport.'

On my ride home – solo – from the Vouvalis building, I logged into my Peregrine Airways account and discovered, thanks to the bright red alert running across the homepage, that a hold has been placed on my previously limitless account. *Indefinitely.*

Sloane clutches at her literal pearls. 'No.'

'Yes,' I say glumly, and take another sip of wine.

She reaches across the table and gives my hand a sympathetic squeeze. 'What did you do?'

'Nothing!' I squawk indignantly. 'It's what I *didn't* do.'

Sloane frowns then seems to remember the flood of increasingly incoherent messages I sent her this morning. 'Right. This engagement thing?'

Just hearing the word *engagement* makes me want to heave. I still haven't quite accepted that this is really happening. That my father would so easily hand me over as a means to get a step ahead in business. A knot starts to form in my throat but I force it away by swallowing down another gulp of wine. Now is not the time for tears.

Now is the time for *strategising*.

Asher and I have agreed to meet up later this week to firm up my admittedly sketchy plan, so I've got just under seventy-two hours to work out the kinks here. And there are a *lot* of kinks. First and foremost: the plan is insane, a fact Sloane helpfully reminds me of as soon as I share it with her.

'You've been watching too many romcoms,' she says. 'Or, you haven't watched enough. It's meant to be fake dating, not fake exes. And even the former is patently ridiculous.'

I wave a dismissive hand in front of her. 'I've thought this through.'

Sloane snorts. 'No, you most definitely have not. You've thought *a* thought. One single, deranged thought. Which was "What if I pretend to be heartbroken over a fake ex so I can get out of marrying a real fiancé I never asked for?"'

'Exactly! You get it.'

'No,' she says flatly. 'I don't. I really don't.'

I sigh and slump back against the booth. She's right. The plan is unhinged. But these are desperate times. 'I don't see you coming up with any bright ideas.'

Sloane opens her mouth, then closes it and bites her lip and looks at me guiltily.

'What?' I ask, narrowing my eyes. 'Just say it. Spit it out.'

'Why don't you just say no? Walk away?'

Ah. I see where the guilt is coming from now. In our almost decade of friendship, Sloane and I have spoken about this more times than I can count.

Why don't I just say no to my father's demands?

It's not like I haven't thought about it. I have. Over and over and over again. But it's not that simple. Sloane is *someone,* even without her family name propping her up. I'm just . . . Imani. Spoiled heiress with no talents or skills or dreams of her own.

At least, that's what the world seems to think.

I remember just after I graduated, I did an internship at Peregrine Airways, hoping to understand more about the business that'd loomed over my life from the day I was born, and maybe find my own niche among it all.

The other interns didn't like me. Don't get me wrong; they were polite and smiled back at me, but it only took me about two weeks to realise that I was never invited to lunch, or drinks after work, or even that they had a separate group chat that was much more active than the one I was officially included in. At the end of the three-month internship, when we were all vying for one of the coveted job spots on offer, they slipped up. Someone messaged the wrong group chat – the one with *me* in it:

> Ugh. What was the point of all this anyway? They're just going to give it to Daddy's Little Princess. Knew I should've accepted the role at BA.

A slew of laughing and exclamation emojis followed before I assume someone realised the mistake and they all silently left the group without another word. None of them would even make eye contact with me for the last week of the internship.

It didn't matter that I'd pulled my weight just as much as the rest of them throughout the three months, that I'd stayed late and showed up early, that my project proposal – an idea to launch a scheme in the countries where Peregrine Airways flies to get the local, and often underprivileged, youth interested in all aspects of aviation – was just as innovative as theirs, and delivered just as high-quality work as the rest of them. To them, I was nothing but a puppet with a name that got me the right connections.

I ended up declining the job offer when it came through, and my proposal, as thoroughly researched and as dear to my heart as it was, never came to fruition.

'Earth to Imani,' Sloane says, snapping her fingers in front of my face. 'You disappeared for a second there.'

I blink and shake my head slightly, grounding myself back

in the present. My wine glass is empty, and Sloane's eyeing me like I've just grown a second head.

'Sorry,' I mumble. 'Just remembering something dumb.'

Sloane gives me a look. It's one of those rare, soft ones that occasionally slips through her sardonic, glamorous diva persona. 'It wasn't dumb,' she says softly.

I shrug because I really don't want to get it into it. Not now. Not when I'm already teetering on the edge like this. I clear my throat and try to get us back on track. 'I can't say no to him. You know that. He's already promised to freeze me out. No more trust fund, no more company access, no more . . . anything. I'll be completely cut off.' I pause. That bloody lump is back in my throat again. 'And I'm not ready for that.'

Sloane gives me a long, considered look. It's the kind of look that says she wants to smack some sense into me and pull me into a bear hug at the same time. 'You shouldn't still have to play these games.'

I shrug again. 'But I do.'

For a moment, neither of us says anything. Then, Sloane straightens in her seat and flashes me a determined grin.

'Fine. But if we're doing this, we're doing it *right*. We need spreadsheets, we need dates, we need photo evidence of this whirlwind relationship. And I want the kind of heartbreak story that'll make Taylor Swift weep.'

A startled laugh slips out of me. 'You're in? You'll help me?'

She nods, her own smile widening. 'Let's fake you a break-up so toxic, your dad won't know what hit him.'

*

'Your guy is irritatingly elusive.'

Sloane is draped across my kitchen island, brows furrowed as she scrolls through her phone with all the intensity of an MI5 agent doing reconnaissance on their next target.

'First of all, he's not *my* guy,' I grumble before leaning over her shoulder to catch a glimpse of the screen. 'And secondly, yeah, I feel like he dropped off the face of the earth after we left uni.'

Though, to be fair, it's not like he was ever really part of my orbit while we were studying in the first place.

Sloane hums and opens up yet another article about Vouvalis Resorts. This one is about the company breaking ground at their soon-to-be newest hotel location in Turks and Caicos. The main image for the article is one of Georgios Vouvalis shaking hands with who I assume is someone important on the island – maybe the mayor? Stood next to them both is a tall, grinning, incredibly handsome man.

'Ugh.' Sloane rolls her eyes and clicks off the article. 'Andreas, *again*.'

Asher's oldest brother, Andreas, seems to be following very closely in his father's footsteps when it comes to the family business. From our thirty minutes of recon work since we got back to my apartment, we've discovered that Andreas has been steadily amassing a healthy portfolio of *Forbes, Fortune* and *Bloomberg* profiles in his own right, and has handled several of the latest Vouvalis Resorts deals himself over the last few years.

'You can tell who Daddy's favourite is to take over once

he kicks the bucket,' Sloane snorts, swiping away yet another article about Andreas and the family business. 'Ah! And here's Teddy.'

Theodore Vouvalis – the middle child.

Sloane taps on a new link, which takes us to a socialite gossip site where we're immediately bombarded with photo after photo of Teddy slinking out of bars and restaurants with a beautiful woman on his arm. Sometimes two.

'Charming,' I mutter, my eyes landing on a photo of him stumbling out of some London club, sunglasses on at night, a cigarette dangling from his lips like he's a cliché from a bad indie film. *My* father would have a heart attack if I'd ever been caught like this in front of a camera, but it seems Georgios couldn't care less.

Sloane nods in agreement. 'He's basically a walking red flag dressed in designer clothes. The stories I've heard about him from girls at shows? Ugh.' She rolls her eyes again. 'Let's pray he doesn't become your brother-in-law.'

Just the thought makes me shudder.

Sloane scrolls to the bottom of the page and hits the **VOUVALIS** tag, pulling up every article about the family hosted on the site. There are pages and pages about Georgios, Andreas and Teddy, but next to nothing on Asher. The closest we get is little more than a footnote about a failed attempt at opening up a new location in Grenada four years ago.

> '... Asher Vouvalis declined to comment on the abandoned plans to bring the Vouvalis name to the famed

spice island. Elsewhere in the Caribbean, plans to open two new resorts, headed up by Vouvalis Sr, in Jamaica and Barbados, are well under way . . .'

And that's it. Not a peep more.

Georgios and Andreas' business dealings are everywhere, Teddy's half-drunken smirk is plastered all over social media, but Asher? Asher is like a ghost. If I hadn't sat directly opposite him myself this morning, I might even be doubting that a third Vouvalis boy even exists.

'It's like he doesn't even exist,' Sloane murmurs, now currently absentmindedly scrolling through an anonymous gossip page on Instagram. 'But I guess his low profile works in our favour.'

She's right, of course. But *why* isn't there anything about him?

I'm probably considered solidly C-list in the socialite world – compared to Sloane's glitzy A-list status, anyway – and even I've got a handful of carefully planted, *tasteful*, stories in the gossip rags. I suppose this is why my father even entertained the idea of marrying me and Asher off in the first place.

No matter how desperate he gets, just the thought of seeing a photo of me on Teddy's arm, drunkenly stumbling out of a seedy club at 3am would be enough to send him into an early grave. Not out of any fear or love for *me* of course, but because of how the optics would affect the Davies name.

I suppose Andreas wouldn't be the worst option in the

world for a scheme like this, but it's clear he's been following in his father's footsteps – and that includes the occasional dodgy business deal or two. I can see why my father would want to keep the Davies name at arms-length away from that.

And then there's Asher.

Graduated from a good university and then seemingly disappeared. I have to assume he works in some capacity in the family business, but otherwise he's a blank slate in our world. No one really knows anything about him, and that means my father and Georgios have the freedom to create whatever story they want when it comes to us.

But that also means *I've* got that freedom as well, and I intend to take full advantage of it.

'Oooh! Got him!' Sloane squeals excitedly before shoving her phone in my face. She's about two hundred posts deep on the anonymous Instagram gossip page and, nestled between an off-guard shot of Sloane herself stepping out of a black cab, and a blurry shot of a reality TV star looking *very* cosy with an up-and-coming singer, is a photo of the three Vouvalis brothers at a charity gala.

Sloane taps on the photo and enlarges it. It's clear the main goal for whoever took the photo was to capture Andreas and Teddy. They're in the forefront, leaning up against the bar, grinning and milking the camera like it's second nature. They look good, too, but my focus isn't on them. Next to Teddy, looking like he's out of his comfort zone and doing his best to shy away from the endless flashing bulbs surrounding them, is Asher.

The photo is clearly a few years old, so he looks slightly younger than the man I met today, but he's no less handsome. Like his brothers, he's wearing an exquisitely crafted tux – Ralph Lauren, according to Sloane – that shows off broad shoulders and a trim waist. His skin is warmer than his brothers, a soft shade of brown where theirs is more golden, and his chocolate-brown curls fall just a little messily across his forehead; a few strands hanging loose directly between dark, green eyes.

And that smile.

It's not confident or cocky like his brothers, but almost a little nervous. Like he's not sure whether he should actually be smiling at all. Somehow it's both charming and vulnerable at the same time.

It suits him.

'You know,' Sloane says thoughtfully, 'he's not bad-looking at all. I mean, I've definitely had worse exes.'

Categorically, she has *not* but I get what she means.

I glance back at the photo and feel my lips start to curve into an involuntary smile. 'Yeah. He's not bad.'

CHAPTER FOUR

Asher

Look up the word *anger* in the dictionary and you'll find a picture of my father scowling up at you. I have very few memories of seeing my father genuinely happy, or expressing an emotion that isn't some form of vague irritation. Even so, I think I've only seen him this furious once before and I, unfortunately, was the cause of that episode too.

'. . . chance after chance and this is how you repay me?'

I glance up just in time to watch my father slam a hand down on his desk, sending a stack of paper and a stapler crashing to the floor.

'Well?' he snarls, glaring at me like I'm the source of every single problem in his life. According to him, I might as well be. 'How are you going to fix this?'

By *this* he means the Imani Davies situation.

I open my mouth to respond but he starts pacing the room and muttering furiously like he didn't just ask me a question.

'Do you understand how hard I've had to work to get Davies to come around to this idea? Months, Asher. I've spent *months* working him. This merger could change *everything* for the business – for the family . . .'

I manage to swallow down a snort. Since when have I been part of any of his considerations when it comes to the family?

'And yet you insist on making things difficult.' He pauses in his ranting momentarily and narrows his eyes. 'As usual.'

I could point out that the reason he's having to go to these lengths to get over the line with Peregrine Airways is because of *his* own less than savoury behaviour over the years, and has nothing to do with me, but he's inching closer to a paperweight on his desk and I don't fancy my chances if he reaches for it and sends it flying.

'If we don't get the Peregrine shareholders and investors on board—' He cuts himself off abruptly and gruffly clears his throat. 'Well, the specifics of the situation don't concern you. Just know that it needs to be done and you need to do your part in ensuring success and securing our family's legacy. Is that understood?'

I run my tongue over the back of my teeth in an attempt to tamp down the maelstrom of resentment and rage I can feel building inside me. All this talk about family and legacy coming from him of all people leaves a bitter taste in my mouth. I'm nothing more than an inconvenient obligation to him; he's made that perfectly clear over the years. There's no love or even a hint of fatherly affection driving him here.

'I *said*,' he grits out, leaning against his desk until he's only mere inches away from my face. 'Do. You. Understand?'

I'm not entirely sure why this, of all my father's schemes over the years, has rubbed me the wrong way like this. He's always treated me as nothing more than a transaction; just a pawn in some game where the prize is always more money and power, so it shouldn't be that difficult to agree to this ridiculous demand. But when I open my mouth to utter out the expected 'Understood', nothing comes out.

Maybe it's because he's involved someone else this time. Someone entirely undeserving of his anger. As much as I'm willing to be his punching bag, I can't do that to someone else.

To her.

I guess he hasn't ground down my backbone as much as I thought he had.

He's still waiting for me to respond, staring at me with cold eyes and a tight jaw. The silence that stretches between us is thick and suffocating. His nostrils flare suddenly, and for a moment, I think he's going to explode again. I eye the paperweight nervously.

He opens his mouth and I flinch, ready for the explosion. But it's not more vitriol that comes out of his mouth. Instead, he sighs and I do a double take, sure I'm seeing things. Because it looks like the fire behind my father's eyes dampens slightly. He looks almost concerned. For me? Surely not.

'This is Grenada all over again, isn't it?' he asks, voice softer than I've ever heard it before. It's not exactly a kind tone of voice by any definition, but there's none of the bite there was just seconds ago.

I frown. It feels like we're in uncharted territory here. My father ranting, raving and throwing things I can handle. I know how to navigate and dodge that. But this? This is new. I don't like it.

'Perhaps I've been too hard on you,' he says softly. He settles into his seat, leans forward and steeples his fingers together. The shock I'm feeling must be painted clear as day across my face because he chuckles knowingly. 'All I've wanted to do is shape you into something – or should I say, into *someone* worth carrying the Vouvalis name. Have I been hard on you over the years?'

Yes, I think bitterly, but I stay silent, knowing he's not looking for a response from me.

'Perhaps,' he says, cocking his head to the side. 'But I considered it a necessary evil. I'd hoped that under my tutelage, you'd eventually grow into a man – into a *son* – I could be proud of. I had thought, naïvely perhaps, that we'd reached a turning point when I gave you the Grenada resort. You'd begun to show promise after all. But we both know how that turned out.'

The soft, fatherly façade slips for a moment, and I get a glimpse of the anger I've become so accustomed to. It's almost a relief to see it.

'I did what I felt was best,' I force out, not that it does any good. In the two years since the Grenada debacle, I've tried and failed to defend myself and my choices there more times than I can count. It never ends up going my way. He doesn't care that the resort location he wanted to open up in Grenada would have displaced hundreds of locals and reduced their access to the beach and the sea. He only care abouts profit and the bottom line, no matter how many people he hurts.

'Yes, yes,' he says dismissively. 'And therein lies the problem, doesn't it? What *you* feel is best is never quite right. But never mind that. Never mind Grenada or all your other missteps over the years. This is your chance to redeem yourself. *She* is your chance.'

My father smiles then and the expression on his face is so foreign, it startles me. 'If you do this for me, I can make sure you're finally seen for what you are, Asher. You'll be more than just the boy who's squandered every chance I've given him. You'll be my son.'

For a moment, I can't breathe. There it is. The hook. The same one he's been dangling in front of me since I was eight years old and desperate for any scrap of affection he might one day decide to toss my way.

I like to tell myself that his approval means nothing to me, and that I'd stopped chasing it years ago, but the lie doesn't hold much weight even in my own head. I was, after all, perfectly ready to say *yes* to marrying Imani just to keep him happy, and even now, I'm not laughing in his face and storming out of his office like I know I should.

Deep down, beneath all the anger and resentment I've built up over the years, there's still a pathetic, broken part of me that's desperate for his approval. The kid who used to hide at the top of the stairs just to hear if my father might say something kind about me to someone else when he thought I wasn't listening. The same kid who'd spend day after day trying to earn a smile, and when it didn't come, decided it was because I hadn't worked hard enough to deserve one yet.

That kid still lives inside me, and as much as I hate to admit it, he wants what my father is offering.

My voice sounds hollow when I speak again. 'If I do this . . .' I start. 'If I do what you're asking, will that finally be enough for you?'

The silence that follows stretches for too long. He leans back in his chair, regarding me with a look that might be pity or maybe disgust. I can never tell the difference with him.

Just as I think he's not going to give me an answer, he exhales slowly and says, 'Well, that depends entirely on you, doesn't it?'

I clench my jaw and nod stiffly. 'Understood.'

A fleeting look of happiness passes over his face, and then he's back to business again. 'I want this deal with Davies signed by the end of the year.'

Seven months. He's giving me a little over seven months to somehow convince Imani to marry me.

'Whatever you did to hurt the Davies girl so badly? Undo it. I don't care how you get her on board, just make sure it gets done.'

'I can't force her to love me.' If I haven't been able to earn my own father's love in twenty-odd years, what hope could I possibly have for a woman I've just met? Well, *re*-met, technically.

Though our interaction was fleeting and it's not like she remembers, so I suppose we are essentially starting from zero.

My father barks out a bitter-sounding laugh. 'Who said anything about love? You just have to marry the girl.'

'I can't force her to do that either.'

He shrugs and it feels like the wind has been knocked out of me. My father is a cruel man. I've known this since the very first day I met him. But this is a new level of callousness. 'You'll figure it out, I'm sure.'

I open my mouth to respond but now that he's got what he wants from me, he dismisses me with a wave of the hand and barely spares a glance in my direction. Not that I need telling twice.

Imani's grateful smile when I agreed to her plan earlier flashes in my mind as I leave the office and I shake my head to dissolve the mental image of her.

She's going to absolutely hate me.

There's a car waiting outside, ready to take me home where I plan to faceplant into bed and disconnect from the world for at least twenty-four full hours. I've decided I'm owed at least that after the morning I've just had.

I open the door to the sleek black car waiting for me, and am immediately met with a loud BANG, followed by a shower of colourful confetti hitting me in the face.

I barely have time to blink before a pair of arms extend from the car and yank me inside. Thoughts of a kidnapping, as misguided as it would be given how little ransom my father would cough up for me, flash through my mind and I feel a beat of panic before—

'Congratulations!' Teddy roars, tugging the door shut behind me once I'm inside. Never mind that I'm currently draped haphazardly across his legs and still not sitting upright. 'Never thought we'd see the day, did we Dre?'

Andreas, sat opposite us, pretends to wipe away a single tear. 'We're so proud. You're all grown up.'

'Ha, ha,' I deadpan, shoving myself away from Teddy so I can scoot into the empty seat beside him properly. 'I see you two have heard the news.'

Teddy signals to the driver to start moving and leans back into his seat, a wide, Cheshire cat-esque grin splitting his face. 'Heard the news,' Teddy scoffs, reaching into the door compartment to pull out a bottle of champagne already missing its cork. 'We've been celebrating. Here, drink up.'

He unearths a champagne flute from God knows where, shoves it in my hand, and immediately begins pouring.

'When do we get to meet your dearly beloved?' Andreas asks as he passes Teddy his own glass. Teddy dutifully begins topping him up.

'Oh yes,' Teddy says, his grin widening to truly ridiculous proportions. 'Our dear new sister-in-law. Can't wait to meet her. I bet she's ecstatic. Tell us how the proposal went down.'

I glare at my brothers. 'This isn't funny.'

'On the contrary,' Andreas says in between sips of champagne. 'This is hilarious.'

'Incredibly,' Teddy agrees. 'Our baby brother is getting

married. To a woman he's not said even one word to. This is peak romance if you ask me.'

Andreas nods. 'The stuff Hallmark movies are made out of.'

I know I shouldn't take the bait, but I'm already on edge from my meeting with our father. 'And what would you know about romance, Teddy? How is Céline, by the way?'

Teddy's smile drops immediately at the mention of his ex-fiancée. His eyes narrow. 'Watch it, Ash.'

I ignore the thinly veiled threat, satisfied that I've got a little bit of revenge for their teasing, and instead ask, 'How long have you both known?'

'Just this morning,' Teddy says.

'About a week now,' says Andreas.

Teddy scowls at him.

Andreas shrugs. 'He'd find out eventually.'

'And neither of you felt like giving me a heads-up?'

The mood shifts slightly in the car. We're all painfully aware that while our father actively loathes me, it doesn't mean he has any real love for Andreas or Teddy. None of us are really safe from his manipulations; they've always just been better at dealing with him than me. Out of the three of us though, Andreas is clearly the favourite – if you can even call not actively hating his eldest son a form of favouritism. So it doesn't surprise me that Andreas has known about my impending forced nuptials for a not insignificant amount of time.

It *does* surprise me that he didn't say anything though. When it comes to our father, the three of us have always banded together and looked out for each other as much as possible. That Andreas would leave me in the lurch like this is uncharacteristic.

He does, at least, have the decency to hold his hands up apologetically and look somewhat ashamed. 'I wanted to tell you,' he says carefully. 'Believe me, I did. But he made it very clear that if either of us intervened that he'd . . . escalate.'

'Escalate how?' I snap before I can stop myself. I'm trying to remember that Andreas and Teddy aren't the enemy here, but my patience for our father's schemes is running thin and they're an easy target right now.

'He said he'd take the French resort from me,' Andreas says.

Teddy grunts and mutters, 'And he threatened to lock me out of the family account. Said something about teaching us what *real* consequences are for once.'

I exhale slowly. Our father has never once given up an opportunity to remind us that everything we have is technically his.

'So we stayed quiet,' Andreas finishes. There's genuine regret in his voice, which irritates me more than an excuse would have. At least I could've had a reason to snap at an excuse. 'I also wasn't entirely sure that he was serious about it. You know how he gets sometimes, throwing out any random idea and seeing what sticks. But then he kept bringing it up over and over again and I eventually realised . . .' He trails off and gives me another apologetic wince.

'There's a pretty big difference between "let's build an underwater hotel" and "I'm going to marry off my son to a stranger in order to get a deal over the line",' I point out through gritted teeth. 'One is slightly more realistic than the other.'

Andreas hums thoughtfully and tips his glass in my direction. 'Debatable. The underwater hotel was a solid concept. Just bad execution.'

'And this is all a moot point anyway, because you're not going to do it,' Teddy chimes in. 'You're not going to marry her. *Obviously.*'

I open my mouth, close it, open it again, and then clamp it shut.

Teddy suddenly looks alarmed. 'Uh, *what*?'

'I'm going to marry her,' I say quietly.

Teddy reels back like I've just slapped him. 'No, you're not. Dre, tell him.'

Andreas just purses his lips and Teddy's eyes widen in shock. '*Andreas.*'

Andreas turns to look out of the window, stubbornly refusing to meet mine or Teddy's gaze. After a beat of silence he says, 'I think he should do it.'

'Have you *both* lost your minds?' Teddy squawks, looking between us both. 'If this is some kind of prank, I'm gonna need you to end it now.'

Even I stare at Andreas incredulously. 'I know I just said that I'm going to do it, but I didn't think you'd be on board.'

Andreas is still refusing to meet my eye. 'Obviously,' he says, and his voice sounds strained. 'I'd prefer you to find love on your own. But, I think, ultimately, this could be good for you. And for your relationship with him.'

'In what way?' Teddy blurts out, still staring at Andreas like he's just sprouted another head. 'Am I seriously the voice of reason here? *Me*?'

Teddy has a point.

Andreas shifts awkwardly in his seat. 'I'm not saying it's an ideal situation—'

'Well, thank fuck for that,' Teddy drawls. 'That means you haven't completely lost your mind.'

'I just mean,' Andreas continues, ignoring Teddy like he's not sitting directly opposite him. He looks up and finally meets my gaze. 'This could be what you've been waiting for. You do this one thing, and maybe he'll finally ack—'

'I get it,' I say bluntly, cutting him off before he can say out loud what we both know he's getting at. An unpleasant mix of shame and embarrassment starts to build inside me.

For as long as I can remember, I've been fighting hard to earn my father's love and recognition and, for as long as I can remember, I've been failing.

When I was younger, it felt like I spent every waking moment trying to prove myself. Every decision I made, every risk I took, it was all in service of that one impossible goal: making him proud. But nothing I did was ever good enough. Every success somehow turned into a failure in his eyes. Every attempt to impress him just made me look more foolish. I thought if I worked harder, learned faster, stayed quieter, maybe one day he'd look at me and see someone worth loving.

He never has. But it's one thing for me to acknowledge how painfully desperate I am for my father's approval; it's a whole other thing entirely to realise that I'm apparently so transparent and pathetic in my efforts that Andreas is starting to pity me.

'No,' Teddy says firmly. 'He'll throw a tantrum and, I won't lie, it'll probably be bad for a while, but it will *pass*. He'll get it over it, move on to the next scheme. You know he will. You've been here before.'

I know exactly what he's referring to: when I ruined the planned Grenada resort by trying to add a caveat in the contract that would mean locals would still be able to access the beach and come and go as they please. My father was furious and, instead of negotiating, he simply cancelled the plans for the resort and blamed it on me. He's never really let it go and regularly uses it as an example as why I'm apparently 'weak' and how I just don't have that 'Vouvalis edge'. I still don't understand the point in opening up new locations in places like Grenada, and then completely sequestering ourselves from the people that make the country what it is. That experience had been what I thought was the peak of my father's rage. Until today, of course.

But the stakes are higher here. If I do this, I can get what I've always wanted. I know it, and Andreas knows it too.

'I have to,' I sigh, taking a leaf out of Andreas' book and avoiding all eye contact with Teddy.

'No, you don't,' Teddy insists.

'I do.'

'Have you both lost your minds?' Teddy asks again. 'Asher, he's not asking you to bribe a local official here or to smooth over some scandal with a timely donation to an orphanage or whatever. He's asking you to *marry someone*. It's insane.'

'You think I don't know that?' I finally snap. Everything about the last few hours of my life is nothing *but* insane. It's one thing to play along with my father's endless parade of half-baked schemes, but this one involves someone else, and she doesn't deserve to get dragged into whatever the hell the mess I call my family life is. I know that.

Teddy rubs a hand over his face. 'Then don't do it.'

'You don't understand,' I sigh.

Teddy studies me for a long moment, his usual easy confidence replaced with a serious look I rarely see on him. 'You really think this will change anything with him?'

'I don't know,' I admit. 'But I have to try.'

I can feel Teddy's frustration radiating off him. His jaw is tight, and I know he's using every ounce of self-restraint he has not to say something cruel, just to try and get through to me.

'I just don't get it,' he says after a long moment of silence. 'Why arc you still playing his games?

Because I'm weak. Because some part of me still believes that if I just do this one thing right, if I can just not screw it up this time, maybe he'll look at me and see more than a disappointment. Maybe he'll finally see his son and the last two decades of rejection will all be worth it.

But I don't say that. Instead, I lift my lips into a dry smile and say, 'Why are any of us?'

Andreas purses his lips. Teddy scowls and turns to stare stubbornly out the window. The celebratory mood is well and truly ruined.

We sit in a stony silence until the car slows as we turn down a familiar road. I glance out of the window and feel a sense of ease and relief as we begin crawling towards my building.

'Alright,' Teddy says heavily. 'Since you've apparently decided to abandon all sense and you're actually going through with this, I guess that means that this is now a real celebration.' He lifts his glass again and allows a grin to take over his face. To his credit, it's only slightly forced.

Andreas nods. 'To family,' he says, lifting his glass.

I lift my glass too, though it feels like my hand's made of lead. 'To family,' I say dryly.

Teddy mutters something under his breath that sounds suspiciously like 'dysfunctional family', but he clinks his glass anyway and then adds, 'And to Asher and – uh – what was her name again?'

'Imani.'

'*Imani*,' he repeats with a nod. 'To Asher and our new sister-in-law, Imani.'

'What is she like, by the way?' Andreas asks. 'Is she okay with this whole situation?'

A dry laugh escapes me before I even have the chance to register it. 'Definitely not.'

That earns a cackle of laughter from Teddy. 'So what's the plan there? You know you can't force her down the aisle?'

'Yes, Teddy,' I say dryly. 'I'm well aware. I'm still working that one out.' I finally tip back my glass of champagne and let the bubbles burn their way down my throat.

'Poor girl,' Andreas murmurs as the car rolls to a stop outside my building.

I agree wholeheartedly. Poor girl, indeed.

CHAPTER FIVE

Asher

I'm quickly learning that Imani Davies is the kind of person who does everything with a sort of fiery intensity.

We meet, three days after our initial reintroduction at the Vouvalis offices, at a member's club in Central London. I've never been here before, preferring the Vouvalis Hotel lounges if I ever need a space for entertaining clients, but Imani has me listed as her guest at the front door and I'm waved in after the host scrutinises my ID and then attempts (and fails) to corral me into a membership of my own.

I find Imani nestled in a comfy-looking armchair, a bottle of sparkling water and two glasses on her left, her laptop, covered in what look like passport stamp stickers from every country from Argentina to Zambia, open in front of her. On her right is what I can only describe as a dossier.

She looks up at me over the top of her laptop as I approach, and her lips split into a soft smile I most definitely don't deserve. I have the sudden urge to commit this to memory, reasoning that this is probably going to be the last time I see that smile, given what I'm about to tell her.

'Oh good,' she says, shuffling her laptop and dossier aside as I drop into the seat opposite. 'I was just starting to wonder if they were giving you any trouble at the door. Drink?' She nudges the bottle and a tumbler glass in my direction, but I shake my head.

'There are very few things in this world I hate more than sparkling water.'

She rolls her eyes and laughs. I try not to think about what a shame it is that I'll never get to hear the sound again. 'Sparkling water haters are always so dramatic. But, noted. I suppose that's something your heartbroken ex should know about you, right?' She wiggles her brows conspiratorially and guilt settles uncomfortably in my gut.

I need to get this over with.

I need to tell her that I can't agree to her plan and that we just need to accept that our fathers are going to do what they want to do.

But then I remember the way she looked at me three days ago – the clear disappointment that flashed over her face when she assumed, correctly I suppose, that I was nothing more than a doormat – and I can't do it. The words get stuck in my throat and I realise that I want to savour this moment, this pocket of time where Imani Davies doesn't hate me, for just a little while longer.

'Right,' I say, forcing a grin onto my face that I hope looks natural.

Imani matches my attempt at nonchalance with an easy smile of her own. 'Great. Okay, let's talk strategy.'

Without waiting for my response – which is probably for the best, considering that the only thing that comes to mind is a strangled *Uhh*? – Imani flips open the dossier with a flourish. The front cover hits the table with a THWACK and the pages inside spill out in an avalanche of sticky notes, printouts and lined paper with a semi-coherent looping scrawl over it.

'So,' Imani continues, apparently oblivious to the stunned look on my face as she flicks through the dossier, 'I figured a good place to start would be our respective backgrounds. Childhood, hobbies, family, friends, stuff like that. Nothing too deep, just enough that if anyone asks any questions, it'll be easy to keep up the façade that we actually know each other and used to date. How does that sound?' She looks up at me, thumb and forefinger lifting up a page where I can spy the words:

ASHER [MIDDLE NAME????] VOUVALIS
AGE: 27/28 [probably]
BIRTHDAY: ???????

I clear my throat and let out the strangled *Uhh* from earlier.

Imani isn't deterred. She ploughs on as if I don't look like a deer in headlights in front of her. 'Don't look so scared,' she laughs. 'I swear I'm not a stalker.'

I raise a brow and look pointedly at the dossier.

She lets out another bell-like peal of laughter and it takes me back to that party nearly ten years ago.

'Okay,' she concedes with a wry grin, 'I'm not a very *good* stalker. You, Asher Middle-Name-Still-Unrevealed-Vouvalis, are a very hard guy to find out anything about. No defunct MySpace page from fifteen years ago, no Facebook profile with a hundred photo albums filled with every single photo you ever took with a digital camera, no cringy comments from the account you unfortunately made with your real name when you were twelve. Sadly, I'm speaking from experience.' She flashes me an embarrassed smile. 'But it's fine, that's what this meeting is for: filling in the blanks.'

She pulls out two sheets of paper, keeps the one with my name on it and slides the other one over to me.

IMANI MAYA DAVIES
AGE: 28
BIRTHDAY: August 12th 1997

I scan through the page and learn that she graduated with a First-Class Honours in Business and Management from the same Russell Group university as me, that she's fluent in French, is a qualified lifeguard, is allergic to pineapple, names a Sloane Chavan (a name that rings a very faint bell but I can't figure out why) as her best friend, and her favourite food is her grandfather's roasted seabass. And that's just all the information I glean from a twenty-second glance.

The page is double-sided.

My respective one is empty.

I put the paper down and decide I've indulged enough in Imani's kindness. Enough is enough. I need to end this now, before Imani gets too into this and we head past the point of no return. Although, worryingly, it does feel like she's already there.

'Don't you think this is a bit . . . much?' I gesture towards the dossier and pile of paper in front of me. 'You're really . . . you're really going all in on this.'

Imani cocks her head to the side slightly, the beginnings of a frown starting to appear. 'Well, yeah? I mean, what's the point of doing something if you don't throw your entire self into it?'

She says it like it's simply a matter of fact, and it kills the retort I had lined up on the tip of my tongue.

Maybe she has a point.

Circumstances in life have forced me to become the kind of person who takes the safe route. Who waits for things to fall into place to avoid rocking the boat. Who slots himself into the preordained spaces made for him without so much as a second thought. But there's something about Imani's focus, the way she dives in headfirst without hesitation, that makes me realise there's a difference between doing and simply letting the world turn around you. The different between existing and *living*.

I realise, with a pang, that I'm not sure if my life up till now can be considered well *lived*. I've been nothing but a passive participant in my own life for the better part of twenty-eight years.

'And I needed a distraction,' she continues, completely

oblivious to the mental warfare going on in my own mind. 'From . . . well, never mind.' She shakes her head and waves a nonchalant hand. 'Anyway, if we're going to do this, we might as well do it properly, no?'

I hate how dry my mouth is right now. Hate how slick with sweat my palms are and how hard my heart is thudding against my ribcage.

Imani Davies should not be eliciting these kinds of feelings from me. I barely know her. Her happiness means nothing to me. I owe her absolutely nothing.

And yet.

'What if we don't do this?' I finally manage to rasp out.

Imani freezes. 'Uh?'

'I've had some time to think,' I say, surreptitiously wiping my hands against my thigh. 'And I don't think this plan is going to work.'

A shadow of disappointment flashes across Imani's face. My heart twists.

'Alright,' she says slowly, voice clipped. 'What's your plan then?'

She's misunderstood; gone ahead and mistaken me for a man rather than a doormat.

I swallow down the newly formed lump in my throat and force the words out. 'I don't have a plan.'

'Well then,' she says, and there's not a single trace of the lightness from earlier in her voice now. Not even a hint of that lovely smile. 'Let's stick with *my* one unless you can think of something—'

'I'm not going to go against my father.' I say it so quickly, the words come out as a garbled mess.

Imani stiffens and I watch as any remnant of goodwill she has towards me evaporates. 'Excuse me? What do you mean you're not going to go against him?' she asks. 'Because it sounds like you're saying t bring hat you want to . . . That you *want* . . .' She can't even herself to finish the sentence. Instead, she just frantically gestures between us, eyes wide with alarm.

'I don't want to marry you,' I say quickly, before her imagination can run wild. 'I mean, I'm not trying to offend you or anything, but—'

Imani waves an impatient hand. 'Don't worry about offending me, just explain yourself.'

I swallow. *Just explain yourself.* How do I explain twenty-odd years of neglect and the father-shaped hole in my life to her without sounding like a pathetic mess?

Imani's gaze is still fixed on me. 'Asher,' she says, voice low, steady. 'Please tell me you're not seriously considering going through with this.'

I rake a hand through my hair and sigh. 'It's not that simple.'

'It is,' she insists. 'You say no. You tell your father you're not going to let him use your life like some bargaining chip in a corporate deal. End of story.'

I let out a hollow laugh. 'Just because it's easy for you, doesn't—'

'It's *not* easy for me,' she snaps, eyes flashing. 'That's why I'm here trying to find a solution to this. I thought we were on the same page here.'

Her conviction burns so bright it almost hurts to look at her. She's armed with nothing but the unshakable belief that sheer willpower can rewrite the world around her. I envy it. I used to think I could be like that, too.

I lean back in my chair, my fingers drumming restlessly against my knee. 'It's different for me,' I say, somewhat defensively.

Imani's brow quirks slightly. She's clearly unconvinced. 'Different how?'

I hesitate. I could lie. Could feed her some vague excuse about the business, or my image, or my family's legacy. I could use the same buzzwords my father loves to throw around to get what he wants. But the truth is simmering just beneath the surface, and as much as I want to keep it buried, Imani's gaze is unflinching.

I owe her that at least, don't I? But how do I explain that I've spent my entire life working to earn my father's love and acceptance, and have always come up short? How do I explain that if I fail this, like I've seemingly failed every other task he's thrown my way, that this might just be it. That this is my last chance to prove I'm worth something to him? How do I explain that, when I don't even know *why* I want to prove it to him in the first place but that his approval is like a lifeline I've been chasing my entire life?

I decide to settle on a version of the truth.

'If I don't go ahead with this, my father will make my life very difficult.'

Imani snorts, crosses her arms tightly over her chest and fixes with me a cutting glare. 'Just to be clear,' she says slowly, 'you'd rather actually marry me, a complete stranger, than pretend we're toxic exes for a few weeks?'

When she puts it like that, I sound like an idiot.

'You make it sound simple.'

'It *is* simple,' she insists. 'We've already been over this, Asher.' She holds up her hand and starts counting off her fingers. 'We pretend we dated. We pretend it ended badly and we can't stand to be in the same room as each other. Our fathers panic, realise merging their companies through a doomed marriage is a PR nightmare, and they call it off. No wedding. No deal. *Simple*.'

I open my mouth to argue, but she barrels on, her words gaining momentum with every breath. She taps her dossier. 'I've already mapped it out: public appearances, controlled leaks to the right people, a few 'accidental' run-ins that end in disaster. We'll stage a few fights, throw in a couple of awkward photos, and BOOM.' She snaps her fingers. 'Engagement over. Merger derailed. Fathers suitably chagrined. I don't see what the problem is here.'

The thing is that her plan relies entirely on our fathers having an ounce of shame between them. And while *hers* might, mine most definitely does not. The Vouvalis name has survived scandals, lawsuits, even a bribery investigation. A few public arguments aren't going to scare my father off a multimillion-pound deal with Peregrine if that's what he's set his sights on.

'Come on, Asher,' she pleads with me. Her eyes are wide and she's looking at me like I'm her lifeline. 'Please,' she says quietly, the word threaded through with a kind of desperation that makes my chest ache. 'You can't actually want this. You can't honestly be okay with marrying someone you don't even know just because your father told you to do it.'

I don't answer her straight away. Mostly because I can't. But also, because if I open my mouth, I'll have to admit the truth – that I don't want this, but I don't see a way around it either. Imani doesn't understand what it's like to grow up with a father like mine. To spend years trying to earn something as small and fragile as approval, only to be met with disdain each time. To realise that love in the Vouvalis household is conditional on your usefulness.

'I just don't think it'll work,' I manage finally. 'The plan, I mean.'

'It will,' she says immediately. 'You just have to trust me.' She looks so sure of herself – shoulders squared, eyes clear, lips pressed into a determined line – that for a moment I want to believe her. I want to believe that a few staged arguments and some photo ops could actually undo decades of my father's ambition.

But I know better.

My father doesn't back down from bad press or public drama. He thrives on it. And when this plan of hers starts to crumble, as it inevitably will, he'll find a way to twist it into something useful for him. He always does.

Still, I can't bring myself to say any of that aloud. I know that if I tell her the truth, that she's wasting her time, that this plan is doomed from the start, I'll see that spark in her eyes snuff out, and I don't think I could stand it. Not when she's looking at me like I'm still capable of impressing her.

I make my decision then and there.

I'll go along with her plan, and when everything inevitably comes crashing down on us and we end up right where my father wants us, maybe she won't blame me. Maybe she'll think we both tried, but it just wasn't enough.

Maybe she won't hate me.

I exhale a slow, shaky breath and say, 'It's Lincoln.'

Imani jerks back slightly. 'Huh?'

'My middle name. And I'm twenty-eight. Birthday is 16th February.'

Realisation dawns on her face and I'm treated to her smile again. 'You're in, then? For real this time?'

I nod. 'I'm in.'

CHAPTER SIX

Imani

'So why did we break up?' I let myself sink into my armchair and tap a finger against my chin. 'It has to be because of something big, hence the lingering hate, but not too big, otherwise people will wonder why they never realised we were ever even together in the first place.'

'Something big . . .' Asher echoes cautiously.

'Cheating is too messy,' I say, ticking it off on a finger. 'And cliché. Plus people will ask who with and then we'll either have to enlist a third person into all of this, which would just complicate things even further, *or* we'd have to invent a whole fake person, and who has the time for that?'

He blinks and I worry that Asher might actually think I'm insane. 'Right. But is the "why" really all that important? I feel like we could just get away with being vague.'

I can't help but snort. 'The "why" is incredibly important, trust me. This needs to be as believable as possible, and if we don't have a genuine reason for why we're at each other's throats, it's all going to fall apart at the first hurdle.'

We've spent the last hour or so piecing together our fake history, and I'm pretty happy with what we've got so far. To my surprise, Asher's the one who gets us going with a backstory. He suggests we keep it simple and say we met at a party and hit it off. Ironic really, given how we did technically meet at a party all those years ago, though I doubt Asher remembers that. The moment was so fleeting, I barely even remember it, so I haven't brought it up.

The story we ultimately decide on is that we met at the party and then kept bumping into each other on campus, eventually going from strangers offering each other polite smiles when we passed in the corridor to lovers within the span of a semester. As for why we kept things quiet, we settle on the admittedly cliché, 'my father didn't want me to date while studying' on top of Asher's well-known reclusive nature for why nobody realised we were together. It's a little bit flimsy, I have to admit, and if my father hears about his apparent input in my dating life back then, he'll know it's a lie but I don't think anyone will prod *too* hard on this aspect of the con. Especially not after we start causing a scene and become the focal point for high-society gossip.

'How about we lean into the whole "I wasn't allowed to date while at university" thing?' I suggest. 'Maybe . . . Maybe you wanted to go public with us and I wasn't ready?'

Asher grimaces. 'My brothers would never believe that. If anything, it'd be the other way round.'

At the mention of his brothers, I can't help but marvel at how different he is compared to them. Not that I personally know Andreas and Teddy Vouvalis, but it's clear that the two of them thrive in the spotlight, particularly Teddy, while Asher actively shies away from it.

'And anyway,' Asher continues, 'won't the whole "wasn't allowed to date" story fall apart if one of your actual exes from back then makes a reappearance?'

'Oh, I actually didn't date at university. Not because I wasn't allowed,' I add quickly, noting the slight look of alarm that flashes over Asher's face. 'As long as I don't involve myself with anyone that could "put the company in jeopardy".' I roll my eyes as I mimic my father's voice, repeating the phrase I've heard too many times in my life to count. 'He couldn't care less who I date.'

The current situation notwithstanding.

'So, why didn't you?' Asher asks, then pauses for a second and lets his gaze flicker over me before he says, 'I can't imagine it was for lack of any interest.'

I can't help but laugh, especially when Asher suddenly clamps his mouth shut, looking very much like he wishes he hadn't said the last part aloud.

'Thank you?' I say.

The highest point of his cheekbones darkens slightly and I realise that he's blushing. He nods jerkily, looking for all the world like he wants the floor to open up and swallow him.

'People *were* interested,' I concede. 'But I guess I just wanted to focus on getting my degree. And—' I cut myself off and shake my head. Asher doesn't want or need to hear this.

'And what?' he says.

'It's nothing,' I say with a shrug.

Asher lifts a brow. He doesn't say anything but the silent *it's not nothing* rings loud between us.

I sigh and then reason that maybe this is something my fake ex should know about me. 'Do you ever feel like you don't have anything for yourself? It's like, our father's, right – sometimes it feels like every door I've ever had opened for me is only because of him. And don't get me wrong, I'm grateful, but . . .

Asher still hasn't said a word, but his expression has softened slightly in a way that makes my chest tighten unexpectedly.

'I guess I just wanted something that was mine,' I say, swallowing down a rapidly forming lump in my throat. 'Completely mine. My grades. My degree. My hard work. I wanted to prove, to myself more than anyone else, that I was actually intelligent and capable and not just another trust fund baby floating through life on my last name. I think I just needed to prove that I could do something on my own. I wanted to earn something, for once. Dating would've been a distraction,' I finish with a shrug.

Asher leans back slightly. His deep brown eyes are locked on me and I can't look away. 'I get it,' he says after a moment, and from the way he's looking at me, I can tell he truly does.

It shouldn't surprise me that Asher of all people understands me like this – we do come from similar backgrounds after all – but it does. The only other person I've shared these anxieties with is Sloane, and as sympathetic as she is, she just doesn't understand why being reduced to my family name bothers me so much. And how could she? Although she's a Chavan and that comes with its own set of unique headaches, she's built something for herself outside of the family name.

I've not been so lucky – though not for the lack of trying.

But Asher? He's a Vouvalis and I have no doubt in my mind that it comes with its own set of insecurities, especially with a father like Georgios.

'Anyway.' I clear my throat and force a bright grin onto my face. 'My not-so-tragic backstory isn't important here.'

For the briefest of moments, his expression flickers with an emotion I can't quite place, and it's gone so quickly I wonder if I imagined it.

'What *is* important,' I continue, 'is figuring out *our* backstory. Why'd we break up?'

'Let's keep it simple,' Asher says. 'We'll say that one of us took the relationship more seriously than the other. Maybe I saw it as just a bit of fun and you were—'

'Imagining myself in a wedding dress from day one?' I snort. 'It's a bit of a stretch, but I guess it *was* nearly ten years ago now. Nineteen-year-old me probably was a little more dramatic than I am these days.' I nod, more to myself than anything else, and reach for my pen and notebook to hurriedly scrawl this new direction down. 'Okay, yeah. I think that'll work. We'll say I wanted more, some real commitment, and you were just in it for a good time for a couple of months.'

Asher lets out a surprisingly melodious burst of laughter. 'Sorry,' he says, catching the curious look I shoot him. 'It's just . . .' He gestures vaguely at me, his cheeks beginning to flush a muted rose. 'The idea of me not wanting more with you is kind of ridiculous.'

My pen stills mid-scribble.

Asher seems to realise, belatedly, what he's just said and his eyes go comically wide. 'I just mean, well, look at you, I would've had to have been stupid to . . .' He winces, shakes his head and starts again. 'You know what? Nineteen-year-old me probably *would've* been dumb enough to let you go. So, yeah. I suppose it's entirely plausible.'

The words tumble out in a tangled rush and by the time he's finished, his cheeks are a dark red. I'm fairly certain mine aren't far behind.

'Oh,' I manage to cough out. 'Right. Well. That's good? I think?'

Asher clears his throat. I clear mine. The air between us feels thick and for some reason I find myself staring at his hands as his long fingers fidget with the edge of a sheet of paper.

'Anyway,' he says stiffly. 'It works. You wanted something serious. I didn't. We broke up.'

I nod slowly, forcing myself to move past the heat still crawling up the back of my neck. 'Okay then. Let's go with that.'

Asher's gaze roves over me. He catches my eye and then glances away just as quickly, as if direct eye contact might make both of us suddenly combust on the spot. As if he's just looking for something, *anything,* to do he reaches for the bottle of sparkling water on the table, then seems to remember that he hates sparkling water, and sets it back down. The sequence of events betrays him far more than the persistent blush on his cheeks ever could.

He's flustered, and it's weirdly endearing.

I shake my head suddenly. Not sure where that thought came from. *Focus, Imani. Focus.*

'Okay, next,' I say brusquely. 'Who ended things?'

'You,' he says immediately.

I frown. 'Me?'

'Yeah.' Some of the earlier awkwardness has melted off him now as he rests his elbows on his knees and leans in slightly. 'If our story is that you wanted commitment and I didn't, then you would'vc walked away. No?'

I see what he's getting at, but . . .'Wouldn't it be more dramatic if you dumped me? That way the bitterness makes sense on both sides. If I dumped you, I wouldn't be this mad all these years later, would I? I'd be relieved that I dodged a bullet. This way, I'm angry because you couldn't commit and yet you're the one who ended things, and you're mad because you're being made out to be the bad guy.'

Asher looks at me like I'm insane. 'No one,' he says, huffing out a quiet laugh, 'would buy that I ended things with you.'

My breath stalls for half a second. 'You're giving me too much credit,' I say weakly. 'I can assure you; I've been dumped plenty of times in my life.'

Well, that's not strictly true. Now that I'm hurriedly combing through my dating history, it hits me that I've always been the dumper, never the dumpee.

Asher shakes his head, and there's a faint, slightly incredulous smile tugging at the corner of his mouth as he does so. 'You've never been dumped.'

I scoff and, even though I'm fully aware he's right, I'm ready to deny it on principle. 'You don't know that.'

'I do,' he says simply. 'You're . . .' He trails off, clearly searching for the right word. His gaze drifts over my face for a beat too long. 'You're not the type of person people walk away from.'

I swallow and force myself to hold his eye. 'And what about you?'

Asher falters ever so slightly. 'What about me?'

'Why would I walk away from you?' Admittedly I know very little about Asher but, on the surface at least, he seems like a good guy. Smart, handsome, kind. Why would I walk?

He lets out a hollow laugh. 'How much time do you have?'

I frown. I don't like that. There's something about the way he says it; the way his mouth tightens and he stiffens ever so slightly, like he's bracing for impact. Like he's used to people agreeing with him when he says self-deprecating things like that.

No, I don't like it one bit.

I lean forward, mirroring the movement he'd done moments earlier. 'Why,' I repeat, softer this time. 'Why would I have walked away from you?'

He stills for a moment and when he finally lifts his eyes to mine again, they're darker than before. Sadder, too. He exhales, long and slow, and I think I can pinpoint the exact moment he decides to abandon whatever lie was about to come out of his mouth and to give me something honest instead.

'I just mean,' he says quietly, 'if we did actually date, I wouldn't have expected someone like you to stay.'

'And someone like me is?'

He looks at me, *really* looks this time, and it shouldn't feel like a touch, but somehow it does. 'You're bright – the kind of person who lights up a room,' he says finally. 'And determined. And alive in a way that I'm just not.' The corner of his mouth twitches, but it isn't a smile. 'You fill space while I actively avoid it. You would've got bored of waiting for me to catch up.'

I don't know what to say to that, so I don't say anything. I just sit there, staring at him, as the words hang between us.

Bright.

Determined.

Alive in a way I'm not.

Asher and I barely know each other so the words shouldn't land the way they do. They shouldn't make my throat tighten or my chest pull in an uncomfortable, unexpected way. But there's something in his voice that's too soft, too apologetic, too resigned, which makes me want to reach across the table and shake him.

Or hug him.

Maybe both.

Because the way he sees himself is bleak, wrong – even I can tell him that from just our limited time together – and deeply, deeply unfair.

I don't know how to respond, not without crossing a line that feels forbidden for two people who are just barely acquaintances, so I pivot towards the only thing that feels safe. Humour.

'You know,' I say lightly, leaning back into my chair as if he hasn't just essentially cracked open his ribcage and shared the most vulnerable part of himself, 'if you keep talking like that, no one is ever going to believe we're exes.'

His brows pull together. 'Huh?'

'We're meant to hate each other,' I remind him. 'And here you are complimenting me every five minutes.' I pull an overly dramatic faux-disapproving look. 'Not very believable if you ask me.'

A startled laugh escapes him and the space between us seems to soften slightly. Things suddenly feel noticeably less heavy.

'Sorry,' he says, though he doesn't sound even remotely apologetic. 'I'll work on being less complimentary, I guess?'

'Please do,' I say. 'Because right now, no one's going to buy the whole *bitter exes* thing.' In fact, if someone were watching us right now, they might think we were on a first date. 'Actually, I'm starting to think we have a bigger problem.'

Asher cocks his head to the side.

I narrow my eyes in mock seriousness and wag my pen in his face. 'I'm not entirely convinced you even have the capacity to be hateful.'

Whatever he was expecting me to say, it definitely wasn't that. Several emotions flit over his face, before settling on bemusement. 'I think I'll be alright.'

I hum in disagreement. 'I'm not sure. And if you can't be convincingly awful to me in front of everyone, then our whole plan collapses. Maybe we should practise. Go ahead.' I fold my arms and nod at him. 'Say something mean.'

Asher just stares at me, his lips parted slightly in disbelief. It's kind of adorable if I'm being honest.

I tap my pen against my notebook. 'Any day now.'

'This is ridiculous,' he mutters.

'It's also necessary,' I counter. 'Come on. Give me one insult. Just a tiny one. I believe in you.'

'I'm not going to insult you.'

'But I've given you permission! Just do it. I promise I won't cry.'

'No,' he says flatly.

I pretend to gasp. 'There! See? *That* tone was perfect. Hold onto it and try again. That's the kind of hostility we need.'

'That wasn't hostility.'

'It was absolutely hostility.'

'It was exasperation.'

'Well, exasperation counts,' I say, feeling a little exasperated myself. 'We can make exasperation work.'

He looks at me with a mix of disbelief and something else

I can't name and then drags a hand down his face. It's a long-suffering motion that ends with him staring at me through his fingers. 'Imani.'

The way he says my name, like he's half pleading, half desperately trying not to laugh, makes my stomach flutter.

I straighten in my chair, as if the movement might literally shove the feeling back down to wherever it came from.

'Yes?' I manage. I'm aiming for breezy and unbothered but can concede I probably land a little closer to breathless.

He drops his hand from his face and looks at me with a tired kind of fondness that makes the flutter intensify tenfold. 'You're impossible.'

'Better,' I say, with a grin. 'Now we're getting somewhere.'

'You're not going to let this go, are you?'

'Absolutely not.'

A sigh escapes him. It's one of those long, extremely resigned ones that suggests he's questioning every single decision he's ever made that's led him to this exact moment. Then he shifts in his chair, squares his shoulders, and looks directly at me as if he's preparing for something utterly monumental.

'Fine,' he says quietly. 'If you insist.'

I brace myself. 'Do it.'

His entire demeanour changes. Gone is the slightly shy, bashful-looking man I was staring at before. Now he looks cold and stern, and I think I could genuinely believe that he hates me.

I realise, very quickly, that I don't like that, but I don't have time to dwell on it.

'Imani,' he begins, solemn as a priest. 'Your handwriting . . .'

I blink. 'My handwriting, what?'

He hesitates for what I'm sure has to be dramatic effect, then delivers the blow.

' . . . is atrocious.'

For a full second I can only stare at him.

Then another second passes.

Then a third.

I glance down at my notebook and take in the admittedly chaotic mixture of loops, half-formed letters, and the slant that changes direction three times a sentence. Hmm. Okay. Perhaps he has a point.

I look back up at him and a laugh bursts out of me.

Asher blinks, like he's startled by the sound, but then the corners of his mouth soften and he's fighting back a bark of laughter of his own.

'Oh my God,' I say between laughs. 'That was your big insult? My handwriting?'

'It's messy,' Asher says defensively.

'It's perfectly legible!'

'Just about. I've seen doctors with neater handwriting than that.'

'Rude,' I sniff.

Asher's answering grin is the kind of grin that steals your breath away. I much prefer it to the sad look in his eyes from earlier.

'Are you still worried we won't be able to pull it off?' he asks.

For a second, I completely forget what he's talking about. I'm still dazzled by the brightness of his smile, but then I remember our plan and quickly shake some sense into myself.

'I mean, my handwriting is pretty low down on the insult ladder if I'm being honest,' I say. 'But it was something. And I can work with something.'

He looks relieved and I can't tell whether it's because I think our plan has a chance of success, or if he's just happy I'm not going to put him on the spot and make him insult me again.

'Next up,' I say, reaching for my laptop so I can pull up my calendar. 'We need to find an event to make our debut. Somewhere with lots of witnesses. Lots of very *chatty* witnesses,' I add.

Not for the first time, Asher looks like he's very much regretting agreeing to all of this. 'Do you have anything in mind?'

I can't help but grin. 'I'm sure we'll find something.'

CHAPTER SEVEN

Imani

'You are going to absolutely destroy that manicure if you don't stop.'

I freeze, caught with the corner of my thumb wedged between my teeth, and shoot Sloane a guilty grimace. She's right, of course. If I keep this up, my nails are on course to become a swollen, bloody mess before we've even arrived.

'You good?' Sloane asks, her gaze sliding over to me. She's sat opposite me in the car, her legs resting on the empty seat beside me to give her toes some reprieve from the silver heels she's wearing.

'Peachy,' I lie. I pull my hand out of my mouth and shove it under my butt in an attempt to stop myself from chewing my fingers raw. I've attended countless galas over the years, but I don't think I've ever been as nervous about one as I am tonight.

Sloane rolls her eyes and whacks my leg with her clutch.

'Ow.'

'Stop stressing,' she says, expertly ignoring the daggers I'm currently shooting at her. 'Everything's going to be fine.'

'That's easy for you to say,' I grumble. 'You're not the one who's relying on tonight to kickstart her master plan to avoid getting bloody *married* to a complete stranger.'

'Well,' Sloane says with a slight smirk, 'he's not a *complete* stranger. Not anymore. At least you know each other now.'

Technically, she's right. Although *know* is doing a lot of heavy lifting here. Asher and I *know* each other the way you might *know* your favourite celebrity in little tidbits of banal information or the kind of safe, dull facts you might learn about a sportsperson from a trading card game.

Asher Lincoln Vouvalis
28 years old; DOB 16.02.1997
Likes: rugby
Dislikes: sparkling water, and being
forced to insult someone on the spot
Fun fact: received a First in International
Relations at university

And he knows about the same level of information when it comes to me. It's nothing real. Nothing substantial. Though, for the purposes of our little con, I suppose it'll have to do.

It does make me nervous though. To be putting this much trust and faith into someone I've spent one afternoon with and know exactly one one-sided sheet of A4 paper about.

Still, I reason with myself, as our car begins to slow, he's putting the same amount of trust in me with equally little information.

Tonight will be the first true test of whether my stupid plan (thank you, Sloane) actually has any legs.

After Asher and I firmed up our fake history, we spent the rest of our evening combing through the social calendar to find an upcoming event the two of us could plausibly be attending at the same time. It didn't take long for us to find tonight's event: a charity gala raising money and awareness for the growing homelessness in our city.

Admittedly, it feels oxymoronic for an event packed with celebrities and socialites, dressed head to toe in gowns and suits that could pay the average Londoner's rent for half a year, to be fundraising for homelessness, but I've become almost numb to the theatrics of my social circle.

My father learned very early on in his career that showing face at these events and being generous with the number on the cheque he hands over at the end of the night is one of the easiest ways to get and maintain friends in high places. My parents still attend the occasional event throughout the year, but I've been going in their place to the vast majority since I graduated. If this were any other night, I'd be fine. After all these years, I know the drill:

Smile for the cameras.

Do the rounds.

Be seen with a few prominent faces – namely, the children of other tycoons in the same orbit as my father.

And make sure to sign away a hefty donation on behalf of Peregrine Airways before the night is over.

It sounds like fun, but it's become a chore. Aside from Sloane, there aren't many regular attendees of these events that I actually enjoy being around. The supposed charity of it all is nothing but an afterthought and instead the evening is filled with two-faced schmoozing, drunken deals and catty gossiping. While I normally hate it, I'm relying on the vapidness of it all tonight. Asher will be in attendance, and it's time to start sowing the seeds of a disastrous failed attempt at love all those years ago.

I huff out a deep breath and sink into my seat, wishing for a moment that it would suck me into a vortex and spit me out into a universe where I mean more than a bottom line or profit margin to my father.

'You know you don't have to do this,' Sloane says.

'Do you have an alternative plan?' I grumble.

Sloane purses her lips and stays mute.

'Exactly,' I sigh. 'For better or for worse, this is the plan.'

Right now, it's starting to feel like the latter. Our car slows to a complete stop and I take another deep breath.

Showtime.

An attendant pulls open the door and Sloane slinks out first, her silver dress glittering immediately with the sudden onslaught of blinking bulbs. Without a doubt, she'll be gracing the top of the best-dressed lists that'll be published in the morning. I might stand a chance of making an appearance too, if the response from the waiting paparazzi as I exit our car is anything to go by. I let a well-practised and suitably demure smile take over my face as I follow Sloane up the marble steps and into the hotel foyer.

Sloane waits for me at the entrance next to the board with the seating arrangements for the night, gives me what I think is supposed to be an encouraging grin but comes out more like a grimace, and then leans into my side as we step into the grand ballroom.

As much as I've come to loathe these events, I can't help but have a kind of reluctant appreciation for the work the behind-the-scenes staff do that goes into decorating them, because the hotel ballroom – already a fairly impressive space on a daily basis – is nothing short of breathtaking. There are chandeliers overhead dripping with crystals, their light casting a soft, warm glow across the room. The marble floors are gleaming underneath a sea of designer shoes, and the walls are lined with lush greenery with ivy spilling out from gold-framed trellises. It's beautiful.

Sloane and I cut across the floor as we look for our table, which are all adorned in white linen and feature centrepieces of towering roses and delicate orchids, every single petal and stem arranged in intricate patterns, which have turned them into floral works of art. There's a string quartet playing at the furthest end of the room, the soft, lilting music just barely rising above the collective hum of conversation.

Guests are scattered in clusters, some sat at their tables, others milling around, greeting friends with loud, obnoxious laughter or sipping champagne from thin, crystal flutes. As we move through the sea of socialites and celebrities, I can't help but overhear snippets of the same conversations over and over again – the beginnings of business deals being made over hors d'oeuvres, thinly veiled critiques about the latest scandals, and promises of 'oh we must catch up properly soon' that feel more like formalities than genuine attempts at rekindling with an old friend.

We're a predictable bunch.

'We're at table eleven,' Sloane reminds me as we move through the crowd. She's scanning each of the little gilded numbers set into the base of each floral arrangement as we pass by. 'Ah. There.' She nudges me with her elbow. 'Front and centre. Your father must be feeling generous tonight.'

I pull a face. 'My father is always feeling generous when there's a camera within a five-mile radius.'

Sloane snorts and I feel a twinge of envy. I wish I could mimic her ease right now. She's gliding across the marble like she owns the place; meanwhile every muscle in my body feels pulled tight and my pulse is like my own personal drumbeat in my ears.

It's silly, I know. Nothing has even happened yet, and I haven't even seen Asher, but knowing that he's on his way and that the next hour or so will determine whether this entire scheme is a masterstroke or will end in a humiliating public disaster is enough to make my stomach churn.

We pass by about twenty people I recognise as we make our way to our table. That's twenty raised hands, clipped smiles, nods of the head and promises to come find them again later in the evening. But I don't see him.

Panic swells in my chest.

He's not here.

Asher isn't here.

My mind starts racing. He must have had second thoughts and reneged on the plan. *Again.*

And why wouldn't he? The plan is, as Sloane has kindly reminded me about a million times since I first told her, patently ridiculous. Of course he'd get cold feet. Of course he'd prefer not to rile up his father because of me, a veritable stranger. Of course he—

'Ow!' I whimper for the second time tonight, yanking my arm away from Sloane before she can pinch it again. 'Are you twelve years old?'

'Relax,' Sloane hisses back through a fake but remarkably believable smile. She is truly a pro. 'You look like you're about to throw up.'

I just might.

'There's still plenty of time,' Sloane continues as she slows to a halt beside a table with two conspicuously empty seats. It's remarkable how easily she can read me and decipher what's currently stressing me out. 'A lot of people aren't here yet. So take a deep breath and get your shit together. It's show time.'

And show time it is. I barely have the chance to school my expression into one of practised ease and elegance before a tornado of silver and blue suddenly appears in front of me. It's only thanks to years and years of conditioning to be the perfect daughter, the perfect representative of Malcolm Davies and Peregrine Airways, which stops me from grimacing.

'Sloane! Imani! I was sure they'd made a mistake with the seating assignments, but here you are. Here you *both* are!'

Emmeline Pittock, youngest daughter of the Earl of Camberley, beams at both of us, bright blue eyes wide and searching. Searching for what? Something juicy.

I chance a sideways glance at Sloane, whose smile has become slightly manic. We have no concrete proof, but we're fairly confident that Emmy is the one behind the current most popular anonymous Instagram gossip page going around our circle. We usually do our best to avoid her at events like this; Sloane still hasn't quite forgiven Emmy for posting leaked photos of her at a shoot where the make-up artist had no experience with darker skinned women and left Sloane looking a regrettably ashy grey sort of colour. If she had her way, we'd not be within eyesight of Emmy, but for tonight being close to Emmy is a must.

'Emmy,' I say smoothly through a gritted grin. 'How lovely to see you.' I descend into the empty seat next to hers. Emmy follows suit and Sloane drops down beside me with barely a nod in Emmy's direction. 'How have you been?'

'Oh just wonderful, wonderful, darling,' Emmy says absentmindedly. She doesn't return the pleasantry and ask how I'm doing. Instead, she leans over me and bats her doe-like eyelashes at Sloane. 'Did I hear correctly that you've got a *veryyyyy* special magazine cover coming soon?'

Sloane's manic smile widens. 'I'm sure I have no idea what you're talking about.'

Emmy's own smile gets a little bigger too, but it doesn't reach her eyes. She shimmies a little closer towards Sloane.

I'm fairly certain that if it were socially acceptable to simply shove me out of the way and steal my seat, she would. As it stands, she has to settle for awkwardly leaning over me.

It's abundantly clear that Emmy has no interest in me. I should be offended, but I suppose I can't blame her. I'm notoriously low drama and she's never been able to mine me for gossip like she does everyone else, so she's learned not to waste any time with me and instead go for Sloane.

That's all about to change tonight.

While Emmy continues to probe Sloane about a certain coveted cover spot (with no success), I scan the room again. The night is officially in full swing. Surely Asher must be here by now. I'm itching to reach for my phone in my clutch to see if he's left me an apologetic message, but Emmy is too close and even if Sloane is currently taking all her attention, I can't chance her eagle-eye reading something she shouldn't.

I scan the room again, ready to call it quits and accept the fact that I've effectively been stood up, and then I spot him.

Dressed in a tailored navy suit that fits as if it was crafted just for him, he enters the room a few steps behind his brother, Teddy, and who I have to assume is Teddy's date for the evening. The cut of Asher's jacket highlights broad shoulders, and tapers down to show off a trim waist. The crisp white shirt beneath it is almost blinding against the darkness of the suit, the only pop of colour being the flash of a dark tie resting against his chest.

His dark curls are tousled and fall slightly across his forehead in an effortless kind of way that makes my pulse jump.

I've never denied the fact that Asher is handsome, but tonight he looks impossibly good, like he's sauntered straight out of the pages of a magazine.

He suddenly looks over in my direction as if he can feel the heat from my gaze boring into him. For a moment our eyes lock and everything around me seems to slow down. Emmy non-stop gossiping beside me, the chattering guests, the clinking of glasses, the string quartet still playing softly in the background . . . all of it blurs into the faintest hum.

Then, without missing a beat, his lips curl into a small, warm smile like he's relieved to see me. It's the kind of smile that makes you feel like you're the only one in the room. It's a soft, reassuring thing and it makes my heart do a quick flip in my chest.

I force myself to look away before I become an absolute mess of nerves, but I swear I can still feel the warmth of his smile lingering in the space between us.

I inhale slowly, trying to remind myself why I'm here. It's time to set this plan into motion.

I clear my throat and say, as obnoxiously loud as I can make it, 'Ugh.'

The effect is instantaneous. As if she's got some kind of preternatural affinity for sensing juicy gossip, Emmy pauses mid-sentence and turns her head ever so slightly in my direction.

'What was that?' she asks.

I pretend to look flustered and wave a frantic hand in front of my face. 'Oh, it's—It's nothing.' I let slip another glance in Asher's direction and, yep, Emmy follows my gaze, her curious blue eyes landing on Asher.

She pulls away from Sloane without a second thought and finally looks at me with a smidge of interest.

'Isn't that Asher Vouvalis?'

'Is it?' I squeak. 'I wouldn't know.'

I think I've got her.

Emmy sidles up as close to me as she can physically get without invading the last inch of personal space I have left. 'He doesn't usually come to things like this, does he?'

She's clearly probing, trying to see what I'll reveal before she has to ask outright. Luckily for her, I've got extremely loose lips tonight.

'And thank God for that.' I pull a face and Emmy suddenly looks like Christmas has come early.

'What do you mean?' Emmy asks, abandoning any pretence of giving me space. She drops her voice low and is practically in my lap at this point. 'I didn't know you two were acquainted.'

'We're not,' I say hastily. 'I mean, we're not anymore . . .'

Emmy looks like she's about to burst. 'Anymore?' she purrs. 'Does that mean—'

'Look,' I say quietly. Not that volume matters here. If all goes to plan, everyone will be aware of my supposed past with Asher within the next twenty-four hours. 'I didn't want to make a big deal out of it, and you know, it's been years so I should really be over it by now . . .' I trail off and make a show of glancing around our vicinity, checking that nobody is listening in, and then I turn back to Emmy. 'Asher and I dated a while back.'

Emmy's thin brows disappear into her silvery blonde hairline. 'You did not.' The unsaid *I would've known* hangs between us.

'We did. Back at university.'

She frowns and I can practically see her mind kicking into overdrive as she combs through years of memories and gossip, trying to remember if Imani Davies and Asher Vouvalis even knew each other nearly a decade ago, let alone dated. 'Really?' she sounds doubtful and I bite back a wince. I'm going to have to up my game.

'You were a year or two above us,' I remind her quickly. Not that something as small as being a few years older would have stopped Emmy from finding out. The girl is a bloodhound when it comes to gossip. 'You'd probably already graduated by the time we got serious. And, well, we wanted to keep things low key. My father didn't want me dating before I got my degree, and you know Asher's father . . .' I say with a shrug, hoping Georgios Vouvalis' general reputation for being a prick will help me out here.

It seems to do the trick because, after a beat of hesitation, Emmy nods and I swallow down a sigh of relief.

'So, what happened?' she asks.

I allow a look of intense displeasure to spread over my face. 'Let's just say it didn't end well.'

Emmy's eyes widen and it's obvious she's fighting off a grin. 'Wow.'

I hum in agreement. 'This is the first time I've seen him in years. You would have thought the hurt would have died down by now but . . .' I trail off again, pointedly leaving Emmy the chance to fill in the gaps with all the potential hurt Asher might have caused me.

She gives me a sympathetic pat on the arm. 'Wounds like that never really heal,' she says sagely.

A burst of satisfaction shoots through me. There. It's done. Without a doubt, Emmy will have let just about everyone who's anyone know all about my alleged past with Asher by the end of the evening.

'You're right,' I say, equally serious. 'But as long as we don't cross paths, I'll be fine. If you could,' I pretend to glance around nervously, 'if you could keep this between us? I don't really like my business being out there and—'

'Your secret is safe with me,' Emmy says solemnly.

I have to hand it to the girl – she's a phenomenal liar. I almost believe her.

'Thank you,' I say breathlessly. Now that Emmy has decided I'm not a useless lump of non-gossipy trash, she brings me into the fold. I spend the rest of the evening listening as she shares information about just about everyone on the scene. I'm barely paying attention as she reveals how Calliope Locke is currently being sued by no fewer than three different designers for failing to pay for outfits loaned for events or how Hugo Frillingsworth was caught in a compromising position with a waitress just two weeks before his wedding to *the* Helena Montswill. Sloane and I aside, everyone else is hanging onto every word, desperate for more gossip about our peers. Instead, my focus is on Asher's table. He's sat beside Teddy and his date, looking like he'd rather be anywhere but here.

He looks up suddenly and I quickly look away, not wanting to get caught staring by Emmy. We can't really keep up the whole 'we hate each other' lie if she catches us grinning at each other across the room every five minutes, can we?

I manage to refocus on Emmy, Sloane and the rest of the table for less than two minutes before I find my attention waning. There are only so many times I can hear Emmy say, 'Well, *I* heard . . .' before my brain short-circuits. I glance back over in Asher's direction and discover, with a jolt that hits straight in my heart, that he's not at the table anymore.

I scan the room in a panic, and I'm not sure what to make of the fact that I can already pick Asher out in a sea of faces with ease. He's leaning against the bar, waiting to be served.

I'm scraping my chair back and pushing myself away from the table before I even have the chance to properly think about what I'm doing.

'Imani?' Sloane calls after me, obviously startled by my sudden movement.

'Bathroom,' I lie.

Once I'm close enough to the door that leads to the restrooms, I glance over my shoulder and heave a sigh of relief when I realise that no one from my table has kept their eye on me. I wait a second or two, checking to see if Emmy will turn her head in my direction – thankfully, she does not thanks to Sloane who is currently distracting her – then deviate from the bathroom route and instead make my way towards the bar, slipping in between increasingly tipsy attendees until I'm about an arm's length away from Asher.

He doesn't notice me at first, and I take the opportunity to appreciate him close up. It's the little details that catch my attention from this close, like the faintest line running across his right cheekbone, a soft scar possibly from some childhood mischief. The way his dark hair falls just above his brows, tousled yet somehow perfect, as if all he did before leaving his home tonight was run a careless hand through it. And speaking of hands …

My eyes wander down and I can't help but notice the veins in his hands curling underneath his warm brown skin as he taps nervously against the bar top. The way the muscle in his wrist flexes slightly every time his fingers drum against the polished wood is almost hypnotic, and I wonder if he even realises what he's doing.

Asher looks over in my direction, and for a split second, it feels like the world has slowed down again. His shoulders loosen, the tension that had been tightening his posture evaporating in an instant. The edge of his mouth curls up into a smile, soft and genuine. He doesn't look away. I think his smile deepens.

'Imani.' He says my name like a lifeline and like he's genuinely relieved to see me. His eyes soften and I suddenly feel very exposed. 'You look beautiful.'

The words hit me like a bolt of electricity. I feel my face heat up almost embarrassingly fast. Despite how often I receive compliments, there's something about the way Asher keeps complimenting me that has me feeling slightly weak at the knees. It feels different coming from him. He's being sincere and it's clear it's not just a random comment or idle flattery in an attempt to get something from me.

I glance away. 'You're not so bad yourself.' I'm trying to keep it cool and light but my voice betrays me. I sound too soft and too flustered.

Asher chuckles and I reflexively look back up. The warmth from his smile hasn't faded a bit. 'Should we be talking like this?'

'No,' I admit sheepishly. 'I wasn't sure if you were going to show up.'

He winces. 'I know it took me a while to get on board with this, but I wouldn't do that to you.' For some reason, when he says that, I know he means it.

I wave down the bartender and order a cocktail in an attempt to distract myself and refocus on the mission at hand. 'I know. I mean, *now* I know. Anyway, I just wanted to say thanks. For coming, I mean.' I'm rambling. *Why am I rambling?*

The bartender reappears with perfect timing and slides my glass across the counter. I pick up the glass and turn, intending on disappearing back into the crowd and back to my table, when someone brushes past me a little too forcefully. I let out a shocked gasp as the collision pushes me forward, liquid sloshing dangerously close to the rim of my glass.

Before disaster can strike and destroy this dress, Asher's hand finds my waist while his other hand steadies the glass in mine. My breath catches.

'Easy,' he murmurs.

I blink up at him, suddenly hyperaware of how near he is. The faintest trace of his cologne invades my senses. I want to lean in closer and press myself into his scent. It's like a perfume no bottle could ever hold. And it's absolutely unfair how good he smells.

'I'm fine,' I whisper, lying to both myself and him. Because I'm not fine. Not with his hand still lingering against my waist, thumb absently tracing circles against my curves. Not with my entire world narrowing down to the heat of his palm and the impossible calm of his eyes.

'Imani . . .'

That voice.

Fuck.

'Since you're already in the queue, could you get me a—' Emmy cuts herself off, her eyes immediately darting between Asher and me.

I fumble to extract myself from Asher's hold, trying desperately not to think about how much I already miss his touch, and get as far away from him as I can manage. Which isn't very far, considering how many people are clamouring around waiting for drinks. Asher frowns at me, looking remarkably like a chastised puppy. But I don't have time to explain.

Emmy cocks her head to the side, brows furrowed as she processes what she's just seen. It's completely at odds with what I've just told her and my heart skips a beat or two under the weight of her stare.

Oh God.

I've ruined everything before we could even get started, haven't I?

I need to do something to salvage the mess I've made of this stupid, stupid plan.

'Imani? I thought . . .' Emmy begins.

When I get home tonight, instead of sleeping I'm going to spend every last waking minute replaying this scene in my head, cringing into my pillow until I combust.

But right now, caught mid-lie with Emmy staring at me, panic takes the wheel. My pulse spikes, my brain short-circuits, and before I can talk myself out of it . . .

The glass in my hand tips forward and I watch in what feels like slow motion as the amber liquid splashes down the front of Asher's perfectly pressed shirt. Gasps ripple through the people nearby. Emmy's mouth goes slack, her eyes wide.

Asher freezes, blinking down at the dripping mess on his chest. A small part of me, the remaining whisper of logic I still have, reminds me that this was *technically* the plan, but guilt still churns unpleasantly in my stomach.

Everyone in the vicinity is staring at us, waiting for either me or Asher to make the next move. I take a deep breath. No turning back now, I suppose. I may as well go all the way.

'I thought I told you I never wanted to see you again?' My voice comes out as a hiss and I make sure to project loud enough to carry over the music and slice right through the sound of any conversation.

More heads turn.

Heat scorches my cheeks.

Mortified is not a strong enough word for what I'm feeling right now.

Asher's eyes snap to mine and for half a heartbeat I think I've broken him. Then the warmth from earlier disappears, his jaw tightens, and he steps into the role like he was born for it.

'You think I wanted to bump into you?' His words are like glass and his voice drips with disdain. 'Trust me, Imani, the last thing I want is to waste another second on you.'

The words hit harder than they should and even though I know they're not real, my chest still squeezes painfully.

He tosses a look of pure disgust my way and then storms off into the crowd. The people around us start to murmur and I want to sink into the floor.

'Imani!' Emmy's hand lands on my arm, her eyes wide with concern. 'Oh my *God*, are you okay? What was *that*?'

I force my lips into a trembling smile. 'I'm fine. It's fine. Everything's fine. *Really*.'

But it's not fine. Not even close. My heart is simultaneously racing *and* feels like it's been caved in.

Emmy pulls me into a comforting hug, speaking a hundred miles a minute, but I'm not paying attention. I can still feel the ghost of Asher's warmth against my waist even as the sting of his words echoes in my head.

It was fake, I remind myself as Emmy guides me back towards our table. *An act. It wasn't real.*

So why do I hate myself for the look on his face when I threw that drink?

CHAPTER EIGHT

Asher

It feels like every single pair of eyes in the room are on me and I can't blame them.

The last thirty seconds are playing on a loop in my mind. One moment, Imani is in my arms, her soft curves pressed against me as I steady her and keep her from falling. The next, her drink – a pink, fruity concoction – is being splashed over my front and she's staring at me like I'm a piece of gum on the bottom of her shoe.

It wasn't real, I remind myself as I purposely avoid Teddy's questioning gaze and dip through a set of double doors that lead me to the restrooms. It was just an act. This is what we wanted to happen. This was the plan.

Sort of.

Really, the plan was to just start sowing the seeds of a failed relationship and a lingering bitterness that's only grown over the last ten years. I wasn't expecting to have to put it into action so soon. And I definitely wasn't expecting to feel so guilty when push came to shove.

I open the bathroom door and step inside. It's blissfully empty, so I can drop the façade of looking furious and irritated. I lean against the basin and assess the damage in the mirror. My shirt is damp, there's a light pink stain blossoming on the front of it, and I smell vaguely of peach and something sickly sweet.

As I drag a paper towel across the sticky mess on my chest, accomplishing nothing except spreading it further, I wonder if this whole thing is finally about to blow up in my face. I've agreed to go along with Imani's plan under the belief that, ultimately, my father won't care about some more bad press but I don't think it really occurred to me just how committed Imani would be to seeing this through.

I thought at most we'd shoot each other glares from across the room and maybe whisper thinly veiled insults about each other. But Imani does everything wholeheartedly, including this.

The memory of her lips parting in surprise as I snapped back at her forces itself into the forefront of my mind, and that sharp sensation of guilt stabbing my stomach rears its ugly head again.

Trust me, Imani, the last thing I want is to waste another second on you.

Logically, I know that she's well aware that I didn't mean it and that it was all part of the act. But I can't get the image of her face crumpling out of my mind. I'm starting to wonder if maybe I played the villain role a little too well. Which is technically a good thing, I remind myself over and over again. It's good that I looked like a complete ass. It's good that it looks like Imani hates me with every fibre of her being. It's even better that everyone saw and that they're all whispering about us already.

The more it seems like we're on the same page and I'm committed to this plan, the less likely it is she'll hate my guts when it inevitably falls through.

The door to the restroom swings open and I barely have the chance to force an irritated look back onto my face before Teddy comes marching in. He closes the door behind him, leans against it so no one can follow him, and then stares questioningly at me, arms folded over his chest.

'Pretty sure that's a fire hazard,' I murmur, still dabbing at my shirt with the useless paper towel in an incredibly see-through attempt to avoid looking at him and having to answer the mountain of questions I'm sure he has for me.

'Pretty sure you've lost your goddamn mind,' Teddy quips back. 'What the fuck was that, Ash?'

Despite everything, I can't help but let out a dry laugh. 'I'm asking myself the same thing.'

I put down the towel and finally face him. He's staring at me like he's genuinely worried I've gone off the deep end. Which is fair, I suppose. Not only did I message him frantically a few days ago, asking if it was possible for him to get me on the guest list for tonight – something I've never done, as I prefer to avoid events like this, or any events really – but now this? I'm surprised he hasn't called for an ambulance to cart me off yet.

'Are you alright?' Teddy asks, giving me a once-over. He's still looking at me like I've sprouted a second head. 'They're saying she shoved you?'

Idly, I wonder if I should be alarmed by the intensity of the anger that suddenly washes through me. Less than five minutes have passed and already the reality of what actually happened has been distorted, twisted and moulded into something a hundred times uglier than it actually was.

'Imani didn't *shove* me,' I say with a scowl Teddy definitely doesn't deserve. 'She just chucked her drink over me.'

'Because that's *so* much bett—Wait.' His eyes go wide and he holds up a hand. 'Imani? As in, the future Mrs Vouvalis, Imani? That Imani?'

My expression turns sheepish. 'The one and only.'

Teddy runs a hand down his face and groans. 'I know marrying you isn't exactly high up on her list of things she's excited for, but why, and pardon my language, the fuck would she do that?'

A very large part of me wants to come clean and tell Teddy everything about my plan with Imani. He'd probably be able to help with it, if I'm being honest. But then I'd have to explain to him why I agreed to go ahead with the plan in the first place and I can't bring myself to do it. It's embarrassing enough to admit to myself just how patheticically I am craving my father's love; I don't need to verbalise it to my brothers.

'Come on,' Teddy pokes at me. 'Why does your future wife hate you?'

This was her plan, I remind myself yet again even as the word *hate* bounces around in my skull like a pinball.

She wants people to think that we can't stand each other. She wants drama.

Tension.

A simmering loathing that everyone can feel the second we walk into a room together. So why does hearing Teddy say it out loud get under my skin so badly?

Why does it bother me so much that right now, people are probably whispering about how much she despises me, or wondering what she could've done to me to inspire such loathing?

I can't explain it.

'We have a history,' I say before Teddy can ask again.

At that, Teddy raises his brows. 'A history,' he repeats, clearly unimpressed. 'So you do know each other?'

I nod, briefly wondering if I'll ever stop feeling guilty about all of this.

'Yes. Kind of. We dated back at university.' I spend the next two minutes going over the fictional past Imani and I concocted, embellishing a bad break-up that left us both wounded and bitter. By the time I'm finished, Teddy looks like I've just slapped him.

'And you didn't think any of this would've been important to mention before?' he asks, looking genuinely offended that I've omitted this piece of information about my life. 'You know, Dad probably wouldn't have—'

'He already knows,' I say bitterly. The idea that my father would do anything to spare me some pain is laughable. 'And he's already said I have to fix things with her.'

Teddy shakes his head. 'And this is your idea of fixing things?'

'No.' I can't help but scowl at my brother, even though this is exactly what we wanted to happen. 'I didn't mean for it to go down like this. He's going to be pissed, isn't he?'

Teddy scoffs. 'It's not him you need to be worried about. It's *her* father. You know what Malcolm Davies is like.'

I didn't until Imani filled me in, but Teddy is right. If my father is angry at how tonight has unfolded, I have no doubt that Imani's father will be practically apoplectic with rage.

In an ideal world, this would be all we need to do to get the marriage called off. Just one embarrassing night at a charity event and that's it. No more wedding. No more Imani. I'm sure that's what she's banking on.

I doubt things will be that easy though. Not when Georgios Vouvalis is involved.

'Wait a second. Is this why you agreed to this stupid plan in the first place?' Teddy asks suddenly, eyes narrowed. 'Because you've still got feelings for her? Even though it's been, what, almost ten years now?'

'No,' I say immediately.

Teddy is clearly unconvinced.

'I *don't*,' I insist. 'If you couldn't tell, we didn't exactly end on a good note.'

'Doesn't mean you don't still have feelings for her.' He

shakes his head and the look on his face morphs from suspicious into sympathetic. 'Look, Ash, I know better than anyone that love can make you do crazy things, but this scheme Dad's got you involved in isn't—'

'I don't love her,' I say firmly. 'And I didn't agree to go ahead with it in some kind of misguided attempt to win her back. You know why I'm doing it. Don't make me say it.'

'A misguided attempt at rekindling your first love would be a better reason than the reality,' Teddy mumbles, quietly enough for me to pretend I haven't heard him.

'Alright,' he sighs heavily after a long pause, dragging a hand down his face again. 'As much as I'd love to keep babysitting you in here, you hiding out isn't helping things. The longer you hole up in this bathroom, the faster the gossip mill spins.'

He's right, of course, but I still groan and mutter, 'I was hoping if I stayed in here for long enough, everyone would just forget.'

Teddy barks out a laugh. 'Not a chance. There are probably at least three different versions of the story floating around by now. One where she slapped you. One where you got on your knees and begged her to take you back. And probably one where you burst into tears. If not, I'm spreading that rumour once we get out there.'

'Thanks for the brotherly support,' I deadpan.

Teddy gives me an overdramatic wink then pushes off the door and jerks his chin towards the hall. 'Come on. Time to face the music.'

The murmur of voices hits me the second Teddy opens the door and I do my best to drown out the whispers and wide-eyed stares as we make our way to our table. Instead, my eyes skim over sequinned dresses and tailored suits, instinctively searching for Imani.

I catch myself mid-search, irritated. The whole point of tonight was to make it seem like I can't stand the sight of her. Yet here I am, craning my neck this way and that, desperate to know where she is, if she's still here, and if she's okay.

It takes me very little time to find her sitting at her table with the blonde girl from earlier, speaking a million words a minute. To be honest, even if I hadn't been specifically seeking her out, I'm fairly certain Imani would've caught my attention anyway.

I meant what I said when I called her beautiful earlier. Imani is nothing short of striking on an average day, but tonight? Tonight she's a golden beacon in a sea of dark blues, silvers and greens.

Her dress is strapless and a soft metallic gold colour that glows like starlight under the low lights without being gaudy. It's patterned with delicate floral embroidery that catches the light when she moves, like she's been stitched together from sunlight itself.

I drop down into my own seat, my eyes still on Imani. I find myself lingering on the way the neckline of her dress dips low enough to show off the gentle swell of her breasts, and on how the fabric of the gown hugs her curves, cinches at her waist, and skims over her hips in a way that is simply just not fair. Against her rich, warm brown skin, everything about the dress is perfection. The kind of perfection that makes it very, very hard to remember that I'm supposed to hate her.

The blonde says something that has the rest of the table gasping and shooting Imani sad, sympathetic looks, before she leans forward and wraps a protective arm around her. Imani hesitates for a fraction of a second and then leans into the embrace just enough to sell the performance, her lips pulling into a trembling smile that doesn't reach her eyes.

God, she's good at this. I wonder if she's ever considered acting as a potential career path. If being the only child of Malcolm Davies stops being so lucrative, I'd say she definitely has the skill for it.

The blonde suddenly looks up and sees me watching. Her eyes narrow and her expression turns tight as she leans into and mumbles something to Imani. Even from across the room, I can tell that she buys it. She believes, one hundred per cent, that Imani and I hate each other.

Imani will be pleased. Every word I spat, every ounce of venom I forced into my voice, it was all worth it.

So why do I still feel like shit?

By the time the final toast is made, everyone's got their donations in (Teddy and I having been instructed to drop in a sizeable amount on behalf of the Vouvalis company), and the orchestra begins winding down for the night, I'm more than ready to get out of here. I hate these kinds of events on a good day, and tonight is most certainly not that.

The back of my neck aches from the weight of curious stares all night, my shirt is still damp and smells like I've run wild in a sweet factory, and the whispers haven't stopped since I walked back into the room. Every time I catch someone's gaze, which is irritatingly often, they practically snap their necks back to pretend they weren't staring.

For the umpteenth time tonight, I tell myself that these are just the signs of a job well done. The plan couldn't have played out better if Imani and I had written a script. Our little spat will fuel the gossip mill for weeks or, at the very least, until someone else does something wild enough to distract their attention.

My phone buzzes as I follow Teddy and his date – a doe-eyed girl called Penelope with wide eyes and a slightly agape mouth who hasn't stopped staring at me since we returned to the table – out to the front of the building to wait for our car.

Imani
Hey.

I very nearly drop my phone down a storm drain as I see her name flash across my screen. I hadn't been expecting to hear from her just yet. Before I can reply, another message comes in.

Imani
Meet me here in 10 mins?

A third message pops up; this one is a pin with a location about five minutes around the corner.

I don't hesitate.

Asher
I'll be there.

'We're heading to an afterparty in Soho,' Teddy says, as he waves down his driver, snapping my attention back to reality. 'You in?'

Even if Imani hadn't just messaged me, my answer would be the same. 'I'll pass.'

Teddy gives me a dramatic faux pout. 'And here I was thinking you'd actually become fun for once. You sure you don't want to join us?' He's got an arm draped around Penelope's shoulders, and I have no doubt at all that the two of them will spend precisely five minutes at this afterparty before deciding it's time to head back to Teddy's place for more private activities.

'No thanks. You guys have fun, though.'

Teddy looks like he wants to argue, but then his car pulls up and it's like he suddenly remembers he has a pretty girl on his arm and having his younger brother follow him around all evening would be a bit of a mood killer. Especially when said pretty girl very clearly wants to gossip about me to Teddy but is thankfully polite enough to hold off while I'm still in the vicinity. Hasn't stopped her from staring though.

He shrugs, opens the car door and gestures for Penelope

to get in. She gives me one last curious, lingering look over her shoulder then disappears into the car.

Teddy doesn't follow her immediately; instead he pulls me in for a quick, one-armed hug. 'Forget about this Imani business for tonight, okay? We'll figure it out and work out a way to spin it with Dad tomorrow.'

'I'm fine,' I say firmly. 'Everything is fine. Honestly, I'm good.'

Teddy doesn't look like he believes me, but then Penelope sticks her head back out the window and whines, 'Are we going soon?'

Teddy gives me another shrug, though this one is coupled with a devilish grin and I immediately know any remnant of concern about me has faded from his mind. 'You sure?'

'I'm sure.' I shove him towards the car. 'Go. Have fun. I'll call a car for myself.'

He doesn't need telling a third time. I watch as Teddy climbs in and mutters for his driver to head off. I don't move until their car has turned the corner and disappeared from view. Once it has, I take off in the opposite direction, glancing at my phone every now and then to make sure I'm heading in the right direction to the location in the pin Imani sent.

The pin leads me to a dark, dimly lit side street. At the end of the street, I see an idling sleek, black car, but there's no immediate sign of Imani. I frown and glance at my phone.

No new messages and it's been about fifteen minutes since her last one. Surely she hasn't left?

Asher
I'm here.

I'm expecting my phone to light up with a message, but instead I hear a loud honk from the car at the end of the street. I squint into the darkness and can just about make out a head poking out of the backseat window and then—

'Asher!' Imani whisper-shouts. 'Over here! Hurry, before someone sees you!'

There's no reason for anyone in our social circle to be hanging around a dark side street at this hour, but I do as she says and half jog down the street over to the waiting car. As soon as I'm close enough, the door slides open, and for the second time this month, a hand roughly yanks me inside a car.

'Took you long enough,' Imani says, shuffling a little to the side so I can right myself and close the door behind me. 'We were starting to worry you weren't going to show up.'

'We?'

'Hey.'

I realise, with a jolt, that there's another person in this car. I vaguely recognise her as one of the other attendees sitting at the table with Imani back at the gala.

'Asher? Sloane. Sloane? Asher,' Imani says briskly. Realisation dawns on me. This must be Sloane Chavan, the best friend Imani highlighted in her dossier pages.

I give her an awkward wave. She responds by slightly lifting her chin in greeting, like this whole sequence of events isn't extremely bizarre and is barely on her radar.

'Don't worry,' Imani says, accurately deciphering the slightly wary look on my face. 'She knows all about our plan.'

'I know all about your *ridiculous* plan,' Sloane corrects her, taking care to put extra emphasis on the ridiculous. I can't blame her. It *is* pretty ridiculous.

Imani shoots her friend a scowl, but there's no bite to it. 'It worked, didn't it?' She turns to me and gives me a sheepish wince. 'I'm so sorry, by the way. God, this is becoming a bit of a habit, isn't it? Me having to apologise because I took things way too far.'

'You didn't take it too far,' I say at the exact same time Sloane mutters, 'Too far is an understatement.'

Imani smacks her cheeks and lets out a pained groan. 'I threw a drink over you. A drink! I threw it! At you! Over you! At a charity event filled with some of the most influential people in this bloody city. And I *threw a drink over you.*' Another groan escapes her lips. 'Look, your shirt is ruined.'

I glance down. The front of my shirt is pink; the stain having grown larger and darker thanks to my useless attempt to dry it.

'Imani,' I start, but she's not listening.

'I'll pay for it to be dry-cleaned,' she says, now nervously picking at the skin around her fingers. This close, I can see that the skin around her thumb and forefinger is red and slightly raw, like she's spent an inordinate amount of time picking at it. 'Or I'll just buy you another one,' she continues, voice taking on a slightly hysterical tone. 'I'll buy you another two to make up for it.'

I glance over at Sloane, who looks vaguely amused and gives me a shrug that seems to say, 'You deal with it.'

'Imani,' I say again.

She doesn't hear, too lost in a spiral of panic. She's still apologising over and over and pulling at the red skin around her thumb.

I reach out, place a hand on her thigh, and give her a gentle squeeze. 'Imani.'

The effect is instantaneous. She cuts herself off mid apology, and stares at me with wide, slightly teary eyes.

'It's fine,' I say softly, and I mean it too. 'It's just a shirt. God knows I've got enough. And this was the plan, wasn't it? I'd say we sold the whole "exes who hate each other" thing really well. So, tonight was a win, wasn't it?'

Imani gives me a shaky nod. 'I know, I know. It's just I'm so embarrassed. I didn't even give you a heads-up on what I was about to do. You didn't sign up to be humiliated in front of all our peers like that. And then, the way you looked at me?'

A dry laugh claws its way out of my throat. 'The way *I* looked at *you*? What about how you looked at me? I've spent the last two hours sure that you actually do hate me.'

She shakes her head furiously. 'No, not at all. Of course not. I guess it was just the shock of it all? Hearing you say—'

'I was just playing the part,' I say, cutting her off before she can repeat the cruel words I spat at her – I don't need to hear them again. 'Believe me, I didn't mean a word of it.'

A little bit of tension seems to ease off her and she relaxes slightly. My hand is still on her thigh, and I can feel the way she seems to relax underneath my touch. 'Sorry,' she says again through a weak grin. 'For the dramatics, I mean. You must think I'm such a mess.'

'Never,' I say, matching her grin with one of my own. Mess is simply not a word I'd ever associate with Imani. Even with tears pricking at the corner of her eyes and her fingers picked raw, she's still as bright and beautiful as she was when I first laid eyes on her this evening.

Sloane clears her throat and we both jump. I hadn't realised how close we'd got to each other. Imani's shifted in her seat, leaning in so her bare arm is brushing against my jacket sleeve, and my hand is still on her thigh. I snatch it away quickly and Imani clears her throat and scootches a little closer to the window, putting some space between us.

'Now we've got that over and done with,' Sloane drawls with a slight roll of the eyes. It's been less than five minutes, but I'm beginning to learn that Sloane has one setting, and it's sarcasm. 'Can we hurry up and debrief so I can get home and out of these?' She wiggles her feet, showing off impressively high heels.

'Right,' Imani is suddenly all business again. She sits up a little straighter. 'You were right, we absolutely sold the whole "we have a history and hate each other" story. Emmy wouldn't stop probing.'

At this, Sloane pretends to gag. 'What else is new with her?'

'Emmy?' I ask.

'The blonde girl I was sitting next to,' Imani explains. 'She's like the queen of high-society gossip.'

'A bonafide modern Lady Whistledown,' Sloane says.

I have no idea what that means, but Imani nods seriously so I assume it must be an accurate descriptor.

'Really, all I wanted to do tonight was get on her radar,' Imani continues. 'And we definitely did that. Sloane, can you check the—'

'Already on it,' Sloane says, phone in hand.

'What're you looking for?' I ask.

Sloane doesn't respond right away. Instead, she taps at her phone and then scrolls for a few seconds. 'Damn,' she whistles, 'I have to hand it to her, she is fast.'

Sloane flips her phone around and shows us the screen. The Instagram app is open and she's paused on a recent story from an account called @TrustFundTea.

I frown. 'Trust . . . Fund . . . Tea? What is this? Someone rich reviewing all the tea they drink?'

Imani bites her bottom lip to hide a smile. 'It's a gossip page.'

'Called . . . what? What does tea have to—'

'Oh my God,' Sloane snorts. 'Do you live under a rock? Actually, don't answer, I guess you do. Just read the damn story.'

I glance back at the phone and squint at the words on the screen:

@TrustFundTea

Well, well, well . . . It wouldn't be an event packed with high-society glitterati if there wasn't a little drama, would it? Tonight's tea involves two parties who aren't normally found at the scene of the crime, which makes it even more juicy, amIright?

Tempers flared tonight when former lovers, Imani Davies and Asher Vouvalis, crossed paths . . . The air was thick with tension and let's just say . . . words and fluids were exchanged 👀

Long story short, the airline heiress tossed a drink in the hotelier prince's face and he stormed off, but not without sending some particularly icy words her way. Brr! Who knew the baby Vouvalis had such a mean streak?

If anyone got any photographic or video evidence of the fight, or some tea on why they broke up (who even knew they dated?!?!), send it my way! DM or shoot me an email (in bio)*!

**all sources will remain anonymous*

xoxo TFT

I reread the post several times, feeling a different emotion every time. On my last read, I settle for thoroughly confused. 'What the hell? Who wrote this? Who runs this page?'

'We're not sure,' Imani says with a shrug.

'Emmy,' Sloane says definitively.

Imani shakes her head. 'It's *probably* Emmy, but no one can actually trace it to her so she has plausible deniability. But anyway, this is good.'

'What's good about this?' I ask, scanning over the post yet again. 'And you didn't throw it in my face.'

'Emmy, or whoever it is who runs the page, doesn't care about accuracy,' Imani says. 'It's all about what's going to generate the most drama and get the most comments. She'll probably have a photo or video on the feed by this time tomorrow.'

Sloane swipes to the @TrustFundTea account page.

416 posts 173k followers 1532 following

Realisation quickly dawns on me: 173,000 people are following this account. 173,000 people will soon be reading all about what happened tonight between me and Imani. And by tomorrow, if Imani and Sloane are right, there will be photographic evidence for them to look at as well.

'Your father isn't going to like this,' I say.

Imani blinds me with a grin that stretches from ear to ear. 'That's an understatement. He's going to lose his absolute mind. If I'm being honest, I thought it'd take us longer to get to this stage, but I'm not complaining. If we're lucky, this will be it. My father will take one look at the photo or video of me throwing a drink at you,' she winces apologetically, 'and he'll call the marriage agreement off. There's no way he'll risk the business's reputation if this is what he's going to get from us.'

Somehow, her smile widens even more. 'After tonight, we'll probably never have to see each other ever again. Isn't that great?'

'Yeah. Great.' I do my best to match her smile and try not to think too hard about why the prospect of never seeing Imani ever again makes my stomach twist.

CHAPTER NINE

Imani

'Have you lost your ever-loving mind?'

I feel sick. And like I'm about twelve years old.

I'm sat on my sofa, hugging a pillow to my chest as my father paces up and down my living room. He's spent the last fifteen minutes alternating between furiously muttering under his breath and outright yelling at me.

We're currently back in the yelling stage.

'I don't know who you are, but you're clearly not my daughter,' he snaps, glaring at me like I've just been accused of murder and not simply causing a scene at a fancy event. 'Because my daughter, the Imani Davies we raised, would never behave like this.'

My mother sits on the armchair opposite me, her face a perfect mask of disappointment. She shakes her head and titters in agreement. 'Never.'

I squeeze the pillow a little tighter.

This is what you wanted, I remind myself. *You knew he'd be angry. Just ride it out. Ride it out for a little longer.*

'Well?' he yells, and I nearly jump out of my skin. In twenty-eight years, I've only heard my father truly lose control and yell a handful of times and it was never once directed at me. The last time was during the pandemic when he first learned that flights were being grounded. 'Explain yourself!'

'I—' I start, but my throat is hoarse from holding in tears. This is the first chance I've had to get a word in since my parents stormed into my apartment fifteen minutes ago. 'I told you that we had a history.'

'And I told *you*,' he growls through gritted teeth, 'that you need to get over it. To make amends. For God's sake, Imani, whatever the boy did to you, it was nearly a decade ago now. Since when were you the kind of person to hold a grudge?'

'He hurt me,' I snap back. Fuelled by my anger, the lie comes easy. 'Since when were you the kind of father who doesn't care about something like that?'

My father reels like I've just slapped him. Even my mother freezes for a moment. 'He hurt you emotionally,' my father says quietly after a few seconds of strained silence. '*Emotionally*, Imani. Those wounds should have long since healed.'

'Well, they haven't,' I say stubbornly.

He stares at me long and hard and I stare, unblinking, right back.

This is the man who entered the aviation industry forty years ago with a dream. The man who has either outlasted or bested every single one of his competitors and built an empire from the ground up. The kind of man who strides into business meetings with the assuredness of someone who knows everything is going to go his way.

This is not my father.

My father has always been driven, has always wanted the best for me and for me to be the best. He's been hard on me over the years, demanded too much from me on occasion, but he's never been cruel.

When did the change happen? Why did it happen? And how didn't I notice until now? Because, looking at him closely, I can see a difference. His frown lines are more pronounced, his eyes look tired and heavy, and even the way he's carrying himself feels different. It's like he's got a weight on his shoulders and it's finally become too much for him to bear.

'You're to contact the organising committee for the gala and apologise,' my father says gruffly. 'It was an uncharacteristic act from you – we'll say you've been suffering from stress, perhaps a medical issue so they won't probe – and it won't ever happen again. We'll also increase our donation to help smooth things over.'

I gape at him. 'You want me to pretend I'm ill so people won't talk?'

'I don't want to be doing any of this, Imani!' he explodes. 'But you've left me no choice. Imagine my surprise this morning when, instead of opening up an email from the committee thanking me for my sizeable donation, I was met with this!' He dives into his pocket, pulls out a piece of thoroughly scrunched paper, and slams it down on my coffee table.

I lean forward, my heart racing.

It's a photo from last night. More specifically, it's a photo of me mid-drink toss. Asher and I aren't the focus of the photo, but we're caught in the background of some posing gala attendees, and someone has clearly cropped it to zoom in on us. It feels strange seeing it from this angle. In the memories I've been replaying since Sloane's driver dropped me home last night, the only thing I can really remember is the adrenaline coursing through my veins as I made the decision and the look of shock on Asher's face. In this photo, I looked crazed. My eyes are wide and frantic, and I'm gripping the glass with such an intensity, I'm surprised I didn't shatter the damn thing in my hands.

'You threw a drink in the man's face, Imani. A drink!'

'Technically, I threw it at his chest.'

My father blinks at me. 'Is this a joke to you?'

'No.'

'Are you sure? Because you're sure as hell acting like it is. Do I have to remind you about what is on the line here?'

'A deal,' I say listlessly. Every time I'm reminded as to why I've had to resort to these lengths, my heart breaks a little more. 'There's a deal on the line. That's all.'

He opens his mouth and then closes it tightly, his lips spreading into a thin grimace.

'I'm assuming you'll make a lot of money if the deal with Georgios goes through,' I decide to continue since he hasn't responded. 'But we already have a lot of money, Daddy. Is my happiness really worth a little more?'

I've never thought of my father as the Jeff Bezos type, the kind of business magnate who hoards money like a dragon. He started Peregrine Airways because he genuinely loves the skies and delivering a service to our customers that no other airline has even come close to replicating. For as long as I've had sentience, I've known that our riches have been a happy, and very welcomed, second-place prize to simply being the best of the best in the industry. But that's changed too, it seems.

'How many lectures have you given me about quality over quantity?' I ask. My father didn't even start flying internationally for the first ten years of Peregrine Airways, preferring to perfect the service we delivered here before he ventured into international airspace. 'How many companies have you watched fail because their founders started chasing profits over delivering a service people actually love to use? And yet you're hellbent on getting this deal with Georgios Vouvalis, of all people, over the line? You're mad at me because of what happened last night, but how many sordid stories are there about Georgios out there? How many times has he had his face plastered over the trade papers because he ripped off a partner or got caught cutting corners in the expansion of his hotel empire? Is that really what you want to be attached you? What you want to attach the Peregrine Airways name to?'

By the time I'm finished my impromptu speech, I'm breathing heavily. The pillow I clutched earlier has fallen to the wayside and my hands are balled into tight little fists by my side. I hadn't even realised this was something I felt so passionate about, but I guess it makes sense. I may not have a real role at the company, but it's been my big sister, looming over my life for as long as I can remember. I love it just as much as my father does, and the thought of him diluting what he's created just for a few extra zeroes on his tax return come April is enough to make my vision blur with unshed tears.

'Imani . . .'

I look up, daring to feel just a smidge of hope. He said my name with some warmth, with respect. That's the father I know and love.

'You just don't understand.'

'Then help me,' I plead. 'I want to understand.'

He shakes his head. 'The less you know, the better.'

Alarm bells start to ring. 'What do you—'

'All you need to know is that the Vouvalis deal will secure not only our comfort for the rest of our lives, but for your children too. And your children's children. Entire generations of Davies' will never have to know what hardship is, as long as you play your part now.'

I turn frantically to my mother, hoping she'll jump in, but she studiously avoids my gaze and is instead pretending like her shoes are the most fascinating thing she's ever seen.

My father lets out a long sigh. 'But I can't have you behaving like this. The damage you've done to the Davies name in just one night?' He shakes his head and I just about manage to resist the urge to grin. This is it. He's about to do a U-turn on this whole ridiculous scheme.

'I'll talk to Georgios.'

My lips twitch. Come on, say it. Say it. Say it! Say you'll

find a different way to get your shareholders and investors on board with a Vouvalis merger. A way that doesn't involve me and Asher.

'And arrange a time and place for you and Asher to do some damage control.'

The world starts to spin. 'Excuse me?' I rasp, because that is definitely not where I thought we were heading.

He nods to himself and begins pacing my living room again. 'You two will meet somewhere public, a restaurant perhaps. Somewhere you'll be seen and noticed by the right people. You'll make amends and begin repairing the relationship.'

'Daddy—'

'We'll float that this was just a lovers' spat, exacerbated by stress. You're both very embarrassed that it played out in public as it did, but you're still committed to one another and—'

'Daddy,' I say, louder this time. My voice comes out weak and wobbly and I will myself to not start crying. I won't give him the satisfaction. 'I am not marrying Asher Vouvalis. Not for you. Not for any imaginary future children. Not for anyone. I won't do it.'

'You will,' he says quietly. 'You'll do it, and you'll do it with a smile on your face. Because if you don't, all of this?' He gestures around my home and it feels like my heart stops for a beat or two. My apartment suite is in a high-rise serviced building in the middle of Central London. My neighbours are celebrities, politicians, athletes and wealthy socialites. He bought it for me on my twenty-first birthday and I hadn't realised there were strings attached. 'I'll take it away.'

I've had access to my very healthy trust since I was eighteen, and I've always been smart with my money in terms of savings and investments, but even I can admit that maybe I've been relying a bit too heavily on the limitless black credit card that's still in my father's name for the everyday.

I deserve it, I've always told myself every time I swiped with his card without thinking. I've treated it like a salary for the arduous job of being Imani Davies 24/7. For being the perfect business representative at all times. For being expected to build on father's success but never have anything to call my own. It never once crossed my mind that he'd ever use his generosity with money as a leash, and tighten that leash if I ever stopped being the dutiful daughter.

Maybe that was naïve of me.

'You wouldn't,' I say, desperately hoping to call his bluff.

'I don't want to,' he says coldly. 'And I'll certainly get no enjoyment out of it, but I will.' His phone suddenly buzzes and he pulls it out of his jacket pocket and scowls at the screen. 'I've got to take this.'

He ignores my strangled attempt at a retort and steps out onto the balcony, leaving me and my mother alone.

'He means well,' she says once the stony silence apparently gets too much for her to bear. 'And I've heard the Vouvalis boy is quite nice.'

'That's not the point!' I hate how whiny and petulant I

sound right now, but I can't help it. 'Asher could be the nicest person on the planet – I still don't want to marry him.'

My mother sighs, then comes to sit beside me on the sofa. She reaches out to place a hand on my arm and I flinch. She pretends not to notice her daughter visibly recoiling from her and folds her hands into her lap instead, like that was always the plan. 'You know your father struggled a lot growing up?'

I nod stiffly. Everyone knows the Malcolm Davies story. How he bounced around from foster home to foster home and beat every single odd stacked against him to create the absolute titan in the aviation industry that is Peregrine Airways. I don't need to hear it again, but apparently my mother is incapable of reading the room.

'There were days when he wouldn't know where he'd get his next meal from. Times he didn't have one single pound to his name. He's been living in fight-or-flight mode since he was a child, and he's worked damn hard to make sure you've never even had a taste of what he went through growing up.'

'I know,' I say. 'And I appreciate—'

'Do you?' she says briskly. 'Because you sound like a child.'

'He's asking me to marry—'

She waves a dismissive hand in the air, silencing me immediately. 'He's asking you to do your part. Arranged marriages are quite common, you know? Every day, men and women all over the world enter into unions not for love, but for financial or social gain. It's not that out of the ordinary. We're not asking you to do anything that hasn't already been a part of the human experience for thousands of years.'

'Well excuse me for wanting to love the person I agree to spend the rest of my life with,' I say with a sniff. 'I didn't know that was such an unreasonable request.'

For a moment, my mother looks sympathetic. She reaches out to touch my hand again, and this time I let her. She gives me a squeeze, but it does nothing to calm me down. It's the complete opposite of Asher's touch from last night. The second he put his hand on my thigh, I felt eerily calm. Now I just feel even more tense.

'It's not unreasonable,' she says softly. 'It's just not feasible right now. As I said, Asher Vouvalis is, by all accounts, quite the gentleman. Your father and I would never have agreed to a match with someone who wasn't.'

'Have you both forgotten that we have a history?' I say desperately. I haven't tried this tack with my mother yet, and maybe there's a chance it'll move her in a way it didn't for my father. 'Asher Vouvalis had his chance with me and he blew it.'

My mother frowns. 'What went so wrong? And if it was so bad, why is this the first we're hearing of it?'

'I was embarrassed,' I say, the lie coming effortlessly to me. 'I just wanted to forget it ever happened. To forget that we were ever a thing.' I turn to her and grasp her hand in mine. 'I want to do whatever I can for the business, you know I do, but surely there has to be some other way. I don't even understand why we so desperately need this deal with the Vouvalis corporation anyway.'

She pulls her hand free and averts her gaze. 'That's not for you to worry about.'

'So you'll ask me to sign my life away to help, but you won't even do me the decency of telling me why?'

She purses her lips. 'Your father . . . We both just want to make sure you're taken care of. That you can live a life of luxury and freedom without having to worry the way we did. Can you just trust us, Imani? Trust that we're doing this, that we're asking this of you, because we know best. You don't see it now, but five, ten years from now, you'll be thanking us.'

'Ha,' I scoff. 'I highly doubt that.'

My mother gives me a sad smile. 'There was obviously something that drew you to Asher in the first place all those years ago. Focus on that and try and rekindle it. You've got time to fall in love again.'

The door to the balcony slides open and my father re-enters the room. He looks even more tired and browbeaten than before.

'Daddy, I—'

He holds up a tired hand. 'I don't want to hear it, Imani. I've already arranged it with Georgios. You and Asher will meet next week and start fixing this mess you've got us into. No arguments.'

I clench my jaw. 'Asher and I just aren't going to work.'

He mimics the same sad smile my mother gave me just a few moments earlier. 'I sincerely hope that you do.'

CHAPTER TEN

Asher

I'm fairly certain my father has forgotten about me. I was summoned to his office with an expletive-filled text message in the early hours of the morning, yet it's currently closer to ten than the intended 9am he asked for, and I'm still waiting in the lobby. Every so often, Natalie, my father's unfortunate assistant, glances over in my direction and winces. I'm not sure she realises she's not as discreet as she thinks she is.

So, yeah. He's either forgotten that he, in a rage, demanded I come in this morning to be yelled at in person, or making me wait is part of my punishment. To be honest, it could go either way with him.

I drum my fingers against the armrest of my seat, the rhythmic tapping the only thing keeping me from going insane.

Natalie's desk phone rings suddenly, startling the both of us. My father's assistants never last very long and, from the wary expression on Natalie's face as she reaches the phone, I don't imagine she'll be here much longer either.

'Yes, sir,' she says softly in the phone once she answers. 'Of course. Coming, right away.' She hangs up, stands up so quickly her chair wheels squeak loudly against the floor, and scurries towards my father's office door. She pauses just long enough to spare me a thin, apologetic smile and then disappears through the frosted glass door.

When she hurriedly opens it, furious-sounding words float out into the lobby before it swings shut. I can't make out a full sentence, but I know that my father is mid-tirade as per usual. It fills me with a perverse sense of relief to know I'm not the only one capable of eliciting this kind of fury from him and I feel a flash of pity for whichever employee is currently on the receiving end of his fury right now.

The door cracks open again and Natalie reappears, this time clutching a thick stack of papers pressed to her chest. She looks on the verge of bursting into tears and I have no doubt that she inadvertently got caught in my father's anger while she was in there.

'Is everything—' I start, but she just shakes her head and marches towards the exit.

'Fine,' she chokes out. 'He'll be ready for you shortly. He's just finishing up a meeting. I need to, to photocopy these.' She nods to the papers in her arms. 'I'll be right back.'

We both ignore that there's a printer and photocopier wedged behind her desk and that tears have already started to roll down her cheeks. I nod and she practically sprints out of the lobby, the sound of her choked sob echoing as she disappears.

It's only once the lobby doors swing shut that I realise Natalie has left the door to my father's office slightly ajar. It sits open a few inches, just wide enough for my father's voice to filter through properly this time. It's low at first, like he's pacing or speaking turned away from his desk, but then it suddenly comes through more clearly, cutting through the silent lobby like a knife.

'—don't care what anyone else thinks, I've made my decision,' my father snaps.

There's a beat of silence and then—

'Isn't last night proof that this isn't going to plan?' says a voice through clearly gritted teeth. It takes me half a second to place the voice. Initially, I thought that my father was tearing into a particularly unlucky employee, and I was right. I just hadn't realised who that employee was.

'Davies won't tolerate this kind of bad press,' Andreas continues. 'He'll pull out of the deal.'

My father scoffs. 'Leave Davies to me.'

'And Asher?' Andreas asks.

I lean closer to the door, fighting the urge to just get up and press my ear against it.

'What about him?'

'I don't understand why you chose him for this plan in the first place,' Andreas says. 'If you needed someone to cooperate, wouldn't I—'

'You and Theodore ask too many questions,' my father

says, cutting him off. 'Asher . . . He wants my approval more than anything. Always has. If I tell him to jump, he'll jump. If I tell him to apologise, he'll apologise. If I tell him to pull himself together and marry the Davies girl, then he'll damn well do it.' He snorts. 'He thinks it'll make me proud of him.'

My chest aches so keenly, I press a hand to it like maybe I can keep my heart from splitting open down the middle. Suddenly I'm not a grown man, I'm eight years old in an unfamiliar home wondering why my father's eyes turn cold whenever he looks at me.

'You think you can control him,' Andreas says.

'I *know* I can control him,' my father says, and I can practically hear the sneer in his voice. 'The Davies deal is crucial, and Asher will get us there.'

'Are you sure?'

'Completely.'

It doesn't escape me that Andreas hasn't defended me. He hasn't pointed out that maybe I deserve a say in my own life. Hasn't reminded him that I'm also his *son*. Suddenly, Andreas' earlier brotherly advice that I go ahead with this whole plan and marry Imani makes more sense. He's been in on it from the get-go.

My father sighs loudly, signalling his deep frustration. 'He's been a disappointment for years, Andreas. I know you have a soft spot for the boy, but you know as well as I do – he barely shows any initiative. No vision. No drive. But he wants so dearly for me to pat him on the head and tell him he's doing a good job, that'll he'll do whatever role I assign him, no questions asked.'

The door to the lobby swings open and Natalie comes hurrying back in.

I straighten up in my seat, hoping that it's not too obvious that I've spent the last few minutes eavesdropping on my father and Andreas. I'm not entirely sure how convincing I am though, because my chest is still tight. Natalie stumbles back to her desk, swiping at her cheeks and trying desperately to look like she hasn't just been crying in the bathroom, but everything is spinning too fast for me to focus on her.

All I can hear, over and over in my mind, is:

He'll do whatever role I assign him, no questions asked.

He thinks it'll make me proud.

He's been a disappointment for years.

None of this should surprise me. None of this should gut me the way it has. But here we are. Maybe it's because it's the first time I've heard him say it aloud; maybe it's because he's saying it to Andreas, who is supposed to be on *my* side. I just don't know. All I know is that for the first time in my life, I feel a sense of sudden and overwhelming clarity.

My father's voice quietens down to nothing in my mind, replaced with one simple, solid thought: I'm done.

Done.

Done chasing his approval and love. Done with trying to anticipate his reactions and twisting myself into someone who fits whatever version of a son he thinks is useful that week.

It's strange how quickly the decision and the certainty of it all settles in. There's no sudden rush of courage or anger coursing through me, I just feel a calm understanding that something has shifted inside me and I'm not interested in shifting it back.

I straighten in my seat and, for a moment, I consider leaving – just walking out and letting him realise that I'm not going to sit here indefinitely to be summoned like a dog. But I know how that will play out. He'll just take it as another example of my supposed irresponsibility, another reason why I'm the 'disappointment' he so casually catalogued to Andreas. And he'll assume that whatever plan he's concocted, I'll eventually fall back in line, complain a little, maybe push back once or twice, but ultimately do what he wants because I always have. I'll let him believe that, because he'll be wrong.

I'm not going in there to comply with him anymore. I'm going in there because he expects a version of me that no longer exists and letting him talk to that version for the last time feels appropriate. He'll hand me instructions to smooth things over with Imani. I'll nod and play the dutiful son role. He'll think he's won and that I'm doing exactly what he wants. And I'll walk out of that office more committed than ever to following through with what Imani and I have already started.

I stand, my chair scraping loudly against the floor as I move.

Natalie jumps a little. 'Um. He's not . . . I don't think he'll be much longer,' she says, nodding to the door behind her. 'If you just sit—'

'It'll be fine,' I say.

She swallows and looks like she wants to say something else but nothing comes out of her open mouth as I walk towards the office door.

For the first time in a very long time, my pulse doesn't spike with nerves or dread at the prospect of being face to face with my father. If anything, what I feel is a new sense of steadiness and surety settling in my chest.

I push the door open and step into a cold silence. My father is sitting behind his desk, his face pinched with irritation as usual. Andreas is standing off to the side, arms crossed, his face tight. My father doesn't spare me a second glance as I enter the room, but Andreas looks up, and for a brief second, guilt crosses his face.

'You're late,' my father drawls, like I haven't been sat outside for close to an hour waiting on him. 'Sit.'

I do, because that's what he expects from me and I'm willing to play my part in this sick routine – for now.

'We have a problem,' he says, once I'm seated opposite him. 'Last night was unacceptable. You need to fix this before Davies gets cold feet.'

I nod silently and his gaze narrows almost suspiciously – clearly he was expecting an objection.

'Right,' he says, clearing his throat. 'You'll contact the girl, apologise, charm her, and get us back on track for a wedding by the end of the year. Understood?'

'Understood,' I say immediately.

My father looks ever-so-slightly unnerved at how easy I'm being with all of this, like although he knew I'd ultimately acquiesce, he was still expecting at least a little fight.

'Well then,' he says gruffly when it becomes clear I've got nothing else to add. 'Get to it.'

I nod again and rise from my seat. Out of the corner of my eye, I see Andreas turn in my direction.

'Ash, can I—'

'Sorry,' I say over my shoulder, already making my way towards the door. 'I'm already running late.'

He calls my name again, but I don't turn around; I keep on walking. I have no idea what I want to say to him, but I know that if I'm forced to right now, whatever comes out of my mouth won't be good.

I don't stop walking until I'm back out in the lobby and the door to his office slams shut behind me.

Natalie glances up at me as I stride past her and her eyes go slightly wide. I wonder what she sees when she looks at me now. Does she see a new man entirely? Because it sure as hell feels that way.

CHAPTER ELEVEN

Asher

Entry into The Opal Vault is by invitation only and I kind of wish I didn't have one. It's 8pm on a Tuesday evening and the last place I want to be is somewhere like this.

For the last decade I've successfully managed to, for the most part, avoid the galas and events, art galleries and parties and exclusive restaurants the entirety of our so-called high society seems to revolve around. Teddy is the one more suited to things like this. Even Andreas, who is also somewhat of a recluse, would be less a fish out of water than me right now.

But it's me standing outside the hidden entrance to The Opal Vault, a charming, ivy-covered façade on a quiet Mayfair side street. If you didn't know the restaurant was here, you'd probably walk right past it and never know that behind this door is a room filled with some of the city's most elite. Celebrities. Politicians. Top models. Business tycoons.

Being able to wrangle an invitation to The Opal Vault means you're a somebody, and there's nothing somebodies love more than being seen in a room full of other somebodies.

I knock twice on the door and it opens immediately. A stony-faced man steps out with a tablet and looks me up and down. Apparently the vibes I'm giving off label me as someone who belongs in an establishment like this, because the stony expression quickly disappears and is replaced with a cloying one.

'Do you have a reservation, sir?'

I nod, tell him my name, and he scans the tablet for a few seconds before nodding approvingly. 'Wonderful, Mr Vouvalis. Please come inside. It says you're expecting a guest?'

'She'll be here soon.'

'Excellent. Follow me.'

He leads me through a dark, dimly lit corridor that smells overwhelmingly of oud. It opens out into a deceptively large dining room with a vaulted ceiling with several chandeliers hanging from it. The room is buzzing with the hum of conversation, soft laughter, and the clinking of glasses and cutlery to plates. I spot a few vaguely familiar faces as I follow the maître d to my table.

There's Sidney Morrow, a social media mogul, talking animatedly with a politician who has recently had his fair share of scandal. At a table near a window, there's a woman I'm pretty sure is a top model (and also pretty sure she once dated Teddy) clinking champagne glasses with Nate Burnstone, a Formula One driver. There are also people I don't recognise dotted around on different tables, but I can tell from the cut of their suits or the way they laugh, or even just the way they carry themselves, that they're from money.

The maître d takes me to a table covered in a white cloth in the middle of the room, which wouldn't have been my first choice but the decision doesn't surprise me. As well as the tables nestled into dark corners in the room, there are also several private booths in the back with velvet curtains closing them off from the rest of us in the main room. If this were any other night, I would've preferred one of those but tonight isn't about confidentiality or discretion. Tonight is all about being seen. Our fathers have made it abundantly clear, and Imani and I are more than happy to oblige.

A waiter appears just as I sit down and places two pristine glasses and a tall bottle of ice-cold water in front of me. He takes a step backwards, ready to disappear back into the shadows, but I stop him.

'Would you mind bringing some sparkling water out too?'

He nods. 'Of course, sir. Iced?'

I try to remember what Imani had in her glass that one afternoon and then nod. 'Please.'

'Very good.' He disappears, leaving me alone. Although it doesn't feel like it.

I fidget uncomfortably in my seat. It's not as bad as it was after the incident at the gala, but I can feel several pairs of curious eyes on me. I wonder how many of these people follow @TrustFundTea – an account I still can't quite believe actually exists – and how many of them saw the photo and then, two days later, the video of Imani throwing her drink over me at the gala. I've rewatched it countless times now, and every time I notice something else.

The last time I watched it, it was the way Imani's eyes widened as the drink made contact with my shirt, as if she couldn't quite believe what she'd just done.

The time before that, it was the way her hips swayed in the few seconds of movement before she threw the drink. Hypnotising.

I pull out my phone to give me something to do while I wait and open my message history with Imani. I scroll up to a few days ago, after we'd both been told, in no uncertain terms, that we needed to fix things. Or, rather, that we needed to make a show of fixing things. I think it was her father who suggested The Opal Vault, so here we are.

Imani
Have you ever been to a restaurant and been sat by the kind of couple that just oozes 'we should've broken up months ago' energy?

Asher
. . . No . . . No, I don't think I have

Imani
Oh come on, you definitely have!

Or maybe you've been sat by a couple on a first date that is going terribly?

I was sat next to a couple once and the guy kept going on and on about how his ex used to do this and do that, and he didn't seem to realise his date was definitely not into it.

Pretty sure he called her the ex's name too.

They got separate cars home, lol.

Imani

Anyway . . . I'm feeling inspired.

Asher

?

Imani

Our fathers want us to be seen together. So let's make them regret that.

No drinks will be thrown this time, I promise, lol.

Her plan for tonight is simple but should hopefully be an effective one. As long as we both play our parts well and, after the morning at my father's office a few days ago, I'm ready to do just that.

The waiter returns with a cool pitcher of sparkling water just as the maître d leads Imani into the dining room. She looks beautiful, as usual. Her eyes meet mine almost immediately and I'm treated to a brief grin that lights up her whole face. It's so brief, most people would miss it, but I catch it and commit it to memory before she remembers she's supposed to be displeased to see me and the smile drops from her face.

Show time.

The maître d guides Imani to our table and I make a pointed show of not getting up from my seat to greet her. The rudeness of it all makes me cringe inwardly but, I remind myself, it's all part of the plan.

'Asher,' Imani says frostily as the maître d, after waiting a beat too long and realising *I'm* not going to step up and do it, pulls out her chair and gestures politely for her to sit.

'Imani,' I say, forcing any warmth out of my voice so it comes out equally as cold.

The maître d looks between us, a small frown puckering his brows in the middle, but doesn't say a word. A true professional. Once Imani's settled in her seat, he bows his head and then trots off back through the door and into the corridor.

'You're late,' I say, taking care not to lower my voice to the same politely hushed levels of the other diners seated around us.

'I had better things to be doing,' Imani says, pointedly not looking at me as she settles into her seat. Instead, she pulls her phone out of her handbag and begins tapping away, seemingly deeming me less worthy of her attention than whatever is on her screen.

Out of the corner of my eye I spy one of the expensive suit-wearing men beside us give our table a disapproving once-over before turning his attention back to his own meal and guest.

'I'm told you wanted to apologise,' I say.

At that, Imani scoffs loudly, earning herself a few pointed glares from some of the tables around us. 'I—' She seems to falter for a second under the weight of the scrutiny from our fellow diners but then picks herself back up right where she left off. 'I have nothing to apologise for.'

'Ha,' I bark, and this time the man in the expensive suit actually snaps his head around in my direction and glares at me for a full five seconds. 'My shirt would say otherwise.'

'I did you a favour,' Imani sniffs. 'That shirt was hideous. If anything, I'm sorry it took that long for someone to do something about it. Though fashion taste was never your strong suit, was it?'

'You embarrassed me in front of just about everyone we know,' I hiss back. 'I think, at the very least, I'm owed an apology.'

The model glances over her shoulder then turns back to her date and whispers in his ear. In the general quiet of the room, her voice travels and I hear *Asher Vouvalis* and *Imani Davies* come from her lips in barely hushed tones.

'I told you I never wanted to see you again,' Imani says, raising her voice ever so slightly. 'After how you treated me, you're lucky all you got was a spilled drink.'

That gets a little more attention. I can even see some of the waiters now, hovering on the sidelines and watching our table with undeniable interest. I wonder who'll be the one to get in touch with @TrustFundTea about this. Will they try and sneak a photo or video? It feels wrong, but I fix a hateful scowl onto my face, just in case.

'After how I treated *you*? The way you were acting, you're lucky I—'

'I'm so sorry to interrupt, but are you ready to order?' Our waiter appears from seemingly nowhere, a bead of sweat trickling down his nose like he had to be forced to come out here and interrupt us mid argument and he's not sure how we'll respond.

Imani turns to him, and her entire demeanour changes almost immediately. She beams up at him and makes eye contact the entire time as she places her order.

It's strange what you can learn about someone when you least expect it. I've gone to countless dinners like this over the years and watched as the people around me treated the staff like nothing. My father in particular is one of the biggest offenders here. I don't think he's ever actually looked a member of serving staff in the eye. But Imani makes a point of actually talking to our waiter like a human being and not a robot programmed to serve her. It shouldn't be refreshing to see, but it is.

The waiter makes a corny, food-related pun and she laughs like it's genuinely the funniest thing she's heard all day.

An unexpected spike of jealously stabs at me. While I'm subject to, admittedly fake, scowls and scoffs, he gets her undivided attention, laughter, and the kind of smile that could put the sun to shame.

'And you, sir?' the waiter asks, reluctantly turning from Imani to look at me. As soon as his attention is off her, Imani's smile drops and she's back to glaring daggers at me from the across the table. I know they're fake and that this is all part of the ruse that I agreed to, but I still squirm in my seat a little.

Being on the receiving end of Imani's ire isn't fun.

I give my order and our waiter – Thomas, I can see from the thin name tag pinned to his lapel – swiftly disappears into the shadows once again, leaving us alone. Or, as alone as we can be given that half the restaurant are unabashedly staring at us now.

Imani's well aware that we have an audience. She crosses her arms over her chest and leans back and curls her lips up into a sneer that doesn't suit her. 'I suppose I shouldn't be surprised you ordered the most boring thing on the menu. Asher Vouvalis, always taking the safe route.'

'I know what I like,' I retort, loud enough that the couple behind her, who have been pretending not to listen, both pause in the middle of raising their forks. 'And I'm not in the habit of wasting my time.'

Her eyebrows arch like daggers, and for a second I could believe I've genuinely offended her. 'This is a colossal waste of mine.'

'And yet here you are,' I shoot back. 'Having dinner with me.'

'Only because I was forced.' She says this with the kind of venom that carries, letting it drop into the room like broken glass. Heads turn. Someone says, 'Goodness.' The man in the expensive suit beside us is practically salivating at the drama of it all.

We hold each other's gaze, both of us simmering in manufactured disdain, until the plates arrive. Thomas places mine down with professional precision, but when he sets Imani's in front of her, she smiles sweetly again, thanking him with warmth that isn't even remotely faked. The contrast is dizzying.

Once Thomas is gone, Imani eyes my plate and then rolls her eyes dramatically. 'Do you ever get tired of being so predictable? So mediocre?'

'Do *you* ever get tired of hearing yourself talk?'

She gasps and clutches at her chest like I've wounded her. 'You're unbelievable.' She leans forward and hisses with a stage-whisper, 'You think you're clever, Asher, but you're not. Everyone knows you're nothing more than your last name.'

That one lands harder than I expect, even though I know it's for show. My jaw tightens despite myself. Around us, whispers ripple across the tables like a current.

Okay, that should be enough for tonight.

'This was a mistake,' I say. 'Clearly you can't be reasonable.'

Imani gives me a humourless smile. 'I was just about to say the same about you.'

We finish the rest of our meal in brittle silence, though every action is still deliberate: her sighs, my cold stares, the way we both pointedly avoid any kind of conversation between us.

When the dessert menus are offered, I wave mine away. 'Separate cheques,' I say loudly.

A scandalised murmur rushes through the dining room as Imani lets out a sardonic laugh. 'You haven't changed.'

When we finally push back our chairs, it feels like half the room is openly watching us and I'm certain I see at least two phones pointed in our general direction.

We walk out in frosty silence.

I keep my eyes forward as we pass the maître d', whose polite 'Have a good evening, Mr Vouvalis, Ms Davies,' comes with the faintest note of relief, as though he's glad the tension is leaving his restaurant with us. I don't blame him.

Our footsteps echo in unison down the narrow corridor until the heavy front door opens and the most exclusive restaurant in the city spits us back outside. A gust of cool air hits my face, clearing away the cloying scent of oud and expensive wine that clung to the dining room.

We barely make it ten steps away from the entrance before Imani breaks. A high-pitched sound bursts out of her and, for a second, I think she's violently sneezing. But then she doubles over, clutching at her stomach, and I realise that it's laughter spilling out of her. Pure, unrestrained laughter. She's in hysterics.

'Oh my *God*. That was—' She cuts herself off with another delighted cackle.

'Yeah,' I agree, a smile tugging at my own lips.

'People were *definitely* filming,' she says, after another bout of unrestrained laughter. A triumphant grin spreads over her face. 'If we're not all over the gossip pages by midnight, I'll eat my shoe.'

'I don't think you need to worry about that. Did you see the guy next to us?' I ask. 'He wasn't even bothering to hide his phone by the end. We'll be on that account within the hour.'

'Excellent,' she says, straightening slightly as she wipes at the corner of her eye. 'They all definitely think we hate each other.'

'Oh, one hundred per cent.'

'I'd say that's mission accomplished then.' She lifts her hand for a celebratory high five.

We're standing beneath a streetlamp, and the warm yellow glow from it softens her face, highlighting the curve of her cheekbones and the glint of pure mischief still sparkling in her eyes. It's a shame I've had to spend the entirety of tonight focusing on the act we're attempting to pull off instead of admiring the woman standing in front of me, because I'd much rather be doing the latter.

I smack my hand against hers and the clap rings out in the quiet street.

Her expression softens, just a fraction. 'I hope I wasn't too harsh in there. I don't like talking like that. Especially not to you. Promise, if I ever take it too far, you'll tell me, okay?'

'Like throwing a drink at me too far, or . . .'

She pulls a face and I get the feeling that if I reached out to touch her cheeks right now, they'd be warm. 'Exactly like that. I'm serious though – I don't like being rude to you.'

'Good,' I say, and for some reason that makes her laugh again. It's a small, quiet laugh this time, but it's no less genuine.

We stand there for a beat, the noise of Mayfair nightlife drifting in from the main road a few streets behind us. I could let us part ways now and both of us could head right on back to our separate worlds, but that feels wrong.

Too abrupt. I remember that afternoon at the member's club and how nice and easy it had been talking to her.

I glance sideways at her. 'How about a walk? Just so we don't end the night on a sour note.'

Imani tilts her head, considering. 'A walk?'

'Yes. That thing people do when they've just caused a minor social earthquake and don't want to go straight back to their living rooms, obsessively refreshing an Instagram gossip page for the rest of the night.'

She snorts. 'You know what? You're right. Let's do it.' She gestures down the street, where the quiet Mayfair side road eventually turns into a busier thoroughfare. 'Lead the way, Mr Vouvalis.'

I start walking and she falls into step easily beside me. For the first time all evening, we're not performing.

And I like it.

CHAPTER TWELVE

Imani

I can still feel the warmth from his hand.

Which is ridiculous, really, given it was just a simple high five. But the echo of it lingers under my skin, pulsing through my palm like my body hasn't quite got the memo that the contact is over. His hand was bigger, warmer, and mine just fitted against it perfectly, like it belonged there. Which is a thought I absolutely do not need to be entertaining right now.

I stuff both hands into the pockets of my coat as if that will help shake away the sensation, but it doesn't. If anything, it makes me more aware of the absence of his palm against mine.

Beside me, Asher walks in steady silence, his stride unhurried, hands tucked casually into his pockets like we're just two perfectly normal people out for a perfectly normal late-night stroll instead of co-conspirators fresh off a very public, very messy, staged fight. Which, by the way, went wonderfully.

I have to admit, I've had my reservations about whether Asher could really pull our plan off but he's pleasantly surprised me with his commitment to the role this evening.

I glance sideways at him. The look on his face is unreadable but the way his shoulders are set looks tighter than usual.

I clear my throat, because I hate the awkward silence almost as much as I hate the way my brain keeps replaying that brief brush of skin.

His gaze flickers over to me, one dark brow lifting, and I fumble for something to say now that I've got his attention. 'Tell me something about yourself that most people wouldn't know.'

I cringe inwardly at the dullness of the question. It feels like the kind of thing a HR rep might ask a group of employees during a team-building exercise. As basic as it is though, it seems to have done the trick because Asher looks moderately amused and the tension in his shoulders seems to have eased a little.

'That's a pretty broad scope,' he says.

'Good. Broad means you've got plenty of options. No rehearsed answers. And I don't want some polished PR soundbite about your favourite charity or whatever either. I want something weird.'

'Something weird?'

'Yeah. Like . . .' I search for an example. 'Did you ever collect anything weird as a kid? Or have an imaginary friend for too long? Or, I don't know, maybe you secretly love trashy reality TV?'

His mouth twitches. 'You're assuming I'd even admit to that last one.'

I grin. 'I think you just did.'

'I didn't.'

'You didn't deny it either,' I sing-song, enjoying the way his jaw tightens like he's trying his hardest not to laugh.

After a beat, he sighs, looks around dramatically like he's making sure no one is around to hear. Then he leans in slightly and says in a conspiratorial whisper, 'I didn't know cactuses were real until I was about nine.'

I nearly trip over my own feet. 'I'm sorry? You didn't what?'

Asher stares determinedly ahead. 'Never mind. Forget I said anything.'

'Oh no, absolutely not. You're not getting away with dropping that kind of lore and then chickening out.' I nudge his side with my elbow. 'Elaborate, please.'

Asher lets out a pained groan, looking like he desperately wishes he'd said something more normal like 'I don't think pineapples belong on pizza'.

'Fine. But this stays between us.'

I make a show of crossing my fingers and holding them over my heart. 'Your secret is safe with me.'

His lips twitch ever so slightly. If I weren't paying such close attention to him, I don't think I'd notice. But I am, so I do.

'I'd only ever seen them in cartoons. Looney Tunes, mostly. You know the ones with Wile E. Coyote and the Road Runner? He'd go crashing into one or get flattened next to one. So I thought . . .' He pauses, and I give him an encouraging nod. 'I thought that cactuses were just another made-up Looney Tunes thing. Like the Acme rockets. Or anvils falling from the sky.'

I have to stop walking for a second because I'm laughing too hard to move. 'You thought cactuses were *fictional*? Like they were just cartoon props? *Cactuses*?'

Asher scowls at me, but there's no malice behind it. 'Yes. Until a holiday in Greece when I was a kid. I was walking back from getting ice cream with my brothers, and I saw one by the side of the road. I remember thinking that it looked so fake. And I thought it was so strange that someone would take the time to make this completely fictional thing from a kid's cartoon and just leave it randomly on the side of the road.'

'Oh my God.' I clamp my hand over my mouth to try to muffle the cackles from coming out. It doesn't work, but I have to hope Asher appreciates the effort.

'So I ran up to it,' Asher continues, the tips of his ears darkening slightly. 'I remember yelling for Andreas to take a photo and then—'

'Oh no,' I say, knowing exactly where this is going. 'Tell me you didn't touch it.'

'Worse, actually,' he says solemnly, looking like he's having war flashbacks. 'I ran up to it and full-on hugged it.'

That sets me off again. I'm bent over in the middle of the street, practically crying. 'You *hugged* it?'

'I didn't think it was real!' he protests, his mouth curving upwards despite himself. 'I thought it would make a funny photo! Anyway, long story short? I spent the next half an hour picking needles out of my arms, face and chest while my brothers rolled around on the floor laughing. I've still got a scar.' He points to the faint scar I'd noticed along his right cheekbone at the gala. Of all the ways I could've imagined he'd got it, deliberately face-planting into a cactus definitely wasn't one of them.

I swipe at my eyes to wipe away the warm tears that are now flowing freely. 'That just might be, and no offence, the funniest thing I think I've ever heard.'

'Glad to be of assistance,' he says dryly.

He very kindly lets me get through the last of my giggles and then we fall back into step and turn down another side street. I'm still smiling and, despite the May breeze, my chest feels oddly warm. He didn't have to tell me that story. He could've made something up or said something boring and generic just to keep me quiet until the end of our walk. He didn't even have to suggest the walk at all, but I'm glad he did.

I like talking to Asher. It's easy. It's been easy from the very beginning, I realise, remembering how easily our conversation flowed back at the members club. When it's just us, I don't have to put on airs and be Imani Davies, dutiful daughter and heiress to the Peregrine Airways empire. I can just be me and apparently, that's enough for him. Ironically, it feels like we've known each other for years.

Suddenly I'm hyper-aware again of how close to each other we're walking and how his stride matches mine like we're old friends who have done this kind of walk a hundred times before.

I clear my throat again. 'My turn now?'

He arches a brow like he's sceptical I can come up with anything that'll top cactus-gate. 'Alright, let's hear it.'

'Okay.' I take a dramatic breath. 'Until I was about, uh, ten? Maybe eleven? I wore a head brace.'

His head jerks towards me. 'What?'

'Yeah,' I say with a wince, as previously squashed memories from my childhood come flooding back. 'I had a pretty strong overbite when I was younger.'

Asher blinks. 'You mean like one of those metal ones? The kind that wraps around your head like some kind of medieval torture device?'

I groan. 'Yes, that exact kind. It even had the chin strap and the neck pad and everything. My mother tried to call it my "robot superhero gear" to make me feel better about having to wear it.'

He lets out a short bark of laughter. 'That's brutal. Did it work?'

'Absolutely not,' I say, already laughing with him. 'I hated every second of it. Thank *God* I didn't have to wear it at school, but I had to wear it whenever I got home, even if we had guests.' I shudder, remembering the time my cousins came to stay for a long weekend and my parents wouldn't let me take a break from wearing the brace. The teasing I endured that weekend was relentless.

'My older cousin once spent an entire weekend chasing me around with her digital camera.'

'There are *photos*?'

I nod sadly. 'Unfortunately.'

His eyes glint dangerously. 'Please promise me you'll show me one.'

'Never.'

'Please.'

'*No.*'

'I'll find them.'

'Over my dead body.'

'Oh, I will,' he says, grinning widely now, and for a second I forget how to walk again. It's not fair that anyone can have a smile that nice.

We round a corner and the streetlights hit him just right, throwing warm gold across his cheekbones and catching the faint scruff along his jaw. I swallow hard and look away.

'Anyway,' I say, trying to distract myself from whatever my heart is doing at this moment, 'that was my weird kid thing. So now we're even.'

'I don't know,' he muses, eyes twinkling. 'Having to wear a head brace is maybe *slightly* worse than not knowing cactuses were real.'

'Definitely not,' I say confidently. 'At least my embarrassing secret has no casualties. Yours ended with you impaled.'

He chuckles again, and the sound sends an odd little flutter through me.

We fall into silence again, but it's different this time and I don't feel the need to say anything to break it up. It feels more comfortable. Like we've found a rhythm neither of us expected to stumble upon tonight. I realise, with a jolt, that I don't want it to end. I want to stay hidden in the quiet back-streets of Mayfair and learn every weird and wonderful fact about Asher Vouvalis he's willing to share, but I'm suddenly acutely aware of the fact that the hum of the busy main road is getting louder and louder with each step we take.

I sigh, feeling the little bubble we've created beginning to pop. 'I guess we should think about wrapping up?'

Asher glances at the watch on his wrist and then at the empty street ahead of us. 'I've got nowhere to be. You?'

I fight down the urge to grin, and instead play it cool with a small nod. 'Let's go.'

And so we do.

As we walk, the conversation flows even more easily than before. I tell him about the time I got stranded in Doha for eight hours and ended up joining a group of elderly Filipino women in a makeshift karaoke session in the food court. He tells me about the month he spent in Crete as a teenager, being the unofficial translator for all the British tourists who wanted to order beer and chips and not much else. We debate the best sandwiches in London; he swears by some hole-in-the-wall deli off Brick Lane that 'does magical things with pastrami' and I counter with the grilled halloumi from a stall in Broadway Market that, I insist, 'has changed my life'.

Somehow that leads to confessions about our comfort foods. His is rice pudding straight from the tin, mine is instant noodles with a possibly ungodly amount of chilli oil. He admits he can't cook anything that requires more than three ingredients and that he's probably exclusively paying the salary for several Deliveroo drivers at this point. I tell him about the time Sloane once set off my building's smoke alarm making toast.

From there, the stories keep coming and each one feels like a little window opening wider and wider. I tell him about the time I accidentally dyed my hair orange trying to go blonde at university – a mistake Sloane has never let me forget about – and he admits he once got a shitty tattoo with Andreas and Teddy to celebrate graduating. He stubbornly refuses to tell me what the tattoo is of or where it is and I make a mental note to try and wheedle it out of him at some point.

We spend the rest of the walk comparing notes on our most questionable life decisions and realise we both hate olives but pretend to like them at dinner parties because it seems sophisticated and like the kind of thing we *should* like.

I make him laugh again. Several times, actually. It feels like I'm playing a game – get Asher Vouvalis to laugh – and I'm winning.

It's easy talking to Asher like this. It's like we've known each other longer than we actually have and we're just stepping back into what is only natural for us.

When it starts to rain and a few drops of water land on my face, I only just about manage to swallow down my groan of irritation. I think I probably could've kept walking with Asher all night long without getting tired or bored.

'We should probably call it a night,' I murmur as the droplets falling to the ground pick up in speed.

Asher nods and I wonder if I'm imagining that he looks as reluctant as I feel. 'Agreed.'

We head towards the main road so we can call for our cars before an umbrella becomes strictly necessary.

'I'm glad we did this,' Asher says as we wait. 'It was nice not pretending to hate you for a little while.'

I laugh softly. 'It was very nice. We should do it again.'

He hums in agreement.

The car I called pulls up to the kerb first, rain misting the windows in soft streaks. I open the door and then hesitate.

'You know,' I start. 'It's a shame that we had to meet under ... well, you know. The *circumstances*.'

He tilts his head, watching me with a quiet, steady gaze that makes my chest tighten slightly.

'I just mean,' I say, shrugging lightly in an attempt to mask how wistful I suddenly feel for a world in which Asher and I could've met with no strings attached, 'if we'd met somewhere else with no drama, no spectacle? I think we'd probably be good friends. I don't know. Maybe even great ones.'

His lips curve into a slow, deliberate smile. The type of smile that makes everything else blur around him. 'Yeah,' he says softly, almost like he's saying it to himself. 'I think I'd have liked that.'

My heart does a ridiculous little flip, and I force myself to nod farewell. 'Goodnight, Asher.'

'Goodnight, Imani.' He doesn't step back from the kerb immediately and walk to his own car. Instead he lingers, eyes locked on mine, and for a moment it feels like the world has shrunk to just the two of us.

I think about stepping closer and offering another high-five or even just brushing my fingers against his, but I get the sneaking suspicion that if I did, I wouldn't want to let go.

So instead, I settle into my car, close the door and watch him through the tinted window. He doesn't look away as my driver pulls off, and neither do I.

CHAPTER THIRTEEN

Imani

It doesn't take long for me and Asher to become regulars on @TrustFundTea, and I'm not sure how to feel about that.

On the one hand, it means that the 'create enough social chaos to force my father to pull the plug on this whole idea' aspect of our plan is working exactly as intended. On the other, I'm not entirely sure how much more humiliation I can take.

My entire life up until now has revolved around maintaining the Davies brand. Perfect grades. Impeccable manners. Supporting the right causes. Being seen with the right people in the right places. Every single move has been over scrutinised and examined to make sure I'm not doing anything to bring the Davies name into disrepute. And in just two months, I've destroyed a lifetime of soul-crushing work.

I guess my father has trained me better than I thought,

because every time I see my face pop up on @TrustFundTea's stories or main feed, I want to crawl into a hole and never come out.

When our evening at The Opal Vault pops up less than an hour after I get home, I watch and rewatch the shaky video of Asher and I trading barbs over candlelight, unable to look away even though I desperately want to.

The caption is straight to the point: *Davies vs. Vouvalis Round Two. Place your bets, darlings.* It gets thousands of likes and comments within twenty minutes of being uploaded.

The horrible, pinching feeling that settles in the pit of my stomach as I doom scroll through the comments doesn't go away. In fact, it only intensifies.

> **@nellie247:** If i was worth £50 mil you can bet your ass i wouldn't be caught dead fighting over appetisers

> **@princesspenny:** Asher Vouvalis finally emerges from his cave and THIS is what he does?

> **@user4232:** are rich people OKAY???

And it only gets worse from there.

Someone snaps a few well-timed photos and videos of Asher and I glaring daggers at each other from our seats at a charity art auction a few weeks later and submits them to @ TrustFundTea before the day is over.

It's the kind of event where you can buy a piece of aggressively conceptual art for less than the cost of a small yacht and still feel like you've done something charitable.

Not my preferred way of spending a Sunday afternoon, but Sloane had heard through the grapevine that Emmy would be in attendance, and it seemed like too good an opportunity for carefully crafted scandal for us to pass it up.

Asher spent the entire event either loudly making snide remarks about any of the pieces I pretended to show an interest in or aggressively outbidding me, which culminated in him buying a ridiculously abstract canvas painting for far too much money (hilarious), as well as a too-loud argument between us in the foyer of the auction house that had all eyes on us (humiliating).

The @TrustFundTea post was up within minutes of me pulling my car door shut. It's a carousel post with *nine* photos, with the final one being an unflattering zoom-in of me raising my paddle and Asher seated several rows behind, smirking as he raises his even higher.

The comments come in thick and fast:

@user198503: These two AGAIN? at this point it must be a humiliation kink because???

@hotboysummer: Why do I ship this?????

@Janet_13486: Ok, I DESPERATELY need to know the backstory here.

@TrustFundTea: @Janet_13486 You and me both, hun! If anyone has the tea, send it my way xo

I know that I shouldn't be obsessing over this and all the gleeful commenters who are parasocially delighted by the public implosion of me and Asher, but I can't stop scrolling.

Not when, a month later, I cause a scene at a glamorous dinner in honour of a designer who is about to retire after sixty years of groundbreaking collections and refuse to be seated next to Asher and @TrustFundTea posts no fewer than *eight* stories about it in a row.

Not when I'm caught, a week or two after that, on video chucking a handbag at the closing elevator doors in Selfridges, with Asher smirking behind them as they clamp shut.

And not even when someone pretends to be a close friend and gives @TrustFundTea the alleged exclusive of what went down ten years ago at university. All lies, of course, but the commenters eat up every word.

Every outing, every event, every fleeting glance over the last few months turns into 'content'. My name and his has become shorthand for 'public meltdown' online. Our faces are plastered across gossip accounts, headlines, memes, even a handful of TikTok edits set to a Taylor Swift bridge. Every time I open up Instagram and check @TrustFundTea, I feel a little worse. It's mortifying and I don't know why I haven't just blocked the page yet, but it's become like pressing on a bruise just to make sure it still hurts.

Spoiler: it does.

My father is furious, of course. He's purpled-faced with righteous indignation, pacing and huffing over every new viral post over on @TrustFundTea. I can get a small sense of satisfaction from that at the very least. Although he hasn't backtracked on his Vouvalis merger plans and my marriage to Asher yet, at least he's feeling the pain of social humiliation from my actions just as much as I am.

Every time a new scandal drops, I get a call or text, summoning me to his office where he spends a good thirty minutes trying to yell and shame me back into submission.

I keep thinking that this is it. That this is going to be the scandal that slaps some sense into him and makes him pull the plug on this ridiculous scheme. But it never is.

We're nearly three months into this, and he's still not wavered. A growing part of me is starting to wonder if he ever will.

'Remind me again where you're going tonight?' Sloane asks, snapping me out of a spiral of increasingly dour thoughts. 'A film premiere, or a funeral?'

'Ha, ha,' I deadpan, glancing over at my phone propped against my dresser mirror. Sloane's face takes up the entirety of my screen, and I can spy the countryside hurtling past her in a whirl of blurred greens in the train window behind her. She's supposed to be here getting ready with me, but she booked a last-minute job in Scotland and is heading there now, leaving me here alone to spiral.

'I might cancel,' I say, brush in hand. My hair is dripping with gel, ready to be pulled back into my signature tight bun, but I can't bring myself to finish the job. Every time I reach for my brush, a wave of nausea hits me and I find something else to busy myself with.

'It's too late to bail,' Sloane says, and she's right. My car is due to arrive in fifteen minutes and Asher is probably on his way already. 'And if you don't show up, they'll probably think you're doing it specifically to avoid Asher, and that'll only make them talk more. You'll get another weirdo pretending to be your friend on @TrustFundTea, claiming that you were too heartbroken to show your face or something.'

'Maybe they'll forget I RSVP'd,' I say weakly. I reach for my brush again, but that same horrible feeling rears its ugly head and instead I reapply my lipstick for the tenth time.

Sloane snorts. 'You're not that delusional.'

I let out an irritated sigh. I wish I *was* that delusional, but alas.

Asher and I have done such a good job with our faux feud, that people have actually started placing bets on what events we'll attend and act the fool at in the @TrustFundTea comment section. Tonight's film premiere was a popular choice and, at the time, feeding into the chaos and rumours had seemed like a good idea. But that was before the reality of being the laughing stock of all my peers had really settled in.

The idea of showing up tonight and knowing that people will be watching me intently, waiting for me to provide the next round of gossip fodder, is enough to make me want to wipe off my make-up, wrap my hair in a scarf, and crawl into bed and forget I'm currently the biggest embarrassment on the social scene.

'I know, I know.' I grab my brush and start reluctantly

scraping my hair back. Ten minutes until my car arrives. 'I'm just tired of this. At what point do we just throw in the towel and—'

'And what?' Sloane scoffs, brows arched in disbelief. 'At what point do you just throw in the towel and get married to a man you barely know?'

'No, not that,' I say quickly, but the protest sounds weak even to my ears. 'Maybe we need to recalibrate, because you were right. Maybe this was a stupid plan.'

Sloane doesn't respond immediately. For a moment, I think that I've lost her thanks to a dodgy connection but then she shakes her head and lets out a quiet sigh. 'This *is* a stupid plan.'

'Yes, thank you.' I scowl at my best friend. 'I've literally just said that. You were right and I was wrong. No need to rub it in.'

'But you've committed to it now,' Sloane continues like I didn't interrupt. 'You can't undo all of this. The damage is done so you may as well lean into it now. Go hard or go home. You wanted to cause enough drama so your dad has no choice but to call things off, and that's exactly what you're doing. As far as asinine plans go, I'd say this one is currently a roaring success.'

'But it's not working,' I say, irritation creeping into my tone. Why doesn't she get this? 'My dad's not budging, and neither is Asher's father. At this point I have to wonder if I'm just delaying the inevitable and embarrassing myself for nothing every time I leave the house.'

Sloane's expression softens slightly. If she were here right now, she'd be pulling me into a one-armed hug. 'It's not even been three months yet.'

'Well, it feels like an eternity,' I interject bitterly.

'I just mean,' she continues, 'did you really think your dad was the type of guy to fold in less than three months? Come on, babe. You're smarter than that.'

I wince. Her words sting slightly because she's right again. She always is.

'I know,' I mutter. I finish pulling my hair into its bun. 'I knew he wouldn't have a change of heart so easily.'

Sloane tilts her head, waiting.

I meet her gaze. 'I just didn't expect this part to suck so much. I thought it would be fun. Funny, even.' I remember that night at The Opal Vault and how I'd all but collapsed in a fit of giggles once we left the restaurant and went on our walk. That night feels a thousand years away now. 'But it's not. It's humiliating.'

The words taste bitter in my mouth, but it's the ugly truth. 'I thought I could handle the whispers and all the comments. I thought I didn't care what people said about me.'

'But you do,' Sloane says gently.

'I do,' I admit, swallowing hard. 'I care way more than I thought I would. I mean, I've always known these people were fake, but now it's like, I walk into a room and I feel it. Everyone looking at me like I'm pathetic. Or crazy. Or both. And you're right, I knew he wouldn't back down this fast. Of course I knew that. But I think some part of me hoped that maybe if I caused enough chaos, he'd snap. Call the whole thing off. Admit it was a bad idea and let me off the hook.'

I let out a laugh that comes out sounding more like a choke. 'God, I was so naïve.'

'You're not naïve,' she says, then cocks her head to the side and gives me a sheepish grin. 'Well, you're a little naïve, but that's not a bad thing.'

I roll my eyes, but my lips twitch slightly. 'I just want it to be done already. I want him to say, "Okay, I get it, you've made your point. This was a bad idea. I'm sorry." I'm tired of feeling like I'm setting fire to my own reputation for absolutely no payoff.'

Sloane leans in closer to her camera. 'Then keep going.'

I blink at her. 'What?'

'If it's not working yet, that just means you haven't pushed him hard enough. If this plan has any hope in hell of working, then he needs to see how committed you are to making whatever arrangement he has with Vouvalis a complete and utter disaster. Make him regret the day he ever entertained a meeting with Georgios Vouvalis.'

I stare at myself in the mirror. The girl looking back at me looks polished and composed. The picture-perfect heiress. But underneath it all, I'm tired. Humiliated. Angry. So very, very *done*.

'I don't know if I have it in me,' I admit.

'You do,' Sloane says bluntly, like it's an uncontested fact. 'Besides, it's either that or, once I'm home next week, we start shopping for wedding dresses.'

Just the thought of that makes my stomach lurch. 'Point taken.'

'Good,' Sloane nods. 'So go to that premiere tonight and cause a scene. It'll suck for a little while but this time next year, when you're tanning on a beach somewhere in the Caribbean *without* a ring on your finger, you'll be thanking yourself. Trust me.'

I can't help but smile a little at that. 'St Lucia, for sure.'

Sloane matches my smile. 'Atta girl. Now—Shit, it's my stop.' There's a flurry of movement as she hops up from her seat and starts pulling her luggage out from the storage rack. 'I've got to go, but you'll be fine. I promise.'

I repeat Sloane's words to myself like a lifeline as I finish getting dressed and make my way to the premiere. They're the only thing keeping me sane – that and scraping the skin around my nails raw – but even her words of encouragement are sounding less and less convincing the closer I get to the theatre and the glittering mob of cameras waiting outside.

By the time my driver opens the door, my palms are slick with sweat and my breath is coming out fast. Way too fast.

I step out of the car and immediately it's like the air has been sucked from my lungs. I freeze as every single pair of eyes in the vicinity seems to snap onto me like vultures spotting fresh roadkill.

I force my chin up and straighten my spine. I can do this.

Out of the corner of my eye I spy a group of women, all daughters of CEOs and founders, who I'm usually fairly friendly with, posing for a photo for a few paparazzi. I watch as their collective gaze slides over to me, eyes widening, lips curling. My stomach sinks and I quickly turn away.

This is good, I tell myself. *This is the point. Let them laugh. Let them talk.*

I hear my name and Asher's hissed and whispered over and over again as I glide down the carpet and make my way into the building. People cover their mouths with their hands as I pass by, like I can't see the way their shoulders are shaking with laughter.

My throat tightens.

My chest burns.

I remind myself that this is the goal. That this is the road to eventual victory. That if I'm feeling the burn of humiliation now, my father will be feeling it too and there's only so much shame he can tolerate.

But my body doesn't seem to care about the plan or logic because my vision blurs and my lungs squeeze in on themselves and no matter how fast I breathe, it feels like I still can't get enough air.

I push through the doors into the theatre's foyer, hoping for some reprieve from the flashing lights outside but it's only worse in here. The space is filled to the brim with already tipsy socialites and it feels like every single head in the room turns in my direction as I step through the doors. My breath gets stuck in my throat.

There's Emmy just a few feet away, her phone already in her hand and aimed in my direction, a sickly smirk on her face. She's surrounded by a group of girls, all with wide eyes looking at me like you might look at a lion at the zoo, desperately willing it to do something so you can get your money's worth of entertainment.

Every bone in my body feels like it's vibrating with panic. My throat is working uselessly around air that won't go in right.

I force a smile, or at least I think I do; my cheeks are too stiff to be certain.

Breathe. Just breathe.

But I can't. My heart claws against my ribs, thudding so hard it's painful, and my hands are trembling so violently I'm terrified someone will notice.

They probably already have.

I hear a pointed laugh from somewhere to my left. A camera flash on the right blinds me. A pair of lips, glossy red, curve into a smirk I just know is aimed at me.

My vision tunnels. The crowd warps at the edges, their faces blurring into grotesque masks, their whispers twisting into barbs I can't quite catch but which I know are about me. My clutch nearly slips from my slick palms, and I have to lock my knees to keep from stumbling.

I don't know what to do.

If I move, I'll fall. If I stand still, I'll suffocate under the weight of their stares.

You want this. You want them to talk. This is the plan. You can do this.

But the words rattle uselessly in my head, drowned out by the roar of my pulse. Everything feels wrong. My chest is tight, my mouth is dry and I feel panic everywhere – under my nails, in the back of my throat, curling around my spine until I'm certain I'll crack open under the weight of it.

I take a deep breath to try and steady myself, but I choke and instead stumble forward. The cry that falls from my lips is more like a croak, and then—

'Imani?'

The sound of my name slices through the fog.

I blink and Asher is suddenly standing in front of me, close enough that I can see the crease in his brow and the tight set of his jaw. His eyes are locked onto me, like I'm the only person in the room.

'Imani,' he says again, softer this time, like he's afraid I'll shatter if he speaks too loudly. I just might. His hand finds my arm and I swear it's the first thing in minutes that feels real.

The crowd is still surrounding us, watching intently, but in this moment all I can focus on is the way his gaze is locked onto mine.

'No,' I manage to croak out eventually. I try to pull my arm away, but his grip tightens. It's not painful, but it's firm and grounding. 'Asher, no. They'll see . . . You're ruining . . .' The words come out in incomplete breathy pants.

Before I can get any more of an argument out, he's guiding me away. I stumble in my heels, but his grip doesn't falter as he pulls me into his side and steadies me. I catch glimpses of camera flashes and curious glances as Asher leads us through the crowd, but all I can really feel is his hand anchoring me, pulling me through the noise and the whispers and the suffocating heat until the cool night air hits my face and I can finally breathe again.

CHAPTER FOURTEEN

Asher

I can tell something is wrong from the second Imani steps into the room. It's like I'm attuned to her presence the same way some people can sense rain before the sky even starts to darken.

For the last twenty minutes, I've been waiting near the bar, half listening to a group of people I barely know and glancing towards the door every time it opens. By the time she finally arrives, I'm ready to go; ready to smirk and throw out some cutting line for anyone close enough to overhear and play my part in our curated feud. But that readiness dissolves as soon as I really look at her.

Something is obviously wrong here.

Imani doesn't look like she's ready to play the part of a scorned ex-lover. She doesn't even look like herself. Her posture is stiff and her face is grey and stricken.

At first I think that maybe she's just nervous being on the

receiving end of so much attention. When she steps inside the room, the crowd ripples, and heads turn towards her like sunflowers chasing the light. I watch her shoulders lock, her grip on her purse tightening until her knuckles go pale. She sways slightly on the spot, eyes unfocused, and then I'm moving across the room. The group I'm standing beside shoot me startled looks and someone even half-heartedly calls my name, but I don't care who's watching. I just know I need to get to her.

People jostle against me as I push through the crowd, too caught up in their own conversation to notice me shoving past them, but my eyes never leave her. She hasn't even looked up yet, too busy staring at the floor, her hand tightening around her purse like it's the only thing holding her together.

By the time I reach her, she looks seconds from crumbling. Her chest is rising and falling in quick, shallow bursts and there's a glazed panic in her eyes when she finally looks up at me.

'Imani?'

She blinks at me, dazed.

I try again, a little firmer this time. 'Imani.'

Her lips part but no sounds comes out. She purses them again and gives me a quick shake of her head.

I slip a hand around her arm and she jerks slightly and tries to pull away.

'No,' she rasps. 'Asher, no. They'll see . . . You're ruining . . .' I know exactly what she's trying to say. I can feel the room filled with curious eyes focused on the two of us. I can hear people whispering and wondering out loud what the hell is going on between us, but I don't care right now. I don't care about our plan and keeping up the act or even getting our fathers to call off this marriage.

The only thing I care about is getting her out of here.

I wrap my arms tight around her and push through the crowd, trying to use my body to barricade Imani from all the stares as much as possible, and I don't stop moving until we get to the exit.

When we burst through the doors and step into the cool night air, Imani gasps like she's been drowning.

I've already pulled out my phone and called for a car before I've even fully thought all the optics through. There's not as big of a crowd out here, but there are enough people milling around that I have no doubt photos of this moment will be on social media before the night's end. Imani winces every time a flash goes off, even if it's not directed at us. She's shivering too, and just as I'm starting to wonder if it might be easier for us to just run in any direction, the car I've called suddenly pulls up. I pull open the door and gesture for Imani to get in.

She hesitates, muttering something about not needing my help, but her hands are still trembling, and I know without a shadow of a doubt that I'm not leaving her like this.

'Come on,' I say as gently as I can. My hand, still on her arm, moves to the small of her back and I'm not sure if I'm imagining the way she seems to lean into the touch. 'We need to get out of here.'

To my surprise, she doesn't argue this time. Just gives me a small nod before she slides into the back seat. I follow after her and pull the door shut on all the noise and the camera flashes and the non-stop staring.

The silence inside the car is heavy after the chaos we've just escaped. Imani doesn't say anything. Sat beside me, our legs brushing slightly, I can feel the tension in her body. Her hands are still trembling slightly, though it's less pronounced now that we're out of the frenzy. For a few moments, the only sound in the car is the low hum of the engine and the faint click of her nails against her purse as she fiddles aimlessly with it in her lap. Then she exhales suddenly, her breath leaving her in a rush like she's been holding it in for too long.

I wait for her to speak, but she just sits there quietly breathing in and out. I'm pretty sure she's grounding herself and I hate to interrupt, but our driver has done the same loop five times in a row at this point.

'What's your address?' I ask.

She winces at the sudden noise and then murmurs it. Her voice is quieter than I'm used to, and I don't like it. It feels hollow. The driver nods and turns the car in the direction of her building.

I keep my eyes on her out of the corner of my vision as we start moving, watching as the colour slowly creeps back into her cheeks and her breathing evens out again. She looks more like herself, but also more embarrassed than I've ever seen her.

'I'm sorry,' she blurts out suddenly, shaking her head. 'God, I'm so, *so* sorry. I didn't mean to ruin everything.'

I frown. Ruin? What could she possibly have *ruined*?

'I just . . .' She buries her face in her hands, pressing the heel of her palms into her eyes so hard I'm sure she must be seeing stars. 'God, I'm just sorry.'

'What are you apologising for?' I ask, genuinely confused. I feel like I'm missing something incredibly obvious.

Imani peeks at me through her fingers. Some of her make-up has started to run down her cheeks, leaving a streaky, black stain. She still looks beautiful. I don't think there's anything Imani could do to *not* be the most striking person in any room she's in.

'What am I apologising for?' she parrots, looking at me in disbelief. 'Was I hallucinating and I didn't just have a complete breakdown back there?'

'Is that what that was?' I ask quietly. 'A breakdown?'

She swallows and looks intently out the window. 'I don't know. I just . . .' She presses a trembling hand to her chest. 'I just couldn't *breathe*. Everyone was staring at me. Pointing. Whispering. Laughing. And I know they've been doing that for the last few months, but I guess . . . I guess it just finally got to me tonight.' She lets out a soft sigh and lolls her head against the window. 'And I've just given them more to talk about, I suppose.'

She closes her eyes and sighs again. For a moment, I just sit there and study her, watching as the tension slowly ebbs from her shoulders and exhaustion settles in its place.

I take her in – the soft curve of her mouth, the delicate fan of her lashes against her cheekbones, the faint shimmer of her tear tracks catching the light from the streetlamps outside as we crawl along. Even unravelled like this, Imani is breathtaking.

My chest tightens in a way I don't want to examine too closely right now.

Then her eyes flicker open. Her gaze is hazy and blurred with unshed tears when it lands on me. I jerk away quickly, feeling like I've just been caught doing something I know I shouldn't, and instead pretend to be fascinated by the blur of light outside the window.

'Thank you,' she says quietly.

I force myself to look at her again. She's staring at me with wide, earnest eyes.

'For getting me out of there,' she clarifies. 'You didn't have to.'

I *didn't* have to, but I know I'd do it every time without hesitation. I shrug in what I hope is a nonchalant manner. 'You needed me.'

Her lips part into a small 'o' shape and she cocks her head to the side, examining me thoughtfully. I wonder what she sees on my face because her lips suddenly twitch into a small but genuine smile. 'I guess I did.'

The car pulls to a smooth stop in front of her building. I get out first, then circle around to her side, pull open her door and offer a hand without thinking. She takes it without hesitation and her palm slips into mine like it belongs there.

Her hand is still slightly clammy but her fingers curl around mine with surprising steadiness.

She doesn't let go.

Not as I help her out of the car. Not as we step through the glass doors of her building, nodding to the concierge as we pass him. Not even as we glide upwards in the sleek lift with only soft jazz music playing faintly over hidden speakers.

I don't let go either. Not that I want to.

Her hand fits into mine the way puzzle pieces are meant to fit together. I tell myself that this is purely platonic and practical; that she still looks slightly shaky and fragile and that I want her to feel safe. But the truth hums beneath my skin.

I like it.

I like the weight of her hand in mine. I like how I can feel the warmth slowly seeping back into her skin with each passing second. I like how natural walking hand in hand with her feels, like we've been doing this forever.

When the doors to the lift open onto the penthouse level, Imani finally looks down at our joined hands as if she's just noticed them. For a second I think she's going to pull away and I ready the apology on the tip of my tongue. Instead, she gives my hand the faintest squeeze and starts walking down the short corridor, tugging me along with her.

Once we reach her door, she rifles through her bag and pulls out her keys. She has one hand still in mine. Her gaze flicks from the lock to me, down again to where our hands are still joined, and then back to me.

'Do you want to come in?' she blurts out suddenly.

'I—'

'Just because you walked me all the way up here,' she says, interrupting me. 'And I ruined the entire evening. Maybe even the whole plan.'

She categorically did not. If anything, the two of us alone without prying eyes and the constant flash of cameras around us is the best possible outcome to the evening.

'I'd just feel a lot less like the worst person in the world if you had something to show for it,' she continues. 'Do you want a drink? I think I've got a bottle left in the wine fridge from the last time Sloane came over. Or tea? I've got a really good collection from when I visited Taiwan, or—'

She's rambling and very clearly flustered. Her cheeks are darker than usual, her palms are getting increasingly clammy, and she's looking anywhere but at me.

It's ridiculous how attracted I am to her right now.

'I've got a decent coffee collection if that's—'

'I'd love to,' I say, and the smile she gives me, soft and shy, might just be one of my favourites yet.

She slips the key into the lock, turns it, and pushes the door open. The action must trigger a sensor because warm light immediately spills out from inside.

Imani steps over the threshold and I follow. The first thing that hits me is how 'hers' her home feels. It screams Imani from the very second you step into it. It's lived-in and curated like a gallery of her life.

My eyes are caught by the wall to the right, where a massive tapestry made of indigo and gold threads hangs. There's a low wooden table beneath it carved with delicate geometric designs that must have been done by hand and taken years and years of dedication.

'Where did you get these?' I'm gesturing to the tapestry and table, but I could ask the same question about just about anything in her home.

She tosses her bag onto a nearby chair and shrugs like it's nothing special. 'It's stuff I've picked up while travelling. The tapestry is from Morocco – it's Berber weaving. I commissioned the table from a woodworker in Bali. He's actually done a lot of stuff for me over the years. I really love his work.' She gestures vaguely around the room pointing towards a dining table and a bookshelf in the same design, but my eyes are already moving from one object to the next.

A cluster of deep ocean blue ceramic bowls line a shelf near the window, each one slightly uneven and with blemishes that show they were handmade. Next to them, there's a brass incense burner shaped like a lotus flower and a scattering of tiny glass bottles surrounding it, each filled with sand and sea glass.

Opposite the shelf, a tall glass cabinet gleams in the warm lamplight. Inside are what look like hand-painted Russian nesting dolls, a delicate porcelain teapot with tiny cranes etched across it, and an assortment of framed Polaroids filled with wide-smiled faces, most of them blurred by movement and bright lights. Imani is centre stage in all of them, beaming from ear to ear.

On the coffee table, there's a stack of art books in a variety of genres – photography, architecture, travel, music, food, and more – and between them, a half-burned candle that smells faintly of jasmine and lavender. A guitar leans against the far wall beside a potted fiddle-leaf fig that's clearly thriving, despite being almost as tall as me. A strand of fairy lights is draped in a lazy curve across the frame of the bookshelf, throwing soft gold sparkles against spines of novels that look well thumbed through and loved. Near the kitchen archway, there's a framed postcard that reads 'Meet me where the air tastes like salt' with a photo of a sprawling white sand beach in the distance.

Imani shrugs again. 'Just souvenirs, you know?'

I scoff. These are not just souvenirs. It's not the kind of plastic, kitschy junk most tourists pick up on their travels. These aren't magnets, keyrings or dishcloths with mass-printed images on them. Her home is filled with intricate, delicate, beautiful pieces from around the world. Things she clearly had to have deliberately sought out from the communities she visited. She's not spending her time in closed-off resorts, sipping cocktails by the pool, only interacting with the locals when she's ordering a meal; she's truly travelling in a way I never have.

It's like every inch of her home is bursting with a story.

I want to know exactly how she came across this Balinese woodworker and struck up the kind of relationship that would involve her commissioning piece after piece from him. I want to know where she found the Berber tapestry and what drew her to it or hear the story behind the hand-painted Russian nesting dolls. I reckon I could sit here for hours listening to Imani tell the stories of her travels.

And then there's the map.

It's huge, taking up the entirety of the floor-to-ceiling windows, and it's clearly a custom job. It's encased in a wooden frame and the countries are painted in with precise, vibrant strokes and the seas are a stormy wash of blues and greys. By each painted country, there's a tiny card pinned beside it with writing in Imani's messy, looping handwriting. They're dates, I realise after a second of peering at one closely. And there's sometimes more than one:

France: 2015, 2018, 2021
St Lucia: 2019
Uganda: 2016
Morocco: 2020
Singapore: 2020, 2021
Bali: 2023, 2024

The map is a crowded kaleidoscope of colour and ink, with more than half the world filled in.

'So what's it going to be?' Imani asks, interrupting my wide-eyed snooping. 'Wine? Tea? Coffee?'

I glance back over to her and watch as she disappears into the kitchen. I follow her and stub my toe on a suitcase that's poking out from behind her large sofa.

'Tea,' I say absentmindedly, then nod towards the suitcase.

It's a dark brown trunk-style case with her name stitched into the top. 'Are you planning on taking off sometime soon?'

Imani pokes her head out, sees where I'm looking and gives me a sad smile. 'Habit. I always keep one packed. Comes with the lifestyle.' She shrugs, like it's obvious. 'It just makes sense. Since I travel so much it's just easier to have the essentials ready to go, you know?' She frowns and lets out an irritated sigh. 'I mean, it *used* to make sense. I've been stuck here for the last three months. Not sure why I haven't put it away yet.'

She's staring wistfully at the suitcase, and it suddenly hits me just how important travelling is for her. I enjoy a break as much as the next person, but it's obvious that it goes deeper for Imani. It's not just a hobby; it's the thing that keeps her going.

'How come you love it so much?' I ask.

She glances away from the suitcase to frown at me, like the question doesn't make any sense to her. 'Huh?'

'Travelling,' I say. 'What kickstarted the love?'

Her frown deepens, like she's never really considered it before. 'I guess it's just in my blood?' The answer comes out more like a question than anything else. 'Peregrine's been looming over me all my life; of course I was going to love travelling.'

I hum noncommittally, not wanting to push it. It doesn't feel like the right answer, the *full* answer, but who am I to say? She starts moving towards the kitchen.

'Where were you supposed to be going?' I ask, pivoting the topic ever so slightly as I follow.

Just like the large, open-plan living area, the kitchen is filled with reminders of all her travels. There's a hand-sewn and embroidered spice bag hanging from what I assume is the pantry door, a stone pestle and mortar resting on the counter, and a row of gleaming knives hanging above the range with Japanese characters engraved into the handles in gold.

'The Seychelles,' she says, forcing a sad smile. 'Have you been?'

I shake my head.

'You have to go one day – it's beautiful. One of my favourite places in the whole world to visit.'

'You've been before?' I ask, leaning against a counter.

'Twice,' she says. 'First time was a trip with my parents in that last summer between school and sixth form. It was amazing, and I had a great time, but travelling with your parents . . .' She pulls a face. 'Anyway, I wanted to experience it on my own terms, so I went back again a few years later and fell in love even more.' She sighs wistfully, crosses her arms, and leans against the counter opposite me. 'I was really looking forward to going back.'

'How do you decide if you want to go back to a place?' I ask, thinking about the countries with multiple entries on her map.

She shrugs. 'Usually there's something I didn't get to do or see the last time I visited, but with the Seychelles . . .' She trails off and suddenly looks shy. 'Nothing. Forget it.'

I frown. 'Tell me. What was it?'

She absentmindedly reaches for a nearby tea towel and

starts picking at it. 'I was meant to go for work this time. Well, not *work* work.'

I tilt my head. 'What does that mean?'

Her fingers wrap around the fabric of the towel, twisting it around and around as she fumbles for the right words. 'I've always wanted to open my own travel agency,' she says quickly, like ripping off a plaster before she can overthink it. Once she's started though, the words come tumbling out. 'A different kind of travel agency. Not like one of those corporate ones that just funnel rich tourists into five-star hotels and pretend like the rest of the country doesn't exist. No offence,' she adds as an afterthought.

I laugh. 'None taken.'

'I mean, I love a bougie hotel as much as anyone, but the best part of travelling is when you step outside the predetermined path. I wanted to start an agency that works *with* the locals – people who actually live there and know the land, you know? I want the experiences to be curated by them, not some random person sitting in an office a thousand miles away, who gets to pocket most of the fee while the person doing the hard work gets next to nothing.' She glances at me, almost like she's bracing for a reaction, and then looks away just as quickly. 'I know it sounds idealistic. Probably naïve. My father certainly thinks so. He keeps telling me it's not scalable enough and there's no real profit in it unless I compromise with the margins.' Her shoulders lift in a small helpless shrug. 'But I don't want to compromise. What's the point of travelling if you're leaving the place in a worse state than you found it?'

I think about the woodworker in Bali she's been commissioning pieces from for years. I think about the tapestries, the ceramics, the hand-embroidered crafts, and the map on her wall. This isn't just a sudden whim for her – this is a dream she's been nurturing for a long time.

'That's why I was going to head back to the Seychelles,' she says softly. 'I've been in touch with a woman there who runs a small eco-lodge. She employs women from nearby villages, sources everything locally, and reinvests as much as she can into marine conservation. I was supposed to meet with her to discuss designing a travel package that would bring in more visitors without destroying the reefs or pricing locals out of their own home.' Her voice drops slightly. 'I was going to use it as a case study for my father. Prove that this kind of model does work and see if he'd be open to letting me advertise on some of our flights.'

I push myself off the counter without really thinking and take a step closer towards her. 'Imani,' I say. 'That sounds amazing. Incredible, really.'

She looks up at me with wide, hopeful eyes. 'You think so?'

I nod. 'You'd be making a difference.'

The light in her eyes dims slightly. 'I'm not doing it though. Even this one thing I wanted to do, to prove that I could do something and have something for myself, I can't do without my father bankrolling it.' She says the last few words with uncharacteristic bitterness, then seems to catch herself. She shakes her head and forces a smile. 'Anyway. First-world problems, right?'

'Don't do that,' I say.

'Don't do what?' she asks. She's turned and started rifling through a cupboard and pulls out two ceramic mugs from a high shelf. I wonder which country she got them from.

'Don't dismiss how you feel,' I say. 'Don't call it a "first world problem" like you're not allowed to feel the way you do.'

Imani freezes, her fingers curling around the handle of one of the mugs like it's the only thing anchoring her in the moment.

I step closer. 'You don't have to pretend you're fine just because you've got things most people would kill for. You're still allowed to be upset when your dream, the thing that brings you joy, gets taken away. Especially like this.'

'No, I know how it sounds,' she says with a wry smile. 'It sounds spoiled. Bratty. I'm here complaining about not being able to take off whenever I want when my life is pretty much perfect here, when there are people out there just trying to make it through the day.' She rolls her eyes. 'Tell me honestly that's not the very definition of spoiled.'

'Imani.' Another step and I'm close enough to see the faint shimmer of the glossy lipstick on her lips. Her breath hitches but she doesn't move to put any more distance between us. 'You don't have to measure your pain or struggle against anyone else's. It doesn't work like that. What matters to you matters. And it's not just about you wanting to take off whenever you'd like. It's your dream. It's part of who you are. Having that taken away would mess with anyone.'

Her lips part like she wants to argue but I keep going.

'It's not spoiled, or bratty, or naïve, or any other word you want to use to dismiss how you feel. It's human.'

Her gaze locks onto mine and the world tilts for a second. I think I could stand here, looking into those eyes for an eternity, and I'd still want more time.

'You miss the thing that makes you feel alive,' I add. 'That gives you purpose. That's not you being selfish by any definition of the word. That's you being honest.'

She lets out a self-deprecating laugh. 'You think very highly of me.'

'I do,' I say with a shrug. 'And you should too.'

She tilts her head slightly, lips twitching like she's fighting a smile. I wish she would. But instead, she shakes her head and presses the mug in her hands into mine. Our fingers brush as she hands it over and the contact zings all the way up my arm.

I don't hate it.

I don't think she does either, because she still hasn't made any effort to move away.

'Do *you* like travelling?' she asks suddenly.

'Not like you,' I admit. 'I mostly just travel for work. Vouvalis Resort hotel rooms and back again. It's nice but it's nothing really meaningful. Nothing like this.'

'Do you want meaningful?'

I think I must stare at her for a solid three seconds before I remember to answer. 'Yeah, I think I do.'

I finally get the smile I've been waiting for. It's soft, almost conspiratorial.

'Alright. One day I'll show you how to travel Imani-style.'

I shouldn't be imagining it, but I do. I can see her laughing in the middle of some crowded marketplace halfway across the world, tugging me through narrow streets. I see her barefoot on some nameless beach at sunset, throwing her head back with laughter as she pulls me into the ocean after her. I see us huddled under a tree in a rainforest, waiting out a sudden thunderstorm.

It's terrifyingly easy to picture myself travelling the world beside her, and from the way she's looking at me, I wonder if she's picturing it too.

'Imani-style sounds good,' I say.

She hums, lips still tilted upwards into that perfect smile. 'I've not had any complaints so far.'

'I don't doubt that.'

Imani laughs and it feels like something has changed between us. She looks up at me through long lashes, her eyes slightly heavier than before. 'You're standing very close.'

I swallow. 'Too close?'

A beat passes between us. Her lips part, but no sound comes out. Instead, her gaze dips to my mouth and lingers there. She runs her tongue along her bottom lip and shakes her head.

I'm not sure who moves first. Me? Her? Maybe it's both of us at the same time. All I know is that one minute there's enough space between us to pretend like this is platonic, like we're just two good friends standing in her kitchen making tea, and then the next—

My hand skims her waist. She breathes out and leans in closer, her breath feathering against my collarbone. I draw her in, pressing her against me until I can feel every deep, delicate curve as her body melts against mine.

She slides her hands up my chest, fingers fisting in the fabric of my shirt. A quiet, desperate whimper escapes her throat and that's all the invitation I need.

I cup her jaw and capture her mouth with mine. Her lips part instantly with a soft sigh and the taste of her rushes through me.

I could easily get addicted to this.

Kissing Imani is nothing like I could ever have imagined it would be. It's not hesitant or slow or the kind of kiss you have with someone when you're just testing the waters, trying to see if there's any semblance of a spark there. Kissing Imani feels like we've been doing this for years. There's no awkward fumbling as we try to find our rhythm; we just fall into it like her lips on mine is as natural as breathing.

Her fingers tighten on my shirt, then slide higher, wrapping around my neck and dragging me down to her. A groan rumbles from the depths of my chest, muffled against her mouth. My free hand finds the small of her back, and I press her even closer, erasing any last sliver of space between us.

She tilts her head, deepening the kiss, and I swear the world falls away. We're not in her kitchen anymore. There are no mugs half forgotten on the counter. We're not in the middle of a fake feud, we don't have scheming fathers, and there are no expectations pressing down on us. It's just her.

Just this.

Just *us*.

I nip at her bottom lip and she gasps. The sound darts straight through me and ignites every nerve-ending in my body. Her gasp fades to a breathless laugh against my mouth. I kiss her once more, just to feel the shape of her smile against my lips, before I force myself to slow down.

Pulling away from her feels wrong, but I do it anyway though my hand is still pressed against her waist and the small of her back, and her fingers stay curled against my chest like she's not ready to let go either.

I'm not sure how long we stay like that. A few seconds? A couple of minutes? An eternity? All I know is that we're still close enough that I can feel her breath on my lips and the steady thrum of her heartbeat against my chest.

Finally, I clear my throat. 'I—'

'No apologies,' Imani says firmly. Her gaze lifts to meet mine. Her eyes are wide and maybe a little dazed, but I don't see any sign of panic or regret in them. I *do* see the faintest twinkle and the curve of a smile tugging at her kiss-swollen lips.

I bring a hand up to her face and brush my thumb along her jaw. 'I wasn't going to.'

'Good. Because there's nothing to apologise for. It was just a kiss.'

'Just a kiss?'

She nods, all fake-nonchalant, even as her fingers linger a second too long against my chest before she finally pulls away and lets her arms swing down by her side. 'A very nice kiss,' she concedes. 'But still. *Just* a kiss. We can be grown-ups about this, right?'

I force a smile, even though every part of me wants to argue otherwise. 'Of course. Grown-ups. Very mature. This was no big deal.'

She swallows and drops her gaze. 'Exactly. No big deal.'

I take a step back, needing the space before I forget what those words mean and lean in again. 'And I guess, for the sake of our plan, we probably shouldn't kiss again, right?'

Her eyes flick back to mine just long enough for me to notice the tiny spark there before the mask goes back up. 'Right,' she says, her voice steady. 'Kissing again would be a terrible decision. Given the circumstances, I mean.'

'The circumstances,' I repeat. 'Exactly.'

A silence stretches between us, thick with everything we're both trying not to say. Finally, I nod and shove my hands into my pockets like that will stop them from reaching for her again. 'Glad we're on the same page, then.'

Imani turns away and starts fussing with the mugs on the counter again, her voice low as she mutters under her breath about putting the kettle on. I nod, but I barely hear her. Because one thought has rooted itself in my head and I can't shake it.

If I'd known that kiss was going to be our first and last, I would've tried to make it last just a little longer.

CHAPTER FIFTEEN

Imani

I haven't seen my father this happy in months.

He's humming what sounds suspiciously like the tune to Bob Marley's 'Three Little Birds' as he opens the door to his office and gestures for me to follow him in. He's even got a little spring to his step. If I didn't know any better, I'd say he was about to break out into a dance number.

For a short while, it feels like things are normal between us again. Like maybe all this Vouvalis madness has just been one long fever dream, and my father hasn't hurt and betrayed me in the worst way possible with this scheme of his.

'Sit, sit,' he says, beaming like he's just discovered our biggest airline rival has filed for bankruptcy. His good mood is unsettling to say the least.

'Is everything okay?' I ask cautiously as I settle into the chair across from his desk. His smile only widens.

'More than okay.' He lowers himself into his large leather

chair and then leans forward with his elbows braced on the desk. 'Imani, my darling.'

I wince internally at the term of endearment. Given everything that's happened between us these last few months, it doesn't feel right. It hits me then that my relationship with my father might never recover from this. Because how do you go back to *normal* once you realise how little you truly mean to your parents? The urge to take off and disappear to some new destination has never felt so strong. I desperately need my flight privileges back.

'I know this has been a difficult few months for you.'

A moderately hysterical chuckle slips past my lips. It's only years and years of social conditioning that stops me from full-blown cackling in my father's face.

Instead, I do my best to compose myself and say steadily, 'That would be an understatement.'

He gives me an apologetic wince. 'And I need you to understand that I'm grateful for your sacrifice and all your hard work here.'

'I don't—'

'Let me tell you,' he says, cutting across me like I hadn't tried to say something. 'I was this close,' he pinches his thumb and forefinger together until they're nearly touching, '*this* close to calling everything off. I could see how badly it was affecting you and the Davies name.' He bristles slightly, like he's remembering every single bit of bad press I've brought our family and business over the last few months. 'Truth be told, I thought you'd never come around to the Vouvalis boy.'

I blink, dumbfounded. Have I misheard? 'You're calling it off?'

My heart soars—

'I *was*,' he says.

—And then crashes back down into the very depths of my stomach.

'As a matter of fact, I was just drafting an email to Georgios this morning, but then . . .' He reaches for a folder on desk, flips it open, and then slides a sheet of paper towards me.

I feel truly sorry for whichever fresh graduate, with bright dreams of entering the aviation world and learning the tricks of the trade, whose job it is to give my father what I assume is a daily debrief on the social media chatter surrounding me and Asher. Because there's absolutely no way that my father searched for @TrustFundTea this morning to print this out himself. At least, I have to hope he didn't. The idea of my father scrolling through the gossip page and reading those comments about me is enough to make me want to dig a hole, bury myself, and never resurface.

The page he slides across is a screenshot from @TrustFundTea's latest post. I'd already seen it this morning but seeing it again in the bright light of my father's office sends a whole new wave of emotions crashing through me. It's a photo of me and Asher at the film premiere last night. Or, more accurately, it's a photo of us *leaving* the premiere. Asher's hand is resting protectively at the small of my back. His brows are knit together in obvious worry and his face a mask of concern. My own expression is pale and drawn. I look like a deer in the headlights.

Just the sight of his hand on me is enough to send my stomach into free fall. I tell myself to stay focused, to keep the memories at bay, but they slip through anyway.

Suddenly, I'm not in my father's office anymore. I'm back in my kitchen, the counter pressing into my spine, Asher's hands firm on my waist, his mouth moving over mine with devastating certainty. His tongue brushes against mine, slow and deliberate, and the memory alone is enough to make my toes curl.

I blink hard and try to drag myself back into the present before my father notices the flush creeping up my neck. He's still talking, words rolling past me in a wave I can't quite catch because my senses are currently going haywire. All I can hear and feel right now is the phantom echo of my own gasp, the rough scrape of Asher's stubble against my skin, and the muscle memory of the way his body fitted against mine like it was made for it.

I cross my legs, uncross them, then cross them again, my fingers tightening around the armrest of my chair. It feels borderline criminal to be having thoughts like this with my father sitting across from me completely oblivious.

And yet I can't stop.

The memory slams back into the forefront of my mind in fragments. Asher's hand sliding higher up my body. The low growl that built up in his chest and vibrated against mine as my lips parted. The molten hot pull between us that made me forget that I'm supposed to be pretending to actively loathe Asher Vouvalis and not be seriously considering jumping his bones.

'Imani?' My father's voice cuts through the haze.

I jerk upright like I've just been electrocuted. 'Yes?'

'I was just saying how proud I am of you,' he says, looking genuinely delighted. 'I knew you wouldn't let me down and you'd find a way to get along with him.'

Get along.

Well. That's one way to put it, I suppose.

I clear my throat and try to inject as much flatness into my tone as possible. 'I mean, I think you're making it a bigger deal than it actually is. He was just being polite. Nothing more to it. We still haven't addressed our, erm, *issues*.'

My father chuckles like I've just said the funniest thing he's heard all day. 'You can say that all you want, but this photo tells another story.' He taps the printout with a finger, obviously satisfied.

I glance down at it again and immediately regret it. My body remembers the warmth of Asher's hand at my back and the exact pressure of his palm against me. And worse, my mouth remembers everything else. The soft insistence of his lips, the slow way he deepened the kiss, even the little noise I made against his mouth. I'm remembering it all now with perfect, excruciating clarity.

I force a laugh and shake the image of Asher's hand slowly drifting upwards to the curve of my breast from my mind. 'You're reading too much into it. Like I said, he was just making sure I got home safely.'

It hits me then that my father hasn't actually asked why I looked like I was about five seconds away from fainting, or why Asher even had to guide me out of the venue and take me home in the first place. He hasn't even asked whether I'm okay *now*.

His eyes are fixed on the photo like it's a quarterly report showing profits soaring into the green. As if the only thing worth noting isn't that I was unravelling in public but that my very public unravelling would ultimately be good for business.

My chest aches suddenly. Has he always been like this? I've always known he's had an unhealthy obsession with optics and reputation, but I'd never realised how unconcerned he truly was about *me*. Did I just never notice because I was too dazzled by the glittering edges of our life – by the penthouses and the constant flights and the limitless bank account?

Or is this new? Is it only now, when he has something big at stake, that he's stopped seeing me as his daughter and started seeing me as a pawn?

I can't decide what's worse. That he's always seen me as nothing more than a commodity? Or that something recently has changed to make him forget that he once loved me the way a father should love his daughter?

Asher's question from last night slams into the front of my mind.

'Travelling? What kickstarted the love?'

At the time, I didn't know why the question made me pause. It's one I've been asked plenty of times before, and my stock answer of just loving, exploring and experiencing everything the world has to offer has never failed me. But last night it did. Because when I opened my mouth to say just that, the words wouldn't come out. Instead, a new answer started to form. One that revolves around the fact that I think I've being lying to myself for most of my life. Because suddenly I'm wondering if my love for travel wasn't in fact sparked by Peregrine looming over me my whole life and stoked by an innate love for exploration, but maybe I've been using it as an escape.

From what?

From *this*.

From my parents, from my legacy, from all the madness of being Imani Davies. And I hadn't even realised it. I'd been operating on a subconscious level, my brain desperately trying to protect me from my father's machinations, that I hadn't even realised how bad things had got until it was too late.

I stare down at the page between us and, once again, take in Asher's hand on my back and his expression etched with real, unmistakable concern. For me.

It's clear that my father only sees this moment as proof of potential for a profitable alliance between Peregrine Airways and Vouvalis Resorts. But when I look at it, all I see is the one person who noticed and cared when I couldn't breathe.

I swallow hard, but the knot in my throat won't budge.

'Imani,' my father says, still smiling, 'I've got a board meeting next week, and I'm going to float the idea of partnering with Georgios Vouvalis. It's a little earlier than we'd anticipated, yes, but the timing is perfect.' He taps the photo again and I don't know whether I want to tear it into little pieces or snatch it from him and keep it pressed close to my chest. 'And when I inevitably get pushback due to Georgios', er, well, due to his *reputation*, I'll casually mention that you and Asher are dating and that, as they can see from this photo, things are getting serious. To them, we'll be two families soon to be united through marriage, so why not make it official in business too? The board won't be able to resist,' he finishes, clearly pleased with himself.

I, on the other hand, choke on my own breath. The room is spinning. I thought we had more time. I didn't think one slip-up would result in him pushing his plans forward like this. 'You can't,' I croak out weakly.

'Remember, Imani,' he says, waving my protests away like they're nothing more than a light breeze, 'this is good for everyone. For the companies. For us. For our family. For our legacy.'

My mind races as I try to come up with a plan to get him to slow down.

'You can't announce it to the board just yet,' I blurt out, forcing my voice to sound calm, even though my heart is hammering like a drum.

My father lifts an obviously unimpressed brow. 'And why is that?'

'Because . . . because . . .' I fumble around for an excuse that won't immediately be brushed aside. 'Because Asher and

I haven't exactly been the picture-perfect example of a stable and happy relationship these last few months.'

He leans back in his seat, eyes narrowing slightly, and taps his fingers against the polished wood of his desk. 'No, I don't suppose you have.'

'If you tell the board about us now, they'll just say the relationship is too volatile. They won't trust that it's stable enough to justify a merger with Vouvalis Resorts.'

His brows furrow slightly and I know I've piqued his interest. I just need to finish the job and reel him in.

'We need to show them that we're in a stable and loving relationship,' I say. 'We can't risk the board thinking we're rushing into this. If they see us as unstable or too volatile, they'll never agree to it. The timing has to be right. You have to wait until Asher and I look unshakable in public. Once we've proven we can be in a room together without things going to hell, *then* you can float the idea of a merger with the board.'

His frown deepens. 'You're suggesting we wait?'

'Yes,' I say, trying to keep my tone flat and businesslike even though my stomach is churning with anxiety. Emotions won't help me here; I need to make it seem like I'm coming at this from a business perspective. I've realised that that's where I went wrong the first time. I tried to get him to see reason as my father, when really I should've been appealing to him as Malcolm Davies the businessman. 'Not forever. Just enough time for us to make this look real.'

He presses his lips together and hums thoughtfully. Finally, after what feels like an eternity, he leans forward again. 'I suppose,' he says slowly, leaning back in his chair, 'that there's some merit to that line of thinking. With the merger already likely to cause trepidation among our shareholders, we don't want to rush and give them cause for concern. Fine. We'll wait.' He nods to himself like this whole thing was his idea in the first place.

Relief floods through me. I've managed to buy myself some time. My father was close to pulling the plug on this plan once – I'm sure we can get him to do it again.

'Great,' I say brightly. 'Thank you for—'

He suddenly snaps his fingers, looking like Christmas has come early. 'I believe Georgios is opening a new location in France next week. What better opportunity to showcase your *stable* relationship and put on a show of unity than that?' He nods again, and I know there's no point in interrupting. 'You'll attend the launch and be seen with Asher *romantically.* No arguments. No drama. A united front. It should be easy. Just build on what you started last night.'

Heat erupts inside me again as my thoughts drift towards last night.

'Got it,' I say through gritted teeth, praying to all that is holy that my neck isn't as red as it feels.

Just build on what you started last night.

He has no idea what he's asking for.

CHAPTER SIXTEEN

Asher

'. . . and he's not even listening.'

A pen flies across the room and lands squarely on the middle of my head, pulling me out of an Imani-induced daydream I hadn't even realised I was drowning in.

Teddy grins at me from across the table. 'Now he is.'

Next to him, Andreas runs a hand down his face and sighs. 'Yes, thank you, Teddy.'

Teddy gives him a mock salute.

'Asshole,' I mumble, lobbing the pen back in his direction. He catches it deftly and winks. 'And I was listening. The new French location is opening next week and our head chef is still refusing to sign his contract until his fee gets renegotiated and has yet to settle on a menu for the launch night. Our father is currently losing his mind and *you're*,' I point to Andreas, 'meeting with three other potential chefs to replace him over the next two days. And *you*,' I nod in

Teddy's direction, 'are meeting with the original chef to see if there's any chance you can convince him to sign without having to increase his fee. Did I miss anything?'

'My bad,' Teddy says, not sounding at all apologetic. 'I guess he was listening.'

Andreas doesn't look convinced, but he mercifully decides to let it slide and turns his attention back to his laptop where a PowerPoint presentation about the launch of the newest addition to the Vouvalis Resorts empire is up on the screen. As soon as his gaze dips to his screen, my attention starts to wander again.

I should be paying attention. I know that.

Though my father will undoubtedly take all the credit, this particular hotel has, from the very beginning, been Andreas' baby. He spent months scoping out the location, negotiating with government and local officials to get the right permits, drawing up marketing and publicity plans, and hiring staff. It's the biggest launch of his career and I can see the pressure eating at him. His jaw is clenched tighter than usual, his eyes are bloodshot and sunken from late night after late night, and I don't think I've ever seen the usually clean-shaven and immaculately dressed Andreas with this much five o'clock shadow *and* wearing a crinkled shirt in my life.

I swallow down the instinctive brotherly concern that rises within me. Before, I would've done just about anything to help him out and try to take some of the stress off his shoulders. Now all I can think about whenever I look at him is how easily he stood in that office and let our father tear me apart without even one word in my defence.

I feel like I'm looking at a stranger when I look at him, so maybe it's a good thing that I'm utterly distracted by thoughts of Imani and last night.

The way she gasped into my mouth, how soft and *perfect* her body felt against mine, even the perfume she was wearing has embedded itself in my memories and I keep getting phantom whiffs of it that send a rush of blood straight to my dick.

I don't think I've ever wanted anyone as badly as I want Imani Davies.

And so of course, I'm doing everything in my power to make sure we *don't* end up together. Life is funny sometimes.

My memories flit from the sensation of Imani's soft lips slanting against mine to a new, and entirely fabricated, fantasy. I'm imagining waking up beside her in the morning – *every* morning – the sun barely peeking through the curtains, casting a soft glow across the room. I imagine the warmth of her skin against mine, the way her breath would slow as she slowly wakes up next to me. She'd stretch, maybe mumble something semi-incoherent as she starts to wake, and I'd get to smile at the simple pleasure of her being there. I'd never tire of it.

'Not again.'

Andreas' tired sigh snaps me out of my reverie. His gaze is locked on me, and it's like he can see the way my mind is wandering, despite my best efforts to hide it.

I blink, suddenly aware of the room again. 'What?' I mumble, pretending like I didn't just let my thoughts, once again, wander into extremely dangerous territory.

'Cut him some slack,' Teddy says, shooting me a knowing

look that immediately has me apprehensive. Nothing good ever comes from Teddy looking at you like that. 'He had a big night last night.'

Ah.

It's suddenly clear to me that Teddy has seen the photo of me and Imani leaving the premiere last night circulating on social media. From the slightly bemused look on Andreas' face, he's seen it too.

'That's right,' Andreas says thoughtfully. 'I'm glad you two are getting along better. I know Father was . . .' He trails off, brows pinching slightly in the middle. '. . . *concerned* about how things were progressing.'

Teddy snorts and I can't help but echo the sentiment. *Concerned* is an understatement.

'And how *are* things progressing?' Teddy asks. 'Will we get to meet our future sister-in-law anytime soon?'

The idea of Imani becoming Teddy and Andreas' sister-in-law and therefore my wife absolutely shouldn't sound appealing to me in the slightest.

And yet . . .

I shake my head, ridding my mind of more delusional visions of Imani by my side. She'd be so disappointed if she knew I was entertaining thoughts like these when we're supposed to be on the same page.

'I'm doing my best,' I grumble. 'But she can't stand me. Not much more I can do there.'

'You sure about that?' Andreas asks, one brow raised.

'Extremely,' I grit out. No part of me mistakes his question as brotherly concern; I know the only thing he's concerned about is the company. Just like our father.

'Can we get back to business?' I ask, gesturing lamely at Andreas' laptop. 'Don't you have a hotel to launch?'

Andreas looks like he wants to say something else about the Imani matter, but then he seems to remember that we're technically in crunch time for this launch and there are still too many loose ends. He clears his throat, turns back to his laptop, and immediately starts reeling off a list of things for Teddy and me to do.

I nod as Andreas tasks me with triple checking the marketing assets before we officially go live with the website, forcing myself to stay grounded in the present. No more daydreaming. No more fantasising. No more replaying the events of last night over and over and over—

My phone vibrates aggressively on the table and my heart stutters as I catch sight of the notification that pops up.

Imani
Guess who's coming to France?

I've never been prone to dramatics, preferring to leave the theatrics to Teddy, but having to see out the workday before I can properly speak to Imani might actually kill me.

It doesn't help that Andreas is getting more and more antsy as the day progresses. Every time my attention ever so slightly starts to drift back to Imani and the bombshell of a message she left me, Andreas is suddenly standing in front of me with more additions to my already bulging to-do list.

I barely have enough time to scarf down a sandwich for lunch, let alone dedicate a spare moment to figuring out what the hell she means by 'Guess who's coming to France?' She didn't respond to the quick '???' I managed to fire off before Andreas descended on me again, and I haven't had the chance to follow up since. By the time the end of day rolls around, I'm more tightly wound than I've ever been in my life.

'Ash?'

I jump as Andreas appears, yet again, seemingly from nowhere, at my door.

'Do you have a minute?'

I glance at the time and start to shake my head. 'I've really got to—'

Andreas enters my office and closes the door behind him without waiting for my response. He slides into the empty seat opposite my desk, crosses his arms over his chest, and lets out a deep sigh.

'Is everything alright?' he asks.

I nod, almost robotically. 'I've done everything on the list. Just waiting to hear back from a few—'

'No,' Andreas cuts me off. 'I mean, with you. Is everything alright with you?'

He stares at me pointedly, the way only an older brother can, like he already knows the answer and is waiting to see if I'll bother lying about it. The realisation ignites a flare of anger inside me. How dare he act like he cares about me now?

'I'm fine,' I say brusquely. 'Is there anything else, or—'

'And Imani?' Andreas asks. 'How are things with her?'

I shrug.

Andreas narrows his eyes and purses his lips. 'You two are getting along better then?'

'Why?' I ask. 'Are you going to tell me again how you think it'll be good for me if I marry her?'

Andreas opens his mouth but I keep on talking.

'Or are you going to man up and tell me what you really mean?'

He frowns. 'What?'

'That the only reason you want me to marry her is because it'll be good for whatever the hell you and our father have planned.'

I don't think I've ever seen Andreas look so stunned. 'I . . .' he starts again. 'Ash, I—'

'I overheard you,' I say. 'A few months back. I heard the two of you talking and he was saying how easily manipulated I am. How desperate I am for his approval and love.'

'Asher—' Andreas starts again, his voice hoarse.

'And you agreed with him.'

'I didn't—'

'You didn't defend me,' I snap, feeling the anger I've been holding onto for the last few months rise like red-hot lava inside me. 'You sat and let him say those things about me and then, when push came to shove, the only thing you cared about was whether he'd be able to use me to get this fucking deal over the line.'

Andreas seems to crumple in on himself. 'You don't understand,' he says, shaking his head.

'Then help me understand! Hasn't it always been the three of us against him? Or have you been playing both sides my whole life?'

'I'm not . . . It's not . . . ' He runs a frustrated hand through his hair. 'You're upset. I get that. I'm not on his side, I'm on *yours.*'

'Sure as hell didn't sound like it.'

'I know,' he says. 'I know.' He leans forward in his chair, elbows braced on his knees and his hands clasped so tightly together, his knuckles have gone white. 'I should've told you sooner. I just . . . There's never been a right time.'

'Told me what?' I ask. 'And there's never a right time to admit you sold me out.'

'That's not what this is,' he says quickly. 'I didn't sell you out.'

'Then explain,' I snap. 'Because from where I'm standing, it looks a hell of a lot like it.'

Andreas drags a hand down his face and groans. 'I've been working with the NCA.'

I blink at him, sure I've misheard. 'You've been what?'

'The NCA,' he repeats, like I don't know what the National Crime Agency is. 'For the last eighteen months or so, we've been building a case.' He swallows then glances nervously around the room like he's half expecting the room to be wired. 'Against him.'

'That's not funny.'

'I'm not joking.' He slumps in his seat and suddenly looks ten years older. 'He's not a good man, our father.'

Despite everything, I let out a snort. That's one thing I *don't* need to be told.

'Bribery, tax evasion, money laundering, offshore accounts that don't match up with any legitimate revenue streams,' Andreas continues. 'There's so much you don't know about because I've purposefully made sure you've been kept in the dark. Both you and Teddy. I've protected you so you can claim plausible deniability when this all inevitably blows up.'

It doesn't surprise me in the least to hear all of this, but it also doesn't make me feel any better. 'So what?' I ask dryly. 'You're the big hero, and I just have to ignore everything I heard?'

'I'm not saying I'm a hero,' Andreas says. 'I'm just saying there's more here at play than you think. I need him to keep trusting me. I need him to think that I'm loyal to him and that I'm on his side.'

'And what about me?' I demand. 'Where do I fit into this master plan? Where does *Imani* fit in with all of this?'

Andreas sighs again. 'If the deal with Davies goes through – or, at least, our father thinks it's about to go through – then we think we can get him on a few of the lesser charges. Not enough to completely bring him down, but enough to get the ball rolling.'

Everything starts to slot into place.

'So,' I say slowly, 'let me get this straight. You tried to encourage me to get married so you could send our father to jail?'

Andreas winces now I've put it so plainly to him, like he can finally see how insane this whole thing is, even if he isn't ready to admit it. 'Don't put it like that. It's more complicated than that.'

'Is it?'

'Yes,' Andreas says firmly, like he's trying to convince himself instead of me. 'I know I'm asking a lot from you, but—'

'You didn't ask me though, did you? You didn't bring me in and tell me your plan.'

'I couldn't,' he insists, sounding more desperate than I've ever heard him. 'I told you. You needed to have plausible deniability for when this all comes out.'

A small part of me sees and understands the logic in his argument, but the righteous fury I'm feeling right now is winning and I can't bring myself to give him the benefit of the doubt. I let out a dry laugh. 'You know something? You're just like him.'

Andreas reels back like he's been slapped. 'I am *nothing* like him.'

'You are,' I say. 'You can tell yourself that it's all for the greater good and that you've been *protecting* me this whole time, but when it comes down to it, you'd happily sacrifice me if it gets you want you want. You used me, just like he does.'

I push away from my desk and stalk past him. He doesn't try to stop me. Out of the corner of my eye, as I pass him by, I watch as he slumps in his seat and drops his head into his hands.

The look on my face must be thunderous as I storm through the office because nobody bothers me on my way out. I spot Teddy in my periphery just as I reach the double doors, but even he seems to sense that now is most definitely not the time.

My car is waiting outside and I climb into it, let my head loll back against the leather headrest, and close my eyes. I'm not sure how long I sit there disassociating but my phone's aggressive vibration in my pocket suddenly pulls me back to reality.

I glare at it as I pull it out, expecting it to be Andreas in another attempt at explaining himself and apologising, but then I see Imani's name appear on the screen and I suddenly forget how furious I am with my brother and the only thing I can think about is her.

As soon as the call connects, I'm met with the sight of those warm, dark eyes locking onto mine from the other side of the screen, and it sends a surge of warm happiness right through me.

'Hey,' she says. There's a softness to her tone that immediately melts away all the tension, anger and irritation. At least, it feels like it does to me. Judging from the way her brows pucker into a frown, I'm not sure I'm entirely successful. 'What's wrong?'

'Nothing,' I say as if on autopilot, and then immediately wince because I can hear the strain in my voice. I clear my throat and try again. 'I'm fine. Everything is fine.'

'Asher.' She says my name so plainly, but there's a heaviness in it that unravels me.

I let out a deep sigh that seems to come from the very depths of my soul.

'That's what I thought,' Imani hums. 'Where are you now?'

'On my way home.'

She thinks for a second and then gives a little nod of her head. 'Do you want to meet up?'

There's nothing I'd like more than that, but I shake my head. 'No, don't worry about—'

'*Asher.*' The way she says my name cuts clean through me. It's ridiculous, really, how she's able to do this. She doesn't raise her voice, but the way she says my name makes it impossible to keep trying to pretend.

I exhale slowly. 'I've had A Day.'

'I can see that.'

The way she looks at me, it feels like she's reaching into my chest and pressing her palm flat against my heart. Like she knows exactly where I'm hurting right now and she can hear the thoughts I haven't even realised I'm thinking yet.

'Okay,' I say finally. 'Yeah, I want to see you.'

The smile that curves her mouth is small but just the sight of it, even through a screen, has one tugging at my lips too.

'Good,' she says. 'There's a restaurant about fifteen minutes from your place that I like. I'll send you a pin. Meet you in twenty minutes?'

My grin widens. 'That's the best thing I've heard all day.'

CHAPTER SEVENTEEN

Imani

'When you said *restaurant*,' Asher starts, plopping down onto one of the bright red, uncomfortable plastic seats opposite me, 'this isn't really what I was expecting.'

I grin and push a flimsy cardboard box filled with greasy chips and several even greasier pieces of chicken between us. 'What's the problem? This is, by every definition of the word, a restaurant.'

Asher lifts a brow, and my grin only widens. Under Top Fry's fluorescent lighting we both look slightly jaundiced, and the walls are a shade of off-white freckled with oil splatter, with faded posters advertising a two-piece chicken and chips combo for the criminally low price of £1.99. I suppose I can't blame him for not expecting me to bring us somewhere like this.

I shrug and dip one of my chips into the small mountain of ketchup the owner kindly squirted into the corner of the box. 'Don't tell me you've never had London's finest culinary offering before?'

Asher thinks for a moment. 'Not since I was about sixteen.'

'Then you're missing out,' I say before digging into the meal, and I mean it too. London's small army of chicken and chip shops can be fairly hit or miss, but in my humble opinion, Top Fry is the best of the best. There's something about the way the chips come out of the deep fryer, perfectly golden and equal parts crispy on the outside and fluffy inside, and the moistness of the mysteriously seasoned chicken, which keeps me coming back for more. It's not the kind of place you'd find boasting a Michelin star, but it's just as good as any white tablecloth restaurant in my opinion. And, as a bonus, it's not the kind of place you'd typically find anyone from our usual social group frequenting. Meaning it's a perfectly safe place to be out in public with Asher right now.

He picks up a handful of chips, dips them into the small mountain of mayonnaise on the opposite side of the box, and then chews thoughtfully for a few seconds.

'Okay,' he says once he's finished and already reaching for a piece of chicken, 'that was pretty good.'

'See?' I say, tearing into my own thigh. 'You've got to trust me. I wouldn't steer you wrong.'

Asher hums noncommittally as he takes a bite of the chicken, but I see the way his shoulders seem to slacken just a little as he chews. It's subtle and I wonder if it were anyone else sitting opposite him right now, whether they'd notice or if I've just become attuned to him in a way I'd never expected to.

It's a strange thought, realising that maybe I'm seeing him in a way other people don't.

I watch the way he eats and take note of the way he pauses after the first bite, or how his jaw shifts slightly to the left when he chews, or even the faint line that appears between his brows when he's concentrating on a flavour and the way it smooths out the moment he decides he likes it. I wonder how many other people have noticed these things about him. Probably not many. The thought both saddens me and makes me feel a strange sense of pride at being one of the few who has got to know him like this.

Asher suddenly catches me staring and lifts a brow. 'Is there something on my face?'

'No,' I say quickly, shaking my head as I reach for another chip. 'I was just thinking.'

'About?'

'You look . . .' I click my tongue, fumbling around for the right word. 'Lighter? From earlier, I mean. When I called you, you looked . . .' I pull a face. 'You know?'

Asher had looked stricken when he answered my call and I'd be lying if I didn't admit I'm extremely glad he no longer looks like he's about five seconds away from breaking down.

'Yeah,' he murmurs.

'Do you want to talk about it?' I ask.

'Not really.' He lets out a deep breath. 'But I probably should, shouldn't I?'

I shrug. 'It might help, and you don't have to get specific.'

He doesn't say anything right away, and I almost think he's not going to and will just clam up, but then he sighs one more time and leans back as far as he can in his chair. 'I'm just tired.'

'Tired?'

'Of never being enough.'

'For who?'

'For everyone.' He says it so casually, the corners of his mouth lifting up into a sad excuse for a smile, like if he says it with enough detachment, it won't hurt as much. He might be able to fool himself, but he can't fool me. I feel the hurt beneath his words, in all that he's *not* saying, settle heavy in my chest.

I look at his hands instead of his face because it's easier that way; if I keep looking at his eyes, I don't know what I'll say. He's fiddling with the edge of the box, tearing little pieces off here and there as a way to distract himself from what he's saying.

'I'm sure that's not true,' I hear myself say.

I think the sound he makes in response is supposed to be a laugh, but it comes out dry and bitter, devoid of any warmth or humour. 'You don't know that.'

'I do,' I insist. I let myself look at him again. He looks tired in a way a good night's sleep couldn't possibly fix. 'And I also know that you don't talk like that unless someone's made you feel it for a very long time.'

He doesn't dispute me and that somehow makes it worse.

'It's like . . .' he says after a moment, staring past me to look at the wall behind me. 'If I'm not useful, I don't really have a place anywhere. Me alone isn't enough – I'm just worth whatever I can do for people in the moment.'

My heart just about breaks. I want to lean across this plastic table, squeeze his hands and let him know that he's more than enough for me.

'Even if you don't ever do anything for another soul for the rest of your life,' I say, 'you're still enough. More than enough.'

He finally looks at me then and there's something raw in his expression, like he desperately wants to believe me but doesn't trust himself to.

I give into my urges and reach across the table to rest my hand over his. His jaw tightens and I think he's going to pull away from me, but instead his fingers curl slightly under mine.

'You don't have to be enough for anyone but yourself. Anyone else is a bonus and they should be so lucky that you're in their lives.'

I know I am.

The thought hits me without warning and I realise that with devastating certainty, I *am* glad that Asher is in my life. These last few months have been chaotic and downright insane and I'm not sure I would've survived if I hadn't had Asher by my side.

He doesn't say anything after that; just nods once and then goes back to picking at the food. My impromptu pep talk hasn't solved anything, I know that, but as he reaches back into the box for a wing, his shoulders look a little less tense and the expression on his face is softer, more Asher-like than before, and that feels like a win.

'I can't believe you insisted on paying,' I snort as Asher and I spill out of Top Fry and into the busy high street it sits on.

'Never let it be said that I'm not a gentleman.'

'It was £4.'

'Like I said,' Asher says, as he steps across me to position himself so he's walking on the outside of the pavement, closest to the cars, 'I'm a gentleman.'

I laugh at that and, after a second, Asher starts laughing too. We fall into step beside each other, bobbing and weaving along the high street. Given the emotional start to this unplanned meet-up, I'd almost forgotten that the last time I saw Asher we were pressed up against my kitchen counter. Now we're walking side by side, his arm brushing against mine every so often, and I'm reminded of what it felt like to kiss him.

It's startling how quickly and vividly it comes back to me. The way his hands had hesitated for just a second at my waist, the warmth of his mouth – soft at first and then not – like he was afraid of wanting too much and then gave in anyway. I can almost feel it again, the quiet intensity of it, the way the world narrowed down to just the two of us and the space between our bodies.

My stomach flips at the thought of it.

I shove my hands into the pockets of my coat, more to keep myself from doing something stupid than because I'm cold. The high street is loud around us with cars rushing past, music leaking from shops, people brushing by in hurried groups, but somehow there's still this bubble around the two of us that feels strangely private.

Asher's arm brushes mine again, this time lingering just a fraction longer than before. I glance at him from the corner of my eye. He's looking straight ahead, jaw relaxed, shoulders loose, like he's not painfully aware of the space between us shrinking and expanding with every step.

Or maybe he is.

I wonder if he's thinking about it too. About my kitchen. About how close we'd been. About how nothing has really been resolved since then; we've just quietly set it aside in favour of more pressing concerns. Like the state Asher was in just an hour ago and—

'Oh shit,' I say suddenly. 'I forgot about France.' I'm not entirely sure how I managed to forget about the thing that's been dominating my thoughts since I left my father's office this morning, but I suppose seeing Asher so close to breaking down took precedence in my mind and shoved all thoughts of ruining our fathers' plan to the very bottom of my priorities list.

'Oh right,' Asher says, blinking dumbfoundedly like he forgot as well. 'I was wondering when I got that text . . .'

'Sorry,' I say with a sheepish grin. 'I wanted to follow up sooner, but I got pulled in about a million different directions today. Long story short, thanks to our little show last night, my father's planning on announcing *us* to his shareholders and board soon. He wanted to do it next week, actually.'

Asher looks alarmed. 'Next week?'

'Mhm,' I hum. Some of my earlier irritation about this whole mess starts to dampen my mood. 'Luckily I managed to convince him that we're still too volatile for a hard launch and he agreed. Unfortunately, he thinks we still need to make one final show of being a solid couple before he can take it to the board.'

Asher's silent for a moment, and then he says, the realisation dawning on him, 'And he thinks you coming to the hotel launch next week is the perfect place for us to put on a show?'

I nod glumly. 'Looks like it.'

Asher comes to an abrupt halt, turns to me, and grins. 'Well then. Let's give him a show.'

CHAPTER EIGHTEEN

Imani

The moment the plane tilts upwards, I feel it.

That familiar, fluttery, weightless rush in my chest that happens every time I take off to a new destination. I've missed it more than I'd ever admit out loud.

It's been months – 102 days but who's counting? – since I've been in the air. Months since I've felt the familiar thrum of engines like a heartbeat through the soles of my shoes. Months since the world dropped away beneath me in that smooth, effortless climb that always feels a little bit like freedom.

And God, I've missed it.

'Should I be worried?' Sloane asks, peeking at me over the top of her sunglasses. She's cocooned in a blush-pink blanket, a glass of champagne in one hand, and her seat already reclined further than technically allowed during take-off. 'We've been airborne for thirty seconds and you look like you're about to marry this plane.'

I grin into my own champagne flute. 'Don't tempt me. It wouldn't be the worst marriage offer I've had recently.'

She snorts. 'You're ridiculous.'

'I'm happy,' I say simply.

And I am. I grew up on planes. Peregrine Airways has been practically stitched into my DNA since birth. My earliest memories are of cabin lights dimming to a warm gold, the soft rustle of attendants moving up and down aisles, and my father's crisp voice telling me to sit up straight and look out the window as the plane touched down somewhere new.

But that was before he clipped my wings.

Now I'm here again, in seat 1A of a Peregrine Airways flight bound for France, drinking my way through the guilt and anger that comes from knowing the only reason I'm flying again is because my father ordered it.

Optics, he'd said. *The board needs to see unity. You and Asher need to present as solid. Romantic. Happy.*

Ugh. I gulp down the rest of my champagne and signal a flight attendant for another.

'I'll admit it,' Sloane says, pulling me out of a potential spiral before I can slip into it. 'As much as I am fully aboard the anti-Malcolm train—'

'Appreciate it.'

'He knows his shit.'

She has a point. Sloane is no stranger to luxury travel, but first class on a Peregrine Airways flight is a different world entirely.

Peregrine's first class is built to rival palaces. Private suites gleam under soft, golden lighting that shifts with altitude; the cream leather seat cushions are stitched with champagne-gold threads and recline into beds softer than the clouds outside. Polished wood panels glint faintly between curved partitions that rise for privacy at the touch of a button. The air smells faintly of oud and vanilla, the scent warm and expensive enough to seep into your bones and make you relax.

On one wall, an inlaid minibar glows amber, stocked with crystal decanters and tiny jars of caviar. A screen larger than should be possible for an aeroplane slides silently out of the panel in front of me. Even the windows are rimmed in brushed gold, each one paired with a plush velvet curtain instead of a standard shade.

The cabin crew glide up and down the aisle like a choreographed dance troupe, smiles all perfectly calibrated, voices soft and smooth enough to calm even the most nervous flyer.

It's decadent. Extravagant. The kind of travel that doesn't just make you feel seen. Every last piece has been designed to remind you that you're not just a passenger – you're *someone important*.

No one does travel like Peregrine Airways and it should feel like home. It *used* to feel like home.

But now, every time I glance at the logo embroidered on the headrest, I'm reminded that I'm only here because my father said so and that he could snatch this from me as easily as he gave it back.

The reminder sours the champagne on my tongue.

This is truly our last chance to pull it off. To show our fathers that Asher and I are a disaster together.

The world's most incompatible couple.

Toxic enough that no amount of corporate spin could possibly sell our 'love story' to their investors and shareholders.

But couples like that don't kiss the way Asher and I did last week.

I keep telling myself that I can still do this. That I can look at Asher and remember the plan, not the way he tasted or the way it felt to press my curves against him. That I can be cold and cutting in public and seemingly impossible to love.

But if I'm being honest with myself, I'm not sure I believe it anymore.

'Okay, so,' Sloane says suddenly, turning sideways in her seat to face me fully. 'What's the plan?'

She doesn't need to elaborate; I know exactly what she's asking.

'Just more of the same really,' I say with a shrug.

'More of the same,' she repeats flatly. 'Well that's the stupidest thing I've heard.'

I scowl at her. 'I don't see you coming up with any ideas.'

She holds up her hands semi-apologetically. 'Fair. But I know you can't just show up and start throwing drinks at each other. Been there. Done that. The people are *bored*.'

I shrug, even though that is pretty much exactly what I'd been planning on doing on this trip. 'Asher's coming up with the plan. We're supposed to meet once we get there to finalise the strategy.'

'And you trust him to think of something good?'

'I have to,' I say. Not just because I'm running on empty when it comes to potential ideas, but because I don't trust myself around Asher anymore.

When this all started, it was almost fun. Matching him glare for glare, insult for insult. Watching the tension build in a way that made everyone else around us uncomfortable.

But then the kiss happened and now every version of this plan feels a little like playing with fire.

Sloane taps a manicured finger against her glass. 'You've got that look again.'

'What look?'

'I thought you were just excited about being airborne again, but now I'm wondering . . .' She tilts her head, studying me like a cat about to pounce. 'What happened?'

A lump forms in my throat. 'Huh?'

She leans in. 'Something. Happened.'

'Nothing happened,' I squeak, and then wince because God damn it, I just squeaked.

Sloane lifts a brow. 'It did.'

I bite my lip. I'm not entirely sure why I didn't tell Sloane about the kiss as soon as Asher left my place. In all the years we've known each other, I don't think I've ever intentionally hidden anything from her.

Sloane studies me for a long moment, her expression caught somewhere between suspicion and concern. 'You're biting your lip,' she says finally. 'That's your tell.'

'I'm not,' I mumble, which only makes her smirk.

'Sure,' she says, taking a smug sip of champagne. 'And I don't occasionally stalk my ex's Instagram to see if he's balding. He is, for what it's worth. Try again.'

I groan and sink lower into my seat. 'You're not going to let this go, are you?'

'Not a chance.' She leans forward, eyes bright and sharp as the diamonds around her neck. 'So spill. What did he do? Or—' Her grin widens wickedly. 'What did *you* do?'

'Nothing!' I blurt. Then I pause and let out a sigh. There's no point in denying it anymore. Sloane knows me better than I know myself. 'Okay, not *nothing*.'

Her jaw drops. 'Oh my God. You slept with him.'

'What? No!' I hiss, glancing towards the aisle in case one of the flight attendants overhears and runs immediately to @TrustFundTea with this information. 'Why would you jump straight to that? Of course I didn't sleep with him.'

I decide not to share that I've spent an inordinate amount of time daydreaming about it over the last week though.

'Then what— Uh-oh. You *kissed* him.'

'It was a mutual kissing.'

'Define mutual.'

'Simultaneous enthusiasm,' I say, waving a hand.

Sloane's grin turns triumphant. 'Oh my God. Please tell me it was bad. Tell me it was awkward and weird and you accidentally head-butted him or burped in his mouth.'

I let out a long breath. 'It wasn't bad.'

Her eyes widen. 'Oh no.'

'Oh yes,' I say miserably.

She stares at me like she's trying to solve an equation. 'So let me get this straight. You're supposed to be fake-hating him badly enough that your fathers call off their merger, and instead you're out here kissing and catching feelings?'

'I'm not catching feelings,' I say too quickly.

'Imani.'

'I'm *not!*'

She tilts her head. 'Why are your cheeks red?'

'It's warm in here,' I mumble, fiddling with my seatbelt like it's suddenly the most fascinating thing in the world.

Sloane huffs dramatically and flops back into her seat. 'You're doomed.'

I glare. 'I'm *fine.*'

'Nuh-uh. You two are going to show up, try to act like you hate each other, and accidentally look like you're about to tear each other's clothes off in the lobby.'

'Not we won't,' I say firmly. 'Asher and I are on the same page. The kiss was a one-time thing. We both know what our end game is here, and we've got our eye on the finish line. We're sticking to the plan. The kiss changes nothing.'

'Sure,' Sloane says with a slight roll of her eyes. 'Whatever helps you sleep at night.'

But that's the problem, isn't it?

It *isn't* helping.

Every time I close my eyes, I can still feel him. His hand at the back of my neck, the low sound he made when he kissed me like a man starved.

I haven't decided which is more worrying. The fact that

I kissed him back with equal enthusiasm, or the fact that I'd gladly do it again.

The captain's voice hums overhead announcing our descent into France. My stomach dips, not from turbulence, but from the sudden, unwelcome wave of awareness that in less than an hour, I'm going to see Asher again.

I have no idea what I'm supposed to do with my face when that happens.

Any thoughts about Asher and how to stop my heart from bursting through my chest the second I lay eyes on him disappear as the plane dips through a sea of pale clouds as sunlight suddenly spills across the cabin in molten gold.

I press a hand to the window as the French Alps come into view, snowy peaks giving way to pine forests and the glittering blue-green of Lake Annecy. It's not my first time visiting this part of France, but the beauty of it all still takes my breath away.

There's a bakery in the small town a short drive from the lake, and I wonder if I'll have time to visit it. It's tucked away on a quiet corner, the kind of place you'd miss if you blinked while driving past. The shutters are a faded green, paint peeling in soft curls like dried petals, and the sign above the door – LA MIETTE – is so weathered it looks like it's simply clinging to the wall out of sheer force of will.

It's not the kind of place that ends up in glossy travel magazines or gets made famous by influencers on TikTok or Instagram, but that's what I love about it. The first time I wandered in, it smelled like butter and sugar and something faintly citrusy. The air inside was warm enough to melt every bit of stress out of my body. The counters were dusted with flour, and the glass case overflowed with pastries that looked too beautiful to eat. There were rows and rows of golden croissants stacked on top of each other, glossy fruit tarts with apricots shining like jewels, and a mountain of buttery *pain au chocolats* filled with creamy, molten chocolate.

I wonder if it's still there. I can picture it now; the low hum of French chatter, the bell that jingles when the door opens, the smell of sugar melting into air, and before I can stop myself, I imagine walking in with Asher.

It's a ridiculous thought. Absolutely unhelpful. Yet it lodges in my mind and refuses to disappear. I imagine him sitting across from me at the corner table, sunlight catching on his hair, grinning my favourite smile over the rim of his coffee cup while butter flakes from his croissant gather on his sleeve.

For one dizzy, traitorous heartbeat, I want that.

I want to see the look on his face when he takes his first bite and he realises that this tiny bakery, nestled off the beaten track in the middle of the French Alps, will ruin every single other bakery for him.

I want to share it with him; this quiet, ordinary thing that feels like home.

The realisation hits me so suddenly, it's like I've been slapped.

I want to share *something real* with him.

Which is insane. Because this whole thing between us, whatever it is, just isn't real. It's all built on lies and strategy and optics.

Still, as the plane dips lower, the clouds thinning into a wash of blue and gold, I can't shake the image I've conjured of Asher laughing in that little bakery, sugar on his thumb, sunlight in his hair.

When we land, the ground staff at the airport staff usher us through a private terminal and before long, we're sliding into the back of a glossy black car with tinted windows and emblazoned with the signature Vouvalis V.

The drive winds us through pine forests and sleepy lakeside villages. It's picturesque. Stunning, really. I wish we had more time here, but we've only got forty-eight hours. As we crest the final hill and the hotel grounds come into view, I can't help but gasp. Vouvalis Resort locations are always beautiful, but this is on another level.

The building rises from the lakeside like something out of a dream. Sleek lines of white stone and glass terraces that curve along the water's edge, sunlight catching on every mirrored surface. I spy an infinity pool in the near distance that seems to spill straight into the lake. Cameras flash near the entrance where a cluster of photographers has already gathered to snap the oncoming onslaught of guests for the weekend.

The entranceway is crowded with cars identical to ours, guests snapping photos on their phones and posing for the hired photographers, and cheerful-looking staff dragging around large, expensive suitcases and taking them up to rooms. I shouldn't be able to find him in a crowd this chaotic, but I do.

He's standing on the steps, a little way away from the crowd. He looks effortlessly handsome, as per usual.

Navy suit, open collar, the faintest hint of stubble along his jawline. His posture is relaxed, but I can tell by the faint tension in his jaw that he's not nearly as calm as he looks.

The sight of him hits me harder than I expect. My pulse spikes, my brain short-circuits, and for a second, I think I genuinely forget how to breathe.

And then his eyes find mine through the car window.

A tiny, knowing smile flickers at the corner of his mouth. It's the kind of smile that simultaneously seems to say *thank God you're here* and *I remember exactly what you taste like.*

I swallow thickly.

Sloane follows my gaze and lets out a low whistle. 'Like I said, *doomed*.'

CHAPTER NINETEEN

Imani

'Imani.'

I swear, the way Asher says my name should be illegal. The way he looks, too.

The French sun has no business being that generous to one man. It paints his skin a beautiful soft molten gold, catches the edges of curls of his hair, throws a glow across his jaw that makes him look less like someone I'm supposed to hate and more like someone I could very, very easily fall for.

Maybe I already have.

I open the door before the driver can, desperate for the distraction of movement, but Asher is faster. He offers his hand as I step out of the car. His palm is warm against mine as I step down, and when his thumb brushes the inside of my wrist, my brain just about short-circuits. It's a soft touch but it feels like being struck by lightning in slow motion.

For a heartbeat, maybe two, everything narrows to just him.

He's close enough for me to see the flecks of hazel in his irises and the faint crease at the corner of his mouth as he fights off a smile.

Then Sloane's voice cuts through and I come crashing back to reality.

'Oh, for God's sake.'

I blink, startled back into my body, and Asher drops my hand so quickly it's almost comical.

Sloane rounds the car, sunglasses perched on her head, expression thoroughly unimpressed. 'Can you two *not*? Honestly, the eye-fucking is getting out of hand. You do remember you're supposed to hate each other, right? Or am I the only one still committed to the plan?'

We both take a step back at the exact same time. When had we become so close?

Asher clears his throat and releases my hand. 'Right. Yes. Can't stand you.'

I nod. 'Loathe you entirely.'

Sloane folds her arms. 'Yeah, I'm not buying it. You're still smiling.'

I glare at her. 'I am not.'

'You are,' Asher says, a hint of laughter in his voice.

I shoot him a glare that I'm hoping conveys mortal hatred, but from the look Sloane gives me, it probably reads more like hopelessly flustered. Sloane groans and presses her fingers to her temples.

'You're doing it again,' she hisses, then leans closer like she's about to hug me and murmurs in my ear. 'People are watching.'

The grand entrance of the hotel is crawling with press and opportunists. The air is thick with perfume, flash photography, and that distinctive hum of self-importance that follows the filthy rich wherever they go. Journalists, influencers and shareholders mingle on the marble steps, everyone pretending not to look for the cameras even as they angle towards them.

And then I see her.

Emmy.

Perched at the edge of the crowd in an impeccably pressed linen sundress, phone in hand, pretending to scroll while her gaze slices through the chaos with surgical precision. Her sunglasses hide her eyes, but I can feel them on me anyway. When she lifts her phone slightly, the camera conveniently pointed in our direction, I can practically hear the @TrustFundTea caption writing itself:

> Vouvalis vs Davies Round … Oh I've lost count! The saga continues 👀

I attempt a scowl, but it's harder than it should be when Asher's standing close enough that I can feel the heat from his arm. His hand brushes briefly against mine again in that infuriatingly casual way that makes my pulse skip.

I lean towards him, voice low. 'We should go inside before we end up on @TrustFundTea before the weekend's even started.' I tilt my chin towards Emmy, who is now loudly pretending to laugh at something no one said. 'Maybe meet up later?'

He nods once, jaw tight. 'Right.'

Then he steps back. I know it's an act and just part of the choreography we've perfected over the last few months, but the sudden distance feels like a door slamming shut. His expression twists into a dirty look and I pretend like it doesn't sting. Voice low, he says, 'I've got a few behind the scenes things to handle now, but I'll come to your room before the cocktail reception. We can go over the plan then.'

'Fine,' I say, forcing my own voice to be terse and clipped in case anyone is listening.

He gives me one last, lingering look and then he turns and disappears into the crowd.

Sloane slips her sunglasses on and sighs dramatically. 'You two are either going to destroy this merger or get married for real. There's no in-between.'

'Not helping,' I mutter, starting towards the doors.

'I wasn't trying to,' she says brightly.

The suite they've given me is on a whole new level.

Floor-to-ceiling windows span the entire wall, framing Lake Annecy in all its impossible glory. The water glitters like liquid turquoise beneath the afternoon sun, rippling with flashes of gold where the light catches. Snow-dusted mountains rise in the distance, their peaks softened by haze, and for a moment I forget that technically, I'm here under duress.

Almost.

There's a marble table near the window with a vase of long-stemmed white roses so symmetrical they look almost fake. Next to them, a silver bucket holds a chilled bottle of champagne, and beside it, a tall glass bottle of sparkling water. A small envelope rests against the champagne bucket. It's made with thick card stock and embossed with Vouvalis Resort's gold crest. It's signed:

Welcome, Ms Davies – we're delighted to have you back with us.
Georgios Vouvalis and the Vouvalis Resorts team.

I've very maturely resisted the urge to draw devil horns over the signature.

Anyway, I have bigger things to worry about right now – like the fact that the cocktail reception starts in less than an hour and I'm still standing in front of the mirror half dressed and already on the brink of a breakdown.

The dress I've decided on for tonight is one of my favourites. It's a black silk slip that manages to toe the line between elegant and dangerous. It skims over my curves, clings where it should and catches the light in a way that makes the fabric look like liquid ink. It's timeless, flattering, and a guaranteed confidence booster.

At least, it's supposed to be. If only I could actually get into the damn thing.

The zipper is on the back, and I've spent the last five minutes struggling to pull it up.

'Perfect,' I mutter through gritted teeth as I reach over my shoulder. The zipper slides up about two inches before catching on the lining and refusing to budge.

I glance around for my phone. Sloane's room is on the other side of the hotel, but I don't think she'll have left for the cocktail reception yet.

Imani
SOS. Can't zip up my dress. Pls help.

Sloane
Lol. Give me 10 mins.

I sigh and keep wrestling with the zipper, muttering under my breath like maybe intimidation or thinly veiled threats will make it cooperate. It doesn't. The metal teeth snag halfway up my back and refuse to budge. I'm halfway through debating whether I can attend the reception wrapped in a towel and a bad attitude when there's a knock at the door.

'Finally,' I groan, adjusting the neckline of my half-zipped dress. 'Come in.' I hear the front door open, then the sounds of footsteps padding along the short corridor. 'Thanks for coming so quickly, I—'

I freeze, because when I look up it's not Sloane standing in the doorway to my bedroom.

It's Asher.

He has one hand braced on the doorframe and he looks disarmingly uncertain. He starts to speak, then hesitates, gaze flicking over me. Over *everything*: the half-zipped dress, the bare stretch of skin along my back, the messy array of make-up and hairpins scattered across the vanity. His expression flip flops somewhere between *I shouldn't be seeing this* and *I never want to look away.* 'Sorry,' he croaks out after what feels like an eternity of silence. 'You said "come in".'

'I thought you were Sloane,' I say weakly.

'Right,' he says, clearing his throat. His gaze moves over quickly to some neutral point on the wall, but not before I catch it linger on me for a fraction of a second too long. 'Should I come back later?'

My stomach does a mortifying little flip. 'No. I mean, yes—Wait, no. It's fine. You can stay. We were supposed to talk strategy anyway.'

'Right,' he says, though his voice sounds a little less steady than usual. 'Strategy.'

He clears his throat, looking anywhere but directly at me, which somehow makes the air between us heavier.

'Okay,' I say, forcing a bright tone as I cross to the table and pour myself a glass of sparkling water. My dress gapes slightly at the back when I move. 'What's the plan?'

He nods, pulling his focus back with visible effort. 'If we're going to convince everyone that we can't be together then we need to lean into the drama more than usual. Maybe . . .' he hesitates, then seems to steel himself and continues on. 'What if we both flirt with other people tonight? Your father can't exactly say we're solid if we're seen getting cosy with other people, can he?'

I take a sip to buy time, trying to ignore the way the idea of seeing Asher flirt with someone else makes my stomach turn. 'So, what, you chat up some other heiress tonight and I laugh too hard at someone else's jokes?'

He gives me a wry grin. 'Something like that.'

'Fine.' It comes out much harsher than I'd intended.

Asher blinks, then tilts his head just slightly. 'You okay?'

'Of course,' I say, too fast. 'Completely fine. Flirt away. I'll find someone equally vapid to laugh with.'

He smiles, but it doesn't quite reach his eyes. 'Do you not want to do this?'

'Yes,' I say with a sigh. 'I do, and I mean it's not like we have any other choice.'

He studies me for a long moment, the kind that makes me feel like he's seeing more than I want him to. Then, slowly, he takes a step closer.

'I didn't mean . . .' His voice drops lower. 'I didn't mean that I *want* to flirt with anyone else.'

I purse my lips. 'I didn't—'

'If I could, I'd skip the whole weekend and just . . .' He trails off, searching for the right words. His eyes find mine again. 'I'd rather spend it with you.'

I ignore the way my chest tightens and shake my head. 'Careful,' I murmur. 'You keep saying things like that and a girl could really start to fall for you.'

Another step closer. 'Would that really be such a problem?'

I swallow. 'Yes, because we're supposed to be pretending like we're incompatible, not . . .' I gesture helplessly between us. 'Whatever this is.'

It hits me that this is the first time I've ever admitted out loud that there is something here between us. I wonder if he realises.

Asher's mouth curves slightly. 'We're not very good at pretending, are we?'

He takes another slow step towards me, and the distance between us shrinks to almost nothing. It's only then that his gaze flicks over to the mirror behind me and catches on the half-zipped back of my dress.

He clears his throat. 'You didn't finish zipping up.'

'Oh. Right.' My hand flies to the back of my neck like I can somehow fix it by sheer force of embarrassment. 'I was waiting for Sloane to come and help, but you got here first.'

He hesitates. 'Do you want *my* help?'

I should say no. I should laugh and wave it off and send him out of the room before this moment turns into something it shouldn't.

But I'm apparently my own worst enemy and my voice betrays me.

'Yeah,' I murmur, turning around. 'Please.'

Slowly, he closes in on me. I can feel his breath ghosting against my shoulder as his fingers find the zipper, the slither of cool metal brushing against the bare skin of my spine.

'Tell me if I'm—'

'You're fine,' I breathe, though my pulse disagrees entirely.

The zipper slides upward with a soft, steady rasp that feels louder than it should in the quiet of my room. His fingertips skim lightly over my back, and suddenly it feels like I'm on fire.

I inhale sharply. His fingertips graze against my skin again and I feel a line of warmth tracing up my spine.

We both look up at the same time. Our eyes meet in the mirror.

The world tilts.

'Asher—' I start, but whatever I was going to say dissolves in my throat when he turns me gently towards him.

'Tell me to stop,' he says quietly.

'No,' I whisper.

His hand slides to my waist, mine finds his shirt collar, and the moment his mouth finds mine, the world tilts again.

This kiss is nothing like our first. This kiss is hungry and all consuming. It's the kind of kiss that steals air from my lungs and reason from my mind all at once. The firm hand on my waist tightens its grip and when I rise onto my toes, he meets me halfway, deepening the kiss until my knees threaten to give out.

He tastes like champagne and heat and every rash decision I've ever wanted to make over the last few months. I thread my fingers through his hair, tugging gently, and the quiet sound he makes in response sends a shiver all the way through me.

'Asher . . .' I breathe against his mouth, though I'm not sure if it's a warning or a plea.

He answers by pulling me closer until there's no space left between us. The movement is effortless; one second my feet are on the floor, the next his hands are beneath me, strong and sure, lifting me up. I gasp, instinctively wrapping my legs around him for balance, the silk of my dress gliding against his shirt.

We stumble back a step, laughing breathlessly into the kiss. The fabric of my dress bunches up to my waist and he slides his palms along my bare thighs tracing slow, reverent patterns against my skin.

He breaks away just long enough to look at me, chest rising and falling, eyes dark and unguarded. 'You have no idea what you do to me,' he murmurs.

I swallow hard, my fingers tightening around the collar of his shirt. 'Then maybe tell me,' I whisper.

He leans forward, brushing his nose against my cheek before kissing the corner of my mouth again in a manner so gentle it hurts. His hand disappears under the hem of my dress and drifts higher, fingers splaying against my back, tracing the outline of my spine.

I can feel every exhale against my skin, every tremor that gives away how hard he's fighting to stay in control. I'm not doing any better.

My hands slide up from his chest to his shoulders, the muscles there flexing beneath my palms. I press closer, until I can feel the steady rhythm of his heartbeat, and the soft sound that escapes him is almost a groan.

I clutch at him, fingers curling in the fabric of his shirt, my breath coming faster and faster.

Then—

A polite KNOCK KNOCK at the door.

We both freeze.

The scene is almost comical. Asher's still holding me upright, my legs are still wrapped around his waist, my dress bunched up to my hips. Our lips are kiss swollen, my make-up is almost definitely smudged, and our hearts are racing.

Another knock, followed by, 'Housekeeping!'

For a long, stunned second, neither of us moves. Then, slowly, like two people realising the punchline at the same time, we both start laughing. Breathless, disbelieving laughter that shakes through us and breaks whatever spell we just fell under.

I press my face into his shoulder to muffle it, still trembling from the adrenaline of our kiss. 'This is not happening.'

Another knock, a little more insistent this time. It's obvious the staff behind the door can hear us cackling away. 'Housekeeping!'

'One second, please!' I call out, trying to sound normal, though my voice comes out half-gasp, half-giggle.

Asher finally sets me down, his hands lingering just a little too long at my waist before he steps back. The space between us feels charged and we're both pretending not to notice.

I smooth my dress down, cheeks hot, and turn to face the mirror. My lipstick is smudged, my hair slightly frizzy, and there's no way I can blame either on the humidity.

Asher clears his throat, running a hand through his hair. 'So,' he says softly, that familiar wry tone creeping back in, 'about the plan for tonight . . .'

I force myself to look at him. 'Right. The plan.'

He hesitates, and then says, 'Do you still want to go ahead

with it? The flirting, the fighting, the part where we pretend to hate each other?'

He's looking at me like he's pleading and I almost say no. Almost tell him that whatever this is feels too real to hide behind another performance. But the image of my father snaps me back into focus.

'Yes,' I say finally, the word coming out quieter than I mean it to.

Something flickers across his face but it's gone as quickly as it appears. Disappointment, maybe? Or understanding.

Then, just like that, his expression smooths out and he's all charm and composure again.

'Good,' he says, slipping his hands into his pockets like he hasn't just completely undone me. 'Then I'll see you downstairs.'

He offers the faintest smile, one that doesn't quite reach his eyes, and then he's gone.

I hear a startled gasp from the housekeeper as Asher exits my suite, some mumbled conversation, and then—

'Ms Davies? I was just coming in to bring you some more towels . . .'

I wave the housekeeper in, pretending I don't still taste Asher on my lips. She bustles about, oblivious, or maybe just polite enough not to comment on my obvious dishevelment – though, thankfully, I've have pulled my dress back down – while I stand rooted to the spot, heart hammering.

The second the door clicks shut behind her, I let out a deep breath and lean back against the table. My reflection in the window looks wrecked – hair mussed, lipstick faded, eyes still too wide. I look like a woman who has very obviously just been kissed senseless.

I wince. There's no doubt in my mind that the housekeeper will be racing back to the rest of the staff with this piece of hot gossip on the tip of her tongue.

Asher Vouvalis was in Imani Davies' suite. Alone. Just the two of them. Absolutely no trouble in paradise.

It'll be on @TrustFundTea by the end of the night.

I came here to wreck my father's plan and to prove that forcing Asher and me together would implode spectacularly.

Instead, I'm doing exactly what he wanted: playing the part of the perfect heiress, the one who can't stay away from the man her father chose.

My father wanted headlines and chemistry and a public image that screams 'Peregrine–Vouvalis power couple'.

And somehow, without even trying, I'm giving him exactly that.

CHAPTER TWENTY

Imani

I can still taste him.

It's maddening the way the memory of him lingers on my lips. I've reapplied my lipstick twice, downed half a glass of champagne while getting ready, and still, the ghost of Asher's mouth against mine refuses to leave my mind.

I tell myself to focus as I step into the lift, heart thudding a little too loudly beneath the silk of my dress as we head down to the reception. I have a job tonight.

Flirt.

Smile.

Remind everyone that Asher and I are a non-starter. And that *everyone* includes me too.

The cocktail hour is already in full swing by the time I make it downstairs. I have to hand it them, the Vouvalis Resort staff have really outdone themselves with this location. The reception room gleams like a jewellery box: soft amber lighting spilling across marble floors, waiters gliding between clusters of people with trays of crystal flutes, and the scent of champagne and expensive perfume hangs heavy in the air.

I straighten my shoulders, paste on a smile, and scan the room for a suitable flirtation candidate. Someone pretty, charming, and absolutely harmless. Someone I can bat my eyelashes at and laugh with for five minutes without feeling my pulse jump the way it does around Asher.

But before I can even take two steps into the throng of the crowd, a voice rings out over the buzz of conversation. It's warm, teasing, and entirely too loud.

'Hi, future sister-in-law!'

I turn, mortification rooting me to the spot, and find myself standing directly in front of Teddy Vouvalis.

The middle Vouvalis boy is grinning like an unruly kid who's just dropped a match into a crate full of fireworks.

His crisp, linen shirt is open just enough to hint at tanned skin and an expensive watch glinting at his wrist. He looks like the human embodiment of a yacht party. He's holding a cocktail in one hand and waving the other enthusiastically like we're old friends and not two people who have never said one word to each other.

'You,' he says, grinning wildly, 'are a very hard lady to pin down.'

'Hello,' I manage, forcing polite warmth into my voice. 'It's nice to finally meet you, Theodore.'

At that, Teddy rolls his eyes and snorts. 'No point in being so formal – we're practically family now, right?'

My smile stiffens, freezing in place. 'I—' I start, but Teddy waves a dismissive hand, already sliding into my personal space like it's second nature. He places a gentle hand on my elbow and guides me through the sea of people. We weave between laughter and perfume clouds until the sound dulls behind us, replaced by the quiet murmur of muted conversation in a tucked-away corner near the balcony doors.

Teddy leans one shoulder against the wall and appraises me. 'You know,' he starts, conversationally, 'you two have everyone *very* convinced.'

My heart trips. 'Excuse me? I don't know what you're talking about.'

If my lie is as obvious as I think it is, Teddy doesn't seem to care. In fact, his grin only widens. 'You and my brother. The whole "mutual loathing" thing. I won't lie. It's pretty good. Pretty convincing even.' He frowns and makes a show of tapping his chin thoughtfully. 'But there's something *off* about it.'

'Off?' I repeat flatly.

'Mmhm.' His tone is teasing, but the look in his eyes is calculated. I get the distinct impression that Teddy Vouvalis isn't someone to underestimate. 'I was watching you two earlier, when you arrived, and the thing is—' He pauses and swirls around his cocktail for what I'm assuming is supposed to be dramatic effect. I'm beginning to think that everything Teddy does is for dramatic effect. 'The thing is, Asher doesn't look at people he hates the way he looks at you.'

I take a steadying sip of champagne. 'You're imagining things.'

'Could be,' Teddy says with a shrug. 'But I'm not. There's something there. You two have chemistry. I saw it.'

I force out a light laugh. 'If that's what you think chemistry is, I'm very concerned about your love life.'

Teddy snorts. 'You two are *both* terrible liars. How can I be the only one who sees this? Or is everyone else just an idiot?'

I roll my eyes. 'Believe whatever you want, Teddy. I'm not interested in your brother.'

'Oh, I will,' he says, all grin again, but the glint in his gaze doesn't fade. 'But you *are* interested in him. So let me give you a tip, since I like you.' He drops his voice slightly and leans in further. 'If you're trying to convince the world that you and Asher are mortal enemies, you might want to stop looking at him like you'd rather be fucking him.'

I nearly choke on my champagne. 'I do *not*—'

He just laughs and holds up his glass in a mock toast. 'Relax, future sister-in-law. Your secret's safe with me. For now.'

I open my mouth to respond, to emphatically deny, deny, deny, but before I can get a single word out, a familiar voice cuts through the air behind me.

'There you are.'

I turn just in time to see Sloane gliding towards us, every inch of her immaculate. Her hair is swept into a half up-do, and her dress is a shimmering bronze slip that hugs and drapes her curves, catching the light every time she moves. Heads actually turn as she passes by. She lifts a brow as she comes to stop beside me. 'I thought you needed help zipping up?' My cheeks warm.

'I . . . figured it out,' I say weakly.

Sloane looks unconvinced but she doesn't have the chance to press the matter because Teddy's eyes have widened like he's just witnessed a divine intervention.

'Well, hello,' he says, straightening from his lazy lean against the wall. His grin transforms into one that could charm the devil himself. 'And who might this vision be?'

Sloane stops beside me and spares Teddy a scathing once-over. 'A vision who isn't interested,' she says, not missing a beat.

He laughs, unbothered. 'That's what they all say at first.'

'They also keep saying it afterwards,' she replies coolly, plucking a champagne flute from a passing tray. 'And during. And forever.'

I bite the inside of my cheek to keep from laughing.

Teddy looks delighted. 'You're funny.'

'I'm not trying to be,' she says, taking a slow sip of her drink.

'Even better,' he says, leaning in slightly, as though her disinterest is a challenge. 'The name's Teddy, by the way. Asher's superior and vastly more charming brother.'

She gives him another clearly unimpressed sideways glance. 'I know who you are.'

'And yet I don't know who *you* are,' Teddy says, shaking his head. 'You'll have to forgive me.'

'Will I?'

I choke on a laugh, earning a quick side-eye from her that says *don't you dare encourage him*.

'I hope so.' Teddy flashes her a smile that shows off a

dimple I would bet money has probably caused at least three women to faint this month alone. 'At least tell me your name so I know what to have engraved on my heart when you inevitably break it.'

She doesn't even blink. 'Sloane,' she says flatly.

Teddy waits a beat for her to elaborate and say something else, but she doesn't. This doesn't seem to bother him though.

'Beautiful *and* efficient,' he says, looking at Sloane like she just hung the sun. 'A rare combination. Tell me, *Sloane,*' he practically purrs her name, 'do you always look like this, or is tonight special?'

Her expression doesn't flicker. 'Depends. Do you always flirt this badly, or is *that* special?'

I nearly snort into my glass but manage to catch myself at the last second. Teddy's eyes flick towards me, then back to Sloane, his unshakable grin still firmly in place.

'Ouch,' he says, pressing a hand to his chest. 'But I forgive you. People usually get nicer once they fall in love with me.'

'I don't see that happening,' Sloane says smoothly, scanning the crowd like she's already bored. 'Might want to focus your efforts elsewhere.'

Teddy laughs. 'Challenge accepted.'

'Not a challenge,' she corrects, taking another sip of champagne. 'A suggestion. You should take it.'

'Ah,' he says, unconcerned. 'You'll come around. They always do.'

'I doubt that.'

'Then maybe you'll be my first exception.'

She sighs and mutters, 'God give me strength,' under her breath.

Teddy, clearly having the time of his life, gestures towards the bar across the room, where bottles of champagne and wine gleam under amber light. 'Alright, alright, since I've been so thoroughly rejected, allow me to offer a peace treaty. Drinks? On me.'

Sloane tilts her head. 'You do realise they're free?'

'My family are footing the bill,' Teddy says with a shrug. 'So technically, they *are* on me.'

I can't help but laugh at his roundabout reasoning, and Sloane shoots me a withering glare.

'Fine,' she says finally. 'Go. Bring back something strong enough to erase this conversation from my memory.'

Teddy salutes her with his glass. 'Coming right up, *Sloane*.' He turns and strolls towards the bar, moving like a man entirely certain of his charm.

The moment he's out of earshot, Sloane lets out a long and dramatic exhale. 'Fucking hell, he's exhausting.'

'Incredibly,' I agree. 'But you have to admit—'

'Well, well,' Emmy drawls, suddenly appearing at Sloane's side like smoke. 'I've been looking for you.'

Every muscle in my body tightens.

'Emmy,' I say evenly, lifting my chin. 'Lovely to see you.'

'Oh, I'm sure,' she says sweetly. Her gaze flicks towards the bar, where Teddy is chatting animatedly with the bartender, his smile as blinding as ever. 'It looked like you were getting quite cosy with Teddy Vouvalis just now.'

I shrug lightly and spot an opportunity to do some damage control. 'He's better company than Asher.'

Sloane snorts. 'No, he isn't.'

Emmy's perfectly sculpted brows lift. 'Oh?' She turns her attention to Sloane, a calculating gleam in her eyes. 'And how would you know, exactly?'

I glance between them and immediately recognise that glint in Emmy's eye.It's the one that means she's found a new thread to pull.

Sloane's expression doesn't change, but I know her well enough to spot the flicker of irritation tightening her jaw. 'I just do.'

Emmy smiles like a lion who's just scented blood. 'Interesting.'

Sloane's mouth curves into a dangerous half-smile. 'Not really.'

I can feel the tension stretching between them, and while they're locked in some kind of silent power struggle, I let my gaze drift over Emmy's shoulder.

That's when I see him.

Asher.

He's standing across the room, surrounded by a cluster of people I vaguely recognise. A daughter of a duke, several athletes, a model or two, a son of a real estate mogul. But standing beside him, and leaning in just a little too close, is a woman I don't recognise. She's beautiful, of course. She's got glossy brown hair, perfect full red lips, and a dress that looks stunning on her but was most definitely not made to sit down in.

She says something that makes him laugh and an unexpected wave of jealously hits me.

I force my eyes away, my throat tight. He's doing exactly what we agreed to do. Flirt. Perform. Sell the illusion that there can never be anything between the two of us. I should be relieved that he's playing his role so well.

But I'm not.

I drain the rest of my champagne and turn abruptly back to Sloane and Emmy, who are still circling each other like rival predators.

'I'm going to get some air,' I say, setting my empty glass on a passing tray before either Sloane or Emmy can respond.

But before I can slip away, Teddy reappears with two champagne flutes in hand, grin still firmly in place. 'Did I miss something?' he asks me in a hushed whisper, glancing between Sloane's frosty expression and Emmy's strained smile.

'I'm not sure,' I say truthfully. Whatever it is that's going on between Sloane and Emmy has been simmering under the surface for a while now and maybe it's all about to finally come out.

Teddy shrugs and then offers me one of the glasses. I take it automatically, grateful for the excuse to look away from the tension radiating between Sloane and Emmy.

Unfortunately, my traitorous gaze automatically drifts back across the room.

To him.

I let out an irritated sigh and Teddy follows my gaze. He's quiet for a long moment, watching Asher and the woman with an expression that's surprisingly thoughtful. Then he makes a soft, sad noise. 'Well, that must suck for you.'

The words hit like a dart, and before I can stop myself, I forget to pretend I don't know what he's talking about.

'Yeah,' I breathe out.

Teddy looks at me for another moment, something flickering behind his easy grin. Sympathy, maybe? Then he clinks his glass lightly against mine.

'Come on, future sister-in-law,' he says brightly. 'Let's get you out of the blast radius.'

I let him lead me away, champagne fizzing on my tongue and jealousy burning in my chest.

CHAPTER TWENTY-ONE

Asher

Harlow is still talking. I think she's saying something about her latest campaign shoot in Paris, or maybe it's Milan? Honestly, I stopped keeping track about five minutes ago. I nod when she pauses, offer a polite 'that sounds incredible' and hope it's close enough to whatever she just said to keep me from looking like a complete ass.

Because the truth is, I haven't heard a single word. I'm too laser-focused on the fact that Imani is currently giggling with my brother.

Teddy is standing close by her side, gesturing animatedly as if he's telling the funniest story in the world. And Imani is smiling at him. Her whole face is lit up, her eyes crinkling in that way that always makes my heart skip a beat.

I force my gaze back to Harlow, who's now recounting how she 'simply had to escape the chaos of London fashion week'. Her hand lands lightly on my arm, manicured nails grazing the cuff of my shirt. The contact barely registers.

Across the room, Teddy tilts his head towards Imani, says something else, and she laughs again. The sound carries even over the low hum of the crowd and the clink of champagne flutes. It hits me square in the ribs.

'Are you listening, Asher?' Harlow's voice cuts through my thoughts. Even in my distracted state, I can hear the hint of irritation in her voice. Can't bring myself to care, though.

'Of course,' I say automatically, though my eyes betray me and drift back to Imani almost as soon as I've got the words out.

She's radiant tonight, but when is she not?

I clear my throat and drag my gaze back to Harlow again. She's looking at me expectantly. Right. Conversation.

'Sorry,' I say smoothly, forcing a smile. 'You were saying?'

Her own smile tightens, as she leans in closer. 'I was saying that maybe we should go somewhere a little quieter to get to know each other? Dinner, maybe?'

'Mm,' I say vaguely, my eyes flicking past her shoulder again.

Imani's laughing with Teddy again and the sight makes my chest ache in a way I don't have a name for.

It's not jealousy, not really. I know Teddy. He flirts the way he breathes: constantly, thoughtlessly and harmlessly. It's second nature for him, and I know there's nothing in it.

But still.

It's not fair.

It's not fair that he gets to stand there with her, make her laugh, draw that soft, unguarded smile from her without even trying. Not fair that he gets to look at her like that, touch her arm, speak to her freely, while I'm expected to play the villain in this story. I'm expected to stand here, feigning indifference, while every part of me wants to be the one standing beside her.

Harlow says something else – I think she's talking about the resort, maybe the décor? – but her voice is just a hum in the background. My focus keeps snapping back to Imani. She's glowing under the soft amber light, the silk of her dress catching and gleaming with every small movement.

'Asher.'

I blink. Harlow's staring at me now, head tilted, an edge creeping into her smile. 'You've barely said two words to me all night.'

'Sorry,' I say automatically, then, realising I've said that at least three times in as many minutes, I add, 'It's been a long day.'

'Mmm,' she says, unconvinced. Her gaze follows mine, and when she spots the source of my distraction, her smile hardens. 'Ah,' she says lightly. 'The infamous Imani Davies. I've heard about your . . .' she clicks her tongue, searching for the right word, '*relationship*.'

'I'm not sure what you mean,' I say, knowing that she won't buy it.

She laughs, but it's utterly devoid of any humour. 'Don't play coy. Everyone's been watching you two for months. It's like watching a bad reality TV show play out in front me.'

Imani's turned around slightly now, creating some space for Sloane to join her and Teddy. Her expression is soft, her shoulders relaxed. She looks happy and at ease, and I hate how much I want to be the reason for it.

Harlow sighs loudly, drawing my attention back to her. 'I don't get it,' she says. 'You could have anyone in this room hanging onto your every word, and instead you're busy staring at a woman who clearly can't stand you.'

I take a slow sip of my drink, mostly to buy myself a second before I say something I'll regret. 'I wasn't staring,' I lie pathetically.

Harlow lets out a dry laugh. 'Please. I'm not an idiot, you know? You've looked at her more in the last five minutes than you've looked at me all night.'

'I haven't—' I start, but even as I'm saying it, my gaze starts to drift again. Imani's still by the corner with Sloane and Teddy. The three of them are deep in conversation – or maybe not conversation, exactly. Sloane's arms are crossed and she looks entirely unimpressed, while Teddy's laughing, his grin as bright and unbothered as ever. Imani stands between them, trying to look neutral but clearly fighting the urge to roll her eyes and laugh as well.

Harlow lets out an exasperated sigh as she takes a pointed step away from me. 'Look, you seem like a decent guy, Asher, but I'm not in the business of being someone's distraction or second-place prize.'

'I wasn't—'

Her tone softens and now she's looking at me with

something I might describe as sympathy. 'You don't need to explain yourself to me. I don't know what's going on between the two of you, but if you like her, maybe stop pretending you don't.' She nods in Imani's direction. 'Because if you keep playing these games, someone else will snatch her up.' She gives me one last sad and slightly bemused smile, before she turns on her heel and walks away.

I should call after her and apologise again, genuinely this time, but then Imani is laughing hysterically *again* at something Teddy says and the familiar pull of envy threatens to take over me.

If you like her, maybe stop pretending you don't.

My feet are pulling me across the room before I register what's happening. One moment I'm staring at the empty space Harlow was just stood in, the next I'm standing in front of Imani and my mind is blank.

Teddy's grin falters as soon as he notices me. Sloane's eyes go wide, like she's watching a car crash in slow motion. But I can't bring myself to care about either of them. It's Imani I'm here for.

'Imani,' I say.

Her laughter fades into nothing and a look of confusion takes over her features as she turns around to face me.

I clear my throat and shove my hands deep in my pockets to hide how tightly they're fisted. 'Imani,' I say again, my voice rougher than I intend. 'Can I have a word?'

CHAPTER TWENTY-TWO

Imani

For one dizzying second, I think I might have imagined it. Asher's voice, low and rough around the edges, cutting clean through the hum of the room. But then I turn, and there he is.

He's standing barely a foot away, hands shoved in his pockets, dark eyes steady on mine. His expression is unreadable and it makes my pulse trip.

'Please?' he adds, quieter this time.

My brain scrambles to catch up. This must be part of the plan. It has to be. *Cause a scene. Be difficult. Keep the tension alive.* That's what we agreed. So, I straighten my shoulders, smooth my face into polite indifference, and channel every ounce of the practised frost I've spent the last few months perfecting.

'Now?' I ask coolly, like I'm mildly inconvenienced by his very existence. I gesture towards Teddy and Sloane. 'Kind of busy, Asher.'

Asher hesitates, and an emotion I can't quite decipher flickers across his face. 'It won't take long,' he says finally.

'Right,' I scoff. 'Because the last time you wanted to talk, it went *so* well.'

That earns a few curious glances from nearby guests. Perfect. All I need now is for him to bite back and to play his part and we'll have something juicy for Emmy to post on @TrustFundTea within the hour.

I stare at him expectantly, ready for him to quip back with some snappy barb or for him to roll his eyes in disdain, but he does neither.

He just stares at me. He looks—God, he looks *wrecked*. Almost exactly like how he was that evening at Top Fry now that I'm really thinking about it.

His jaw works like he's trying to find the right words and keeps losing them. In my periphery, I can see both Teddy and Sloane frowning, and I wonder what I'm missing here.

I lower my glass a fraction. 'What? Are you—'

He shakes his head once. 'Nothing,' he says, and the word lands heavily between us. He looks like he wants to say more, like the words are right there on the tip of his tongue, but he swallows them down and takes a step back instead.

I don't know why but panic suddenly spikes inside me. Asher turns to walk away from me and I get the horrible, sinking feeling that, if I let him go, I'll regret it.

Before I can think better of it, I'm hurrying after him.

'Asher,' I call, trying to keep my voice low, but the sound still carries. A few heads turn. I can practically feel the collective gaze of half the room turning to focus on us. Sloane hisses my name behind me.

'Imani, wait!'

But I don't wait. Right now, I don't care about the optics of this.

Asher slips through one of the side doors and I follow him out into a quiet corridor. When the door shuts behind me, Asher stops and glances over his shoulder. He seems genuinely surprised to see me standing there.

'What the hell was that about?' I demand, crossing my arms over my chest.

Asher drags a hand through his hair. He's looking anywhere but at me. 'I don't know. I'm sorry.'

'You're sorry?' I repeat flatly, one brow raised in disbelief. 'Have you forgotten that this is our last chance to—'

'I was watching you,' he says quietly. 'With Teddy.'

I frown. 'Okay?'

His jaw flexes. 'And I guess I got jealous.'

'You what?' A nervous laugh bubbles out of me. 'Asher, come on. You have no reason to be jealous of me and Teddy. He's your *brother*.'

'I know,' he says quickly. He takes a few steps closer to me. 'And I didn't mean it like that.'

'Then how did you mean it?'

He hesitates for a second or two, then seems to deflate a little as the truth comes out. 'I wasn't jealous because I thought you liked him. I was jealous because he gets to be around you like that. Because he gets to stand next to you, make you laugh, touch your arm, look at you without anyone whispering about it. He gets to be friendly with you. And I—' He huffs out a dark laugh and my heart trips over itself. 'And I can't,' he continues softly, closing the last few inches of space between us. 'I have to pretend like I can't stand the sight of you, when all I want is—'

He stops himself and I realise I've been holding my breath.

'All I want is to stand beside you like it's the most natural thing in the world. I want to make you laugh. I want to be the reason your face lights up the way it does when you smile. I want that privilege, and if I ever got it, I'd never take it for granted.'

The corridor we're standing in suddenly feels too small for both of us.

'Asher,' I start, but my voice comes out like a croak. 'You don't . . . You *can't* . . .'

'I mean it,' he says softly. 'I'm tired of pretending. Of acting like I don't want you when every time you walk into a room, I forget to breathe.'

My heart feels like it's trying to burst free from my chest.

'I want to be the one who gets to stand beside you, Imani,' he says quietly. 'Not because I've been told to by my father. Not for a deal. Not for a stupid social media gossip page. But just because I can't imagine *not* being near you.'

Something inside me splinters. For a moment, I let myself want it: the way his voice drops when he says my name, the way he looks at me like I'm something sacred. I want to reach for him. I very nearly do.

But then reality slams back into place and I remember where we are. I remember how much is riding on this.

I take a shaky step back. 'You can't say things like that.'

'Why not?'

'*Because*,' I splutter, my mind racing.

'That's not a reason.' He closes the gap I just made between us. 'Tell me, Imani. Tell me why I'm not allowed to be in—'

'I want to choose it,' I whisper, cutting him off before he can finish that sentence and upend my entire world. 'If we ever do this, if I ever choose you, I don't want it to be because we were forced into it just to help our fathers get a deal over the line. I want it to be my choice. On my terms. And right now, it's not. Everything is about *them* and if we were to do this, we'd just be their puppets. I don't want that, Asher. As much as I—' I swallow and shake my head, not willing to say aloud what I'm pretty sure he already knows.

Asher nods slowly, his eyes still locked onto mine. 'Then I'll wait,' he says quietly. 'Until it's on your terms.'

My breath catches. 'What does that even mean?'

'It means,' he says, voice rough and honest, 'that I'll stand on the sidelines if that's what it takes. I'll play my part, keep pretending that I can't stand you, like there's nothing between us but years of animosity, until you're ready. Until you want this as much as I do. Until you feel like you can choose it.'

I swallow hard. My throat feels too tight, my chest too full. 'Asher . . .'

He smiles faintly, but it's soft, almost sad. 'You don't have to say anything,' he murmurs. 'I just needed you to know.'

And maybe it's the way his voice dips, or the way he's looking at me like he's memorising my face, but my resolve crumbles.

My hand twitches at my side before I even realise what I'm doing. His fingers graze mine and although the touch is fleeting, it's enough to send a current straight up my arm.

'Asher . . .' I whisper, though I don't even know what I'm trying to say.

He takes another step closer until the heat of him fills the space between us. His gaze drops to my mouth, and I hold my breath.

He tilts his head and it's the tiniest movement, but my heart leaps into my throat as the realisation hits me. He's going to kiss me.

I *want* him to kiss me.

The door at the end of the corridor bursts open, and then there's a rush of laughter and chatter spilling out into the hall. A pair of guests stumble out, half drunk and giggling, their champagne glasses sloshing as they jerkily make their way down the corridor.

I jolt back like I've been caught doing something criminal. My hand flies to my chest. 'Shit,' I say. 'I—sorry. I didn't—'

Raw emotion flits across his face for the briefest of moments before he smooths it over. 'It's fine,' he says quietly, though it doesn't sound like it.

'No, I—' I start, reaching out before I can stop myself, fingers brushing his wrist. 'I didn't mean to—'

He catches my hand before I can pull it back. His grip

is warm, steady. 'Come on,' he says, his voice lower now, gentler. 'Not here.'

Before I can ask what he means, he's already leading me away from the noise. We stop outside a lift, and I know where this is heading before he even presses the button. My pulse thrums in my throat, and I should stop him. I *should*, but I don't.

The doors slide open.

When we step inside, the music and laughter fade completely, replaced by the soft hum of the lift. Asher doesn't look at me as he presses the top-floor button, but his thumb is still tracing slow circles against the back of my hand.

Every part of me knows I should pull away.

That I've already let this go too far. That it isn't fair to him, not after what he just said, not when he's standing here with all that sincerity laid bare between us like an open wound.

But I don't pull away.

Because I'm selfish.

Because I want him.

Because tomorrow, we'll have to step back into that ballroom and start the performance all over again – the bickering, the pointed looks, the perfectly staged loathing. And right now, I just want something real.

The elevator hums softly as it climbs, the only sound between us the faint rush of air and the quick, uneven rhythm of my breathing. His thumb still moves absently against my skin, and it's ridiculous how such a small thing can unravel me completely.

When the doors slide open, he finally looks at me. 'Do you want to come in?' he says quietly, his voice rough like he's forcing the words out. 'You don't have to. If you want to go back, you can. We can pretend like this never happened.'

I know I should say no.

I should remind him that the lines have been blurred too much today and we should stick to the plan.

But then I think about tomorrow, about putting the masks back on, about pretending like this spark between us doesn't exist, and the thought physically hurts.

I think I deserve a little joy before the performance starts again.

'Yeah,' I say softly. 'I'd like to.'

CHAPTER TWENTY-THREE

Imani

Asher's suite is identical to mine, just on the other side of the hotel. While I have a picturesque lakeside view, his balcony opens onto the French Alps. But even with that kind of beauty just metres away, the only thing I'm focused on right now is Asher.

The second the door clicks shut behind us, the rest of the world falls away until the only thing I can hear is the sound of blood pounding in my ears.

'Do you want—' Asher starts, shifting slightly so he can gesture to the kitchen area to the right of the corridor.

'No,' I say, without waiting for him to finish his sentence. It doesn't matter anyway. I know exactly what he's going to say. He's going to ask if I want a drink or something to eat or some other banal social nicety, and then we'll awkwardly dance around the real reason I'm here in the first place. We'll pretend like we don't feel the heat crackling between us every time we catch each other's eye.

I'm tired of pretending.

And from the way he's looking at me? I think he is too.

I step forward, feeling bolder and more like myself than I have in months, and cup his face in my hands. I run my thumb along his cheekbone and he tilts his head into the touch, eyes fluttering shut ever so slightly. 'The only thing I want right now, is *you*.'

His eyes snap wide open and he makes a noise that sounds halfway between a whimper and a desperate groan. It takes me a second to realise he's saying my name. '*Imani*.'

'Please,' I murmur, and I don't need to elaborate. He knows exactly what I'm asking for.

Without a hint of hesitation, we pick up where we left off earlier this afternoon. It's as if the hours between then and now were just one long inhale we're finally letting go of.

There's nothing tentative about this kiss. There's no hesitation, no room for second thoughts or self-doubt. It's the kind of kiss that steals every rational thought from your mind and replaces it with something raw and fevered.

I need more.

I grip the front of his shirt just to stay upright as he backs me towards the wall, his lips tracing fire down the side of my throat. His hands find my waist; mine slide up his chest, popping off the buttons on his shirt as I go.

I drag my nails down his chest and enjoy the way he breathes my name against my mouth like a prayer. I slide my hand back up to his collar and tug him closer until there's no space left between us, until I can feel the rapid thrum of his heartbeat against mine.

It feels like I'm pouring every last emotion that's been building up inside me these last few months into the kiss; the ache of pretending, the frustration, the impossible pull towards him that's been coiling tighter and tighter in the pit of my stomach every day. I want him to feel what I can't say out loud.

That I like him.

That I like him so much it's starting to terrify me.

That I wish things were different and we actually had a chance at being something together.

That I'm sorry.

Asher kisses me back like he already knows all of it. Like he's already forgiven me. His lips trace the corner of my mouth then the curve of my jaw and then the space just below my ear. I let out a soft moan when his nose grazes the line of my throat. He pauses there for a second, and I feel the way his lips curve slightly against my skin before he bites down on the spot where my pulse is racing the hardest.

I let out a cry and arch against the wall, as he goes seamlessly from biting the spot to sucking at it gently. His tongue laps at the sore spot and the sensation of it sends a jolt of arousal shooting through me. I can feel my nipples hardening to tiny, pointed peaks through the fabric of my dress and I squirm underneath him.

Off, I think. *I want them off. My clothes. His. Off. Off.* Off.

I open my mouth to voice the thoughts running circles in my mind, but Asher takes the opportunity to slip his tongue inside and I melt against him, all my thoughts and words dissolving into a breathy whimper. My hands find his shoulders, then his hair, and I tug just hard enough to make him groan into my mouth again. It's a sound I want to bottle and play back on every lonely night when I'm up late wondering, *what if we ever had an actual chance*?

He grinds into me and I gasp as I feel, for the first time, the weight of his firm dick pressing against me. *God*. I lift a leg and wrap it around his waist and have to bite back a moan of pleasure as he slides against the fabric of my panties.

Have I ever wanted anyone this badly before? Have I ever been so desperate? So wet and ready? I don't think so. There's something about him – something about the way his hands dig into the curve of my ass as he effortlessly carries me like I'm weightless across the room – that seems to set every nerve ending in my body alight.

'You,' he groans, face buried in the crook of my neck, 'are going to be the end of me.'

So we're on the same page, then.

He comes to a stop at the foot of the bed and sets me down gently in front of it. Before I have the chance to question him and ask why he didn't drop me down onto the soft duvet and ravish me like I deserve (and desperately want), he reaches behind me and finds the zipper of my dress.

He doesn't drag it down right away; instead, he toys with it, letting it slide a few millimetres before he tugs it back up again. Each slow inch feels deliberate, and I realise he's giving me a preview of what's going to come later.

I make an irritated sound and he laughs. 'Alright, love.'

Love.

After everything we've done so far, I'm not sure why this in particular makes my heart skip a beat. Maybe it's the gentleness with which he's touching me. Maybe it's the way he's staring at me, refusing to break eye contact as his finger plays with my zipper. Whatever it is, my breath catches in my throat.

He finally tugs the zipper all the way, then hooks a finger beneath the strap of my dress and slides it gently downwards, his lips chasing the path his fingers just took.

'Ash . . .' I start, squirming on the spot. My legs feel like jelly and I want to move onto the bed, but his mouth drifts lower, to the curve of my shoulder and his name evaporates on my tongue.

He tugs at my dress with his other hand and it slides down my body, pooling at my feet in a waterfall of black silk. I kick it to the side, suddenly acutely aware that I'm standing in front of him wearing only a thong and some heels. I have no urge to cover up though. Not while he's staring at me like *that*.

It feels like his gaze alone could set me on fire. My skin prickles and warms in quick succession as he reaches out and traces a finger around the swell of my breast. He circles my nipple with his thumb and every single coherent thought I've ever had evaporates in an instant.

I reach for him and then step backwards, pulling him down onto the bed with me, my legs automatically wrapping around his waist to keep him close. The point of my heels scrape against his back, but he doesn't seem to mind.

He groans my name again and again like a mantra as he rocks into me. His dick is straining against the soft fabric of his trousers and I reach down to unbuckle his belt.

The metal buckle slides loose in my hand and suddenly it feels like we're both teetering at the edge of something massive and inevitable. I can feel the heat of his body pressing into my palm as I push his trousers down over his hips. He shoves them the rest of the way, kicking them off with a shuddery exhale, and now it's just his boxers between us.

The outline of him straining against the dark fabric is insane and I don't even bother pretending to be shy. I reach for him. He groans, low and rough, when my knuckles brush against the hard outline of his dick beneath his boxers.

He's so hard it's almost obscene.

He leans in, mouth hungry on mine, and the kiss is all teeth and tongue and a desperate, frantic need that matches my own. I can taste the *yes, yes, yes* in every slide of his mouth and the pressure of his hands on my body.

'Tell me you want this as much as I do,' he manages to rasp out, voice so raw I barely recognise it. There's a searching look in his eyes that makes my stomach drop. He looks like he's terrified this isn't real. I answer by arching my back and pushing my breasts against his chest. He cups them in both hands, thumbs circling my nipples until they're pebbled and aching until I'm seconds away from actually begging for more. Warmth blooms everywhere he touches.

He hovers over me and flicks his tongue over my nipple before pulling it between his lips.

I let out a deep, keening cry, but he doesn't stop. His mouth is hot and hungry and every pull and lap of his tongue makes my breath come out in ragged, high-pitched bursts. I arch my back, offering more, *desperate* for more, and his hands pin my hips to the bed like he's afraid I might float away.

'Asher, I . . .' but I don't even know what I'm asking for.

He moves to the other breast, lavishing the same attention on that peaked, over sensitive bud until I'm nearly seeing stars. My hips tilt up, searching for friction, and his free hand finds my thigh, stroking up, up, up until he's gripping right beneath where I want him most.

I'm seconds from combusting.

He palms at my hip then hooks his thumb around the delicate lace of my thong and pulls, not slow this time but a rough, urgent tug that has the flimsy piece of fabric sliding down my legs in record time.

'Look at you,' he rasps, voice half shattered. 'You're perfect.'

I want to laugh, but it comes out as a whimper instead. I want to say, *you make me like this*, but there's no spare air in my lungs for words. His mouth drags up my chest, along my collarbone, licking and kissing, until he finally takes my mouth again.

He kisses me like he's starving. Like he's falling apart and I'm the only thing holding him together. It's dizzying, wild, and nothing like anything I've ever felt before.

My hips grind against his, desperate for the sweet release of friction, and I swear I can feel how wet I am without even touching myself. I want him so badly it actually hurts.

'*Please.*' I don't even realise I'm begging until the word breaks loose from my throat.

'Tell me what you want, love.'

'*Anything*,' I plead. 'Anything. Just— Just *touch me*.'

His grin is hungry as he moves lower, trailing heat down my body until he's crouched between my thighs at the edge of the bed. The way he looks at me then, every muscle in his body coiled and focused, that sends a bolt of pure electricity through my body.

His hands run along my thighs and then he's spreading me open, knees wide, gaze locked on the throbbing, aching heat between my legs. I think I might actually die if he doesn't touch me, and he must know it because he laughs lowly, and presses a kiss to the inside of my knee.

His fingers slide up, coaxing my thighs wider, and then he drags one slow, torturous finger along the soaked heat of me. I jolt, hips canting up on instinct. His thumb brushes gently against my clit. I nearly see stars. My whole world narrows to that one point of contact.

He moves his thumb in slow, torturous circles and then speeds up, keeping rhythm even as two of his fingers tease at my entrance, stroking so slowly it's almost cruel. I whine, nearly bucking off the bed, and he shushes me softly, still watching me as I twitch and gasp beneath him.

When he finally slides his fingers inside, I swear I nearly lose it.

He fucks me with his fingers, curling up to hit the spot that lights me up like a live wire. Every twist and stroke is maddeningly perfect. I grind against his hand and gasp, barely holding myself together.

He watches as I come undone beneath him, his eyes dark and hungry like he wants to eat me alive.

And then he does.

Asher pulls me right to the edge of the bed, spreading my thighs wide. He kneels down, pushes my hips up with his hands, and just stares for a second, like he's memorising the sight of me ruined and shaking. His breath is hot against my inner thigh.

Then he licks me.

One long, slow swipe that makes my vision blur. I moan, loud, desperate, and he groans back, like he can't get enough. His tongue circles my clit, flicks over it, then sucks it into his mouth and everything explodes.

I jerk, breath catching in my throat, as pleasure spreads hot and fast through my body. He sinks in a finger alongside his tongue and I think I see white for a second. I'm soaking, shamelessly wet and messy around him, and I know he can feel it because he lets out a filthy groan.

Every messy, obscene lap of his tongue coaxes another desperate sound from my lips. He makes it impossible to be quiet – I'm gasping, keening, breathless, and I don't give a damn if anyone can hear through the hotel walls.

'Asher— Fuck. Please, I need—' But I don't even know what I'm begging for because he's already giving me everything.

He hums against me, sending another jolt straight to my core, and then he's plunging his fingers in and out, curling up as his tongue circles my clit, faster, harder, pulling me right to the edge . . .

I come so fast, the sensation crashes into me like a meteor. Every muscle locks, every nerve goes white hot, and I shatter apart on his mouth, legs trembling, my nails digging into the sheets for dear life. My vision actually goes a bit blurry. There are sparkles behind my eyelids. I'm not entirely sure my body is even capable of processing this much pleasure in one go.

Asher groans against me and it sends another aftershock through my body. I gasp. 'Fuck. Fuck. *Fuck*.'

I shatter on his tongue again and my mouth falls open in a helpless, guttural moan. I don't even care how ridiculous I must sound. I want everyone in this entire fucking hotel to know it's Asher Vouvalis making me come undone like this.

When I finally come back to myself, I'm limp and wrecked and shaking, sprawled across his bed. Asher climbs up over me, his mouth shining, his jaw clenched, and he's looking at me like a starved man and I'm his last meal.

I barely get my breath back before he's hauling me up, crushing my lips against his and letting me taste myself on his tongue.

I want him inside me. Now.

I don't even bother to be coy. I fumble desperately at the waistband of his boxers. His dick springs free, hot and impossibly hard, heavy in my palm and *God*, he's perfect. I wrap my hand around him and he bites out a ragged curse. The tip is already wet. He grinds against my thigh and I can feel how badly he needs this.

I hook my legs around his waist, heel digging into his back, pulling him closer until the head of his dick is lined up perfectly with my soaking entrance. He hesitates, just for a second, eyes searching mine.

'Please,' I beg. 'Just—'

He doesn't make me wait. He lines himself up, presses in, and I swear I nearly come again right then and there.

He's hard and warm and so, so big, every inch stretching me perfectly, filling me in a way that I know will ruin me for anyone else. I arch into him, rolling my hips to take him as deep as possible.

The stretch is perfect. It's a slow, heady burn that blurs pain and pleasure into one, and I can't help the broken cry that rips from my throat as he bottoms out, buried to the hilt of me.

'Oh, fuck. *Imani*.'

He moves, slow at first, letting me adjust, but I don't want patience. I want to feel this for days. I want to be *ruined*.

I clutch at his shoulders, digging my nails into his skin, and rock my hips up to meet every thrust. I rake my nails down his back and gasp his name in time with each stroke. 'Asher, harder . . .'

He groans and I can tell I've just shattered whatever last scrap of restraint he's clinging to. He pounds into me, fast and brutal now, and the sound of skin slapping skin echoes through the quiet of the room. Each thrust drags another increasingly loud moan from my lips.

He grabs my thigh, hooks it high up on his hip, and the new angle leaves me seeing stars again. His dick hits that perfect spot with every snap of his hips and I can't think, can't breathe, can't do anything but yell his name and beg for more.

Every thrust knocks the breath from my lungs; every smack of his hips grinds against my clit and winds the tension in my stomach tighter and tighter. I want to hold on and make this last even longer, but it's impossible. I come hard again, my body locking around him, squeezing him so tight I hear him curse.

He doesn't slow down. His pace gets frantic. Desperate. I feel him shudder inside me and then he pulls out with a guttural moan, stroking himself once, twice, three times, and then—

He spurts hot and thick across my stomach and breasts then hovers over me, placing his still shaking arms on either side of my waist. He's staring at me like he's never seen anything so perfect.

I love it.

Asher's still leaning over me, hands braced on either side of my head, chest heaving as he takes in the mess he's made of me. I never want him to look at me any other way.

I pull him down, wrap my arms around his neck, and drag his mouth to mine. It's messy. Feverish. Still so hungry.

My hands roam, greedy and demanding, nails raking down his back, then sliding to his chest, his stomach. I want to map out every muscle. I want to memorise the heat of his skin, the way he shudders when I touch the spot just below his ribs. *Everything.* I can't stop touching him. I graze his jaw, his throat, ghost my hand over his stomach, loving the way he shivers under my palm. He presses open-mouthed kisses along the curve of my collarbone, the side of my neck, like he's drunk on my skin and can't get enough.

I don't know how long we lay there, stealing lazy kisses and touches, but when we finally break apart, it's only to collapse in a tangled heap, his weight pinning me to the bed, both of us covered in sweat and sex.

For a while, there's just the slick, sticky heat of our bodies. My skin buzzing, heart still stampeding, his arm heavy yet perfect where it's slung across my waist. I don't want to move. Ever. I want to melt right here into the mattress and let Asher watch me with that dark, shattered look on his face forever.

But then he sits upright, pressing a kiss to my shoulder as he moves. I shiver at the gentle scratch of his stubble against my skin. I could drown so easily in this feeling.

He mutters something I don't catch before he slips out from underneath me and disappears into the darkness of the room. For a second, panic spikes – I don't want this to end. Not yet. I'm not ready, but then I hear the soft click of the bathroom door and water running. I watch him from where

I'm sprawled, boneless, on the bed: Asher, gloriously, gloriously naked, back and shoulders gleaming in the half-light of the bathroom.

He returns a moment later with a towel, warm and steamy from the tap. He doesn't say anything. Just kneels over me, gaze locked to mine, and wipes the mess off my stomach and chest with the gentlest touch I've ever felt. Like I'm precious. Like he wants to worship every part of me. Like he'd never get bored if we were to stay locked up in this room for the rest of our lives.

When he finishes, he tosses the towel aside and crawls back into bed beside me. 'Come here,' he says quietly, opening his arms. I shuffle up next to him and curl around his body. His arms wrap around me and pull me in close and it feels like coming home.

Finally.

CHAPTER TWENTY-FOUR

Imani

Sunlight breaks through a tiny gap in the blackout curtains, rendering them absolutely useless. I groan and tug the thick duvet over my head. There's a slow, delicious ache pulsing through my thighs as I move. Not pain, exactly, but the floaty, slightly raw feeling that comes from being thoroughly fucked.

I can't help the grin that tugs at my lips as I stretch out in the bed, every muscle in my body singing with the memory of last night. Every time I close my eyes, memories of last night and the way Asher braced himself over me or how perfectly his body fitted against mine take over my mind.

How many times was it in the end? I lost count somewhere around 2am.

I roll onto my side and stretch out, expecting to come into contact with Asher's body and see if he wants to give round five (or is it six?) a go before we have to face reality again.

But my hand just hits empty air. I sit upright abruptly and frown as I peer around the bedroom.

There's no sign of him.

His side of the bed is empty and cool, like it's been some time since he was last wrapped up in these sheets with me. The door to the bathroom is open, but it's dark and there's no sound of running water to suggest he's in there.

For a second – or maybe it's longer than a second, who knows, time suddenly doesn't feel real – I just sit there. I'm naked and alone in this enormous bed with its million-thread-count sheets and I can't shake this sick, sour panic that's spreading through me.

I open my mouth to call out his name, but the sound of raised voices makes me freeze in place.

'I don't want to hear another pathetic excuse.' Georgios Vouvalis' cold snarl is unmistakable. 'Just get it *done*.' I can practically see the sneer of disgust on his face.

'I don't—' Asher clearly tries to cut in to defend himself, but he abruptly stops talking and I imagine Georgios holding up a hand to silence him.

'You don't what?' Georgios' voice is sharp enough to slice through glass. 'You don't think you can do it? You don't think you're capable? Is that what you're trying to tell me now?'

The words are ice-cold, laced with so much venom it's hard to believe this is a father talking to his son. Even after everything my father has put me through these last few months, I don't think he could ever bring himself to talk to me like *this*.

Like he hates him.

Truly, *truly* hates him.

I slip out of bed carefully to keep my movements quiet as I reach for something to wear. There's a pile of our clothes on the floor, but the idea of contorting myself back into my dress from last night isn't an appealing one, so I opt for Asher's shirt. The shirt is huge on me and the sleeves hang halfway over my hands, but at least I'm not stark naked anymore.

I creep to the door, push it open a smidge as quietly as I can, and press my ear to the crack. I can't see them from here, but I don't need to. Every venomous word Georgios spits out carries perfectly across the suite.

'You're an embarrassment, Asher.' His voice is low now. 'Nothing but a constant reminder that no matter how much I invest in you, no matter how much I try to teach you or how many chances I give you, you will always find a way to disappoint me.'

There's a beat of silence that feels like it stretches on forever, then the deep scrape of a chair being pushed back.

'I'm doing everything you've asked,' Asher says tightly. His voice sounds strained, like it's taking everything in him not to break. 'Everything. I've done everything you told me to.'

'And yet,' Georgios hisses, 'you still find new and creative ways to fail. Tell me, how exactly am I supposed to trust you with anything important when you can't even keep a woman in line?'

I flinch.

Keep a woman in line.

Fury rears inside me violently, but I will myself to stay silent.

Asher lets out a deep exhale, and when he speaks next, I can tell he's talking through gritted teeth. 'I told you when this all started that we didn't have a connection. I can't force—'

'And I told you I didn't give a damn,' Georgios roars. He lets out a disgusted noise. 'I give you chance after chance, time and time again, and every time you prove that my initial assessment about you was correct. You're dead weight. Nothing but a liability with my last name unfortunately attached.'

My heart pounds painfully in my chest. I should go back to bed and pretend I'm not here and that I didn't just hear what I just heard.

Asher doesn't say a word, and Georgios doesn't seem to care. He continues on with his tirade undeterred.

'You're weak. You always have been. You think anyone respects you? They laugh at you behind your back. They see you for what you are – a charity case I keep around out of pity.'

Enough.

I can't stand listening to another second of this. Subtlety be damned, I slam the door open with zero finesse and storm out into the living room.

Asher is slumped in the armchair, hunching in on himself like he wishes he could just disappear while Georgios stands over him, face contorted with rage.

Both their heads snap up to look at me as I enter the

room. I wish I could say that Georgios' face becomes a mask of embarrassment or even shock once he sees me, but that would be a lie.

Instead, his lips curl upwards into a satisfied, smug little smirk.

He takes in the rumpled shirt, my bare legs, the way I'm very clearly freshly bedded, and his eyes practically light up. He doesn't even bother to hide it.

'Asher,' he purrs, 'I see you've finally managed to get something right.'

Asher flicks his gaze over to me and offers a small, apologetic smile. It's the kind of smile that says *kill me now* and *I'm so sorry you had to see this* simultaneously.

Georgios clocks the glance, and that smug expression on his face only deepens. He sweeps his gaze over me again. 'Good. This is good,' he says, almost to himself. 'I'll call Malcolm and get the ball rolling. There's no sense in waiting, now that the two of you have clearly, *finally*, found the right chemistry.'

I don't even care that he's talking about us like we're not standing right here in front of him. I just know that I want him out of here and far, far away from Asher.

'I think you should leave,' I say coldly.

There's a long, loaded silence. For one glorious moment, I think Georgios is about to actually bristle with embarrassment, maybe even mutter an apology for embarrassing his son like this. But, of course, that would require some basic human decency and I'm starting to realise that it's a trait neither of our fathers possess.

He glances at Asher, at me, and then at his phone. 'I'll see myself out.' His smile is deeply unsettling. 'Don't disappoint me.' And then, just like that, he's gone. The door clicks shut behind him with all the finality of a guillotine.

It's quiet in the suite. Too quiet. For a second, neither of us move. Asher won't even meet my eye.

'I'm sorry,' he finally gets out, voice roughened at the edges. 'You shouldn't have had to hear that. I didn't want to let him in but . . .' He trails off and shrugs helplessly.

It's laughable, really. The idea that I could possibly care about my own discomfort when he looks like he's about to vanish into thin air.

I cross the space between us and wrap my arms all the way around his shoulders. At first he's so tense it's like hugging a statue, but then he exhales, drops his head against my shoulder and melts into me.

After last night, I would've said that we had reached the heights of intimacy between us. Asher's head between my legs and his tongue rolling torturous circles around my clit certainly feels like the very definition of it. But this? My arms wrapped around him while he breathes into the crook of my neck feels like another level entirely.

He takes in a few more shuddery breaths and then pulls back slightly. I take this as my cue to step away and give him some space, but he snakes an arm around my waist and pulls me onto his lap.

'Thank you,' he murmurs, dragging his thumb absent-mindedly along my hip, tracing slow arcs through the fabric of his shirt. He tips his head back against the chair. He looks tired. And it's not just the *I haven't slept enough because I spent last night getting to know every inch of Imani Davies' body* kind of tired, but the deep, soul-level exhaustion of someone who's spent his entire life trying to brace for the impact of having Georgios Vouvalis as his father.

My heart lurches like it doesn't quite know if it's supposed to ache or flutter in this moment, so it settles for doing both.

'You don't have to thank me,' I say, and I mean it too. I'm not sure whether he's thanking me for interrupting Georgios' tirade before he became even more cruel, or for sending Georgios away, or even for just sitting in silence with him. All I know is that I'd do it again in a heartbeat. Anything to stop him from looking like he's seconds away from crumbling.

'He's wrong, you know,' I say. 'Everything he said. Every last word.'

Asher huffs out a dry laugh. He doesn't let go of me though. If anything, his fingers grip a little tighter, like I'm the only thing anchoring him in this moment. 'You want to know why my father hates me so much? It's not just that I'm a disappointment to him. If it were that simple, I don't think he'd even care too much. It's that I remind him of the biggest mistake he's ever made.'

He inhales shakily, and I can't help but wonder when he last said this aloud, to someone other than himself during his darkest moments. 'My mum was twenty-five, broke, and sick as hell when she showed up on Georgios' door and told him I existed. I'm not even sure he remembered her at first. They'd had a one-night stand seven years before and hadn't said a word to each other since.'

I can't help but wince. 'How did he take that?'

Another dry puff of laughter. 'He looked her in the eye and denied it. Said she was nothing but a liar out for a quick payday and there was no chance that I was his kid.' His hand tightens on my leg. 'But she was pretty sick and didn't have any family or any friends she could trust me with, so she did the only thing she could. She went to his wife.'

Oh.

I blink, trying to process the scale of nuclear disaster this must have kicked off in the Vouvalis household. I risk a glance at Asher's face. He's not looking at me. He's staring blankly somewhere just over my shoulder, his jaw set, but I can see the tiniest tremor in the muscle just beneath his cheekbone.

'She explained the situation, told her that she was sick and didn't have anyone else to turn to. She said she didn't want money. Just wanted to know that I'd be looked after and that Georgios was the only option she had left.'

'What happened then?' I breathe.

For the first time since I walked out into the room, there's a hint of humour in Asher's expression. 'Everything went to shit. Maria – that's Andreas and Teddy's mother – was obviously furious. Not at my mother though, who'd had no idea who Georgios was when they met, or that he was married. She was furious at *him*. Demanded a divorce immediately and then she told *her* father.'

I frown, not understanding the significance.

'Georgios doesn't come from money,' Asher explains. 'He needed a lot of seed money to get Vouvalis Resorts started back in the day, and he got a large chunk of it from his father-in-law, Nicholas. Ex-father-in-law,' the last part he adds with an unmistakable smirk. It's subtle, but it's the first real flash of satisfaction I've seen on his face this morning.

'Nicholas essentially forced Georgios to take me in and raise me alongside Andreas and Teddy as his son. If he refused? Nicholas said he would pull out from the company and take his money with him. He was a majority investor and it would've bankrupted Georgios before he ever really got started. Don't get me wrong,' he says quickly. 'Nicholas didn't do any of this out of care for me. He just saw how hurt his daughter was and knew this was the best way to essentially punish Georgios for what he did to her.'

I let it all wash over me for a second. All I can do is stare at Asher and try to imagine what it must've felt like to be a literal living, breathing expense on someone's balance sheet.

Suddenly Asher's attitude when all this started makes more sense to me. No wonder he never fights back. Someone taught him from day one that the only way to keep existing was to make as little noise as possible.

I try to find the right thing to say, but the words don't come. I just keep thinking about the way Georgios treated him five minutes ago, how absolutely merciless he was. And for what? Because Asher exists? Because he's a casualty of Georgios' own poor judgment?

'And he blames you for that?' My voice comes out rougher than intended. 'I mean, he's the one who made those choices. You were literally a child.'

He shrugs like it barely matters, but I can see the flush creeping up his neck. 'My father doesn't believe in blaming himself. He's spent the last two decades trying to buy out his ex-father-in-law and never have anything to do with him again, but it's never worked out. I think he'll hate me until he finally manages it.'

There are a million things I want to ask, but all that comes out is, 'And your mum? Is she . . .'

The silence that follows feel charged and heavy. Asher toys with the hem of my shirt on my thigh, like if he keeps his hands moving, the words will come out easier. 'She died when I was nine.'

'I'm sorry,' I say, and I mean it with every fibre of my being.

He shakes his head. 'Don't be.' There's a forced lightness in the way he says it. 'She did what she could. She knew Georgios was a shit option, but he was the only option. So she made sure I landed somewhere and I'd be taken care of.'

Taken care of physically, I suppose, but somehow I doubt she had the kind of scene I walked into this morning in mind when she turned up on Georgios' doorstep.

I tuck myself closer against Asher's chest. There's another question clawing at the back of my mind and I blurt it out before I have the good sense to stop myself. 'Do you hate him? Your father. After everything he's done? After how he's treated you all these years?'

He's quiet for so long I start to regret voicing the question. But then his hand moves, his fingertips tracing lazy lines over my bare thigh. 'I used to,' he says at last. 'But it takes too much energy. Mostly I just try to avoid making things worse.'

'And that's what we've been doing, haven't we?' I ask. 'We've been making it worse.' It hits me suddenly that the last few months of scheming and blowing up at each other in public has probably made Asher's home life an absolute misery and yet he hasn't brought it up once. Because of me.

For me.

I swallow. 'Asher, if you don't want to do this anymore, we can—' I cut myself off, because I'm not even sure what I want to say. That we can find another way of getting out of this marriage? And what would that be? If it were that simple, we would have thought about it months ago.

'No,' he says firmly. 'We're going to do this. We're not going to let them win. Not without a fight.'

And then he kisses me.

Slowly. Deliberately. Like he needs me to understand that this moment is real, no matter how much the rest of our lives is built on performance right now.

His mouth is warm and soft, and he tastes like toothpaste and something bitter at the edges, maybe the aftermath of that conversation with his father. I wrap my arms around his neck and tug him closer. He palms my thigh, fingers tightening as he pulls me even further into his lap. I let myself melt into him. I can still feel the ache from last night in my bones, but I don't care. I want more.

I want him.

I *want* him.

Truly. Wholeheartedly. With every fibre of my being. *I want him*.

The realisation slams into me.

I want Asher and my father has handed him to me on a silver platter. So why am I still fighting this?

CHAPTER TWENTY-FIVE

Asher

I want her.

It's as simple and as complicated as that.

I kiss her like I'm trying to say everything I've never actually managed to put into words. I let my hand slide up her thigh, her breath hitches, and for a second everything falls away: my father, the merger, the unrelenting pressure to be someone my father might one day love.

It's just me and Imani.

She's soft against me. I lose myself in the taste of her, in the way she shivers when I run my tongue along her jawline, in the way her fingers curl tight in my hair like if she lets go even for a second, we might both disappear.

I'm not sure how long we stay like this, but it's long enough for her lips to become swollen and her pupils to go wide and dark.

It's dangerous, how easy this feels. We're supposed to be

at each other's throats but the truth is, right now, I'd do anything to keep her here.

And then reality comes crashing down on us in the form of a knock on the door. Both Imani and I freeze.

Another knock, this time harder than the first. And then a voice that's painfully familiar to us both.

'Imani, I swear to *God*—'

Relief floods Imani's face before she springs out of my arms and sprints to the door. '*Sloane*!' She yanks open the door, tugs Sloane over the threshold, and then slams it shut. 'What the hell are you doing here?'

'What am *I* doing here?' Sloane drawls, one brow raised. Her gaze sweeps over Imani's state of dress (or should that be undress?) and then to me on the armchair. 'I should be asking what *you're* doing here, though I guess that one's easy enough to figure out.'

Imani's expression turns sheepish and she doesn't make any attempt to deny what Sloane is so obviously alluding to. 'Long story,' is all she says.

Sloane rolls her eyes. 'I don't doubt it.' She walks further into my suite's living room and drops into the nearest chair. Once she's settled in, she doesn't waste any time. 'Alright, so, quick debrief since apparently we've forgotten how to use our phones.' She shoots Imani a pointed look.

Imani deliberately looks away.

'People noticed when you left last night.'

'Who?' I ask.

'*Everyone*,' Sloane says. 'And that's not an exaggeration.

Literally everyone is talking about it. I spent the rest of last night and most of this morning doing damage control for the two of you. You're welcome.' She takes out her phone and spins the screen around so we can both see the @TrustFundTea story currently splayed across it:

> Multiple sources tell us it was *not* all love and synergy at last night's launch event. Asher Vouvalis and Imani Davies were overheard having a *heated argument* after the airline heiress spent most of cocktail hour flirting up a storm with *another* Vouvalis . . .
>
> My sources say Asher Vouvalis was not pleased to see his former flame hitting it off with his brother of all people and the two had strong words for each other as they took it outside and away from prying eyes . . .

Imani and I exchange a look. While it was just the two of us in here, it was easy to forget that this is our reality: pretending we hate each other and causing scene after scene in public.

'You owe me big time,' Sloane sniffs. 'I am now officially an @TrustFundTea source.' She shudders dramatically. 'I'll never recover.'

'Thank you,' Imani says stiffly. 'We, um—'

'Don't want to hear it,' Sloane cuts her off.

'Is this why your father was in here this morning?' Imani asks me.

'I think so,' I say. It makes sense and explains why he came storming in so furious and red-faced.

This should be a good thing. A *great* thing, even. Imani's plan has worked spectacularly, exactly as she wanted it to.

And yet, there's no rush of satisfaction. No moment of triumph, or at least not the kind I used to crave. Instead, all I feel is this low-grade dread, like we've set something in motion that can't be shoved quietly back under the rug.

I think back to last night and wish we could've had more time together, just the two of us. I catch Imani's eye again. I'm not sure if it's just wishful thinking or what, but for a fleeting moment, I get the feeling that she's wishing for the same thing.

CHAPTER TWENTY-SIX

Imani

I'm late. Again.

It's become something of a recurring theme in my life lately – running late, running away, running from things I don't want to face. Mostly Asher.

I've become an expert at avoidance, perfecting the art of pretending I'm suddenly, tragically, extremely busy every time his name flashes across my phone screen. It's cowardly, I know, but I don't know what else to do. Because how do you go back to pretending to hate someone when you've had their mouth on your most intimate parts, and their voice in your ear whispering sweet nothings that made your heart forget how to function?

You don't.

At least, not gracefully.

Sometimes, in my more delusional moments, I tell myself that I'm not avoiding him because I'm scared but because it's practical. Strategic, even. The @TrustFundTea crowd has certainly noticed our absence from the social scene these past two weeks, which makes it easier to pretend like avoiding Asher has some kind of ultimate purpose. It's not quite as socially devastating as having an argument in public, but it's something and I'll take what I can get right now.

My driver pulls to a stop and all thoughts of Asher evaporate from my mind, replaced with a slightly more pressing issue.

I used to look forward to meals with my parents. That was back when dinner meant echoing laughter and real conversation. Now, dinners with them feel like a performance review for a job I never even applied for, one where the promotion comes with a husband I didn't choose and a future that doesn't feel like mine.

Anxiety settles in the pit of my stomach as my driver opens the door. It's been two weeks since France and every time I've been in contact with my father since then, I've expected him to drop the bomb that he's finally done it: told his board and investors all about his plans to merge with Vouvalis Resorts and that me and Asher will be marrying to sweeten the deal.

For some reason, he hasn't yet and it means I've spent the last two weeks in a permanent state of anxiety-fuelled anticipation waiting for the ball to drop.

Surely this has to be it, I think to myself as I climb out of the car and walk towards the restaurant. I've been summoned to No. 12 Blythe, the upper echelon's current favourite restaurant of the month, under the guise of a simple family dinner.

The text message I received last night simply read *It's been too long* followed by a calendar invite, but I know he must have an ulterior motive.

A hard lump lodges itself in my throat as a doorman pulls open the door. He gives me a look of barely concealed alarm as I stride past him and I know the expression on my face must look like I'm walking to the gallows and not one of the most exclusive restaurants in the city. I can't be bothered to pull up the façade and fix a polite smile onto my face though. This meal signals the beginning of the end for any kind of autonomy in my life, and I can't bring myself to pretend otherwise.

The maître d greets me with a polite smile and does a better job than the doorman at pretending I don't look like I'm seconds aways from tears. 'Ms Davies,' he says smoothly. 'Your parents are already seated. This way, please.'

I nod shakily and he leads me through the main dining room to a frosted glass door tucked away in the back, then scurries away.

A private room. Of course.

I swallow thickly, reach for the door handle, and then freeze. I can hear my mother's soft murmur from here.

'—can't hide this from her forever.'

Eavesdropping on my parents feels like a cardinal sin, but I don't move. Instead, I get a little closer to the door just in time to hear my father let out a heavy sigh.

'And what would you have me tell her? That we're one bad quarter from going under?'

My breath catches.

'It can't be that bad,' my mother says.

'It is,' my father responds grimly. 'We're still haemorrhaging from the routes we had to cut during lockdowns and the investments I made during that period haven't panned out like I'd hoped.'

'What about the government loan?' my mother asks. 'When are we supposed to hear back on that?'

'I heard back last week,' my father says, his voice strained in a way I've never heard it before. 'They aren't going to go through with it.'

My mother draws in a quick breath.

'If this merger doesn't happen, Peregrine Airways won't make it to the end of the fiscal year.'

For a second, I'm sure I've misheard him. My father, the man who built Peregrine Airways out of nothing, who's spent his whole life lecturing me about stability, about perception and control, is saying that the company is broke. I press a hand against the wall to steady myself, but it's no use. The world tilts.

'That's why you should tell her,' my mother insists. 'If she knew, she'd—'

My father lets out a brittle laugh. 'I'm *protecting* her. The less she knows, the better.'

'She'll never agree to marry him if she doesn't know why.'

'She doesn't need to know the truth,' my father snaps. 'She just needs to get it done.'

'Malcolm—'

'Don't,' he bites out. 'Do you think I want this? You think

I wanted to barter our daughter's future like a corporate asset? But Peregrine is hanging by a thread. This merger is the only thing that keeps us in the air. Without it, we're finished. She needs to do her part.'

I don't remember backing away from the door, but suddenly I'm halfway down the corridor, my heart pounding so hard it hurts. The maître d glances up as I pass, and I force my face into something neutral, nodding politely like my entire world hasn't just shattered around me.

Once I'm outside, I stand on the kerb and try to breathe past the sting in my throat. I breathe in too fast and too hard, trying to keep the tears from spilling.

All this time, I thought I was being used just to help get a deal over the line, and that was bad enough on its own. But the truth is much, much worse.

My father isn't just using me to strengthen a business alliance; he's using me to *save* the company and he doesn't even have the decency to tell me the truth. Every fight we've had since the day he demanded I marry Asher, every reminder of my 'duty' suddenly snaps into awful, perfect focus.

This is nothing but desperation. This is a man trying to keep his empire from crumbling, even if it means selling off his daughter like she's an asset on a balance sheet.

A deranged laugh slips past my lips as I wrap my arms around myself and stare out at the street, headlights blurring through my tears.

I have no idea if I'm angry or heartbroken.

Maybe it's both.

CHAPTER TWENTY-SEVEN

Asher

I haven't seen her in sixteen days. Not that I'm counting. Except, of course, I am.

Sixteen days, three hours, twenty-four minutes, and an admittedly embarrassing number of unread messages from me sitting in her phone. At least, I have to assume they're unread because I haven't had a single response from her.

At first, I told myself to be patient. She needed space. Time. Breathing room. France had blurred lines we weren't supposed to cross, and we both knew it. It would make sense for her to want distance after that – after *us*. But the thing is, space has never felt this loud before. Every time my phone buzzes, I hope it's her. Every time it isn't, I feel like an idiot.

I know exactly why she's avoiding me, and I can't even blame her for it because we both know what's coming. Our fathers are gearing up to announce the merger and, alongside it, our engagement. Of course she wouldn't want to be anywhere near me right now. Not when she's about to be forced to do the one thing she's been fighting against this whole time.

I drag a hand through my hair and stare out the window of my office. If I had it my way, I'd take her far from here, to some quiet place by the water, where it could just be the two of us again. My mind drifts back to the weekend in France like a reflex. I've replayed it more times than I can count over the last sixteen days (three hours, thirty-nine minutes) and I crave it more than I've wanted anything else in my life. I want to see her smile and laugh and look at me the way she did back in my suite – as if I wasn't part of the problem.

A thought takes root in my mind. Maybe I can't fix everything, but maybe I *can* remind her of what it felt like when it was just us in that suite. When the world fell away around us and it was just me and her.

The thought quickly turns from wishful thinking into something real and tangible. I reach for my phone and do something I don't think I've ever done once in all my life.

I call my father.

I've sat in meetings with investors who could ruin the company with a single sentence. I've stood behind podiums, delivered speeches that have decided the fate of entire projects. I've even stared down my father when he was at his angriest.

Somehow, none of it compares to the feeling of waiting in the lobby of Imani's building right now.

The concierge keeps giving me wary glances over the top of his computer screen, probably wondering why I've been pacing a dent into the marble floor for the last twenty minutes. I don't blame him. With my sweaty palms and the way I keep jumping and nervously looking over to the door whenever it opens and closes, I know I look suspicious. I'm pretty sure the only reason he doesn't call security to shoo me away is because he recognised my last name when I showed him my ID.

Being a Vouvalis does have it perks; I just wish it didn't come with the strings attached.

Every tick of the clock above the concierge desk sounds louder than the last. My nerves are already stretched thin, pulled taut like I'm waiting for a verdict instead of a woman. I've rehearsed what I'll say at least a dozen times in my head, each version worse than the last. Currently I'm at: *Hi, Imani, surprise, I'm here to kidnap you—temporarily, of course.* Not exactly my smoothest opening line.

When the entrance doors slide open again, I turn too fast and relief hits me square in the chest. There she is. I knew I'd missed her, but I hadn't realised just how much until this exact second. Just seeing her, even across the lobby, feels like finally coming up for air after weeks underwater.

The feeling of relief doesn't last long though, because something is wrong. Just like that night at the film premiere, I can spot it almost immediately. Her shoulders are drawn tight, her eyes rimmed red, and there's an exhausted stillness to the way she carries herself that makes my heart sink.

She looks like she's sleepwalked through a natural disaster and only just realised what happened. I try to catch her eye, but her gaze is fixed on her phone, her mouth pressed into a thin, unhappy line. It's only when she gets within a few steps of me that she finally looks up. For a second, I think maybe she doesn't even register that it's me standing in front of her.

Then she blinks, like she's coming back into focus.

Her lips part. 'Asher?'

My carefully prepared lines are gone, wiped clean by the reality of Imani standing in front of me looking like she's seconds away from breaking. I have to stop myself from closing the distance and pulling her into my arms right here, right now.

'Hey,' I say, trying to keep it light, easy, like nothing's wrong and I haven't spent the last sixteen days doing little else but thinking about her.

She cracks out a ghost of a smile, but it doesn't reach her eyes. 'Hey.'

I offer her a soft smile, hoping it hides the panic thrumming under my skin. 'Rough day?' It's a pathetic attempt at casual, but I'm desperate for anything that might make her laugh or at least remind her she's not alone. Not anymore.

She gives me a quick nod. 'Family stuff. It's nothing. You don't need to worry about it.' She says it like a reflex, but I get the impression that Imani could be bleeding out and she'd still insist it's just a scratch.

Don't worry about it.

How can I not?

Every instinct in me screams to demand answers, to fix whatever has put that look on her face. But I stop myself.

Imani doesn't need fixing; she needs someone who will stand beside her while she finds her footing again.

I nod and, on realising that I'm not going to push, she relaxes ever so slightly.

'What're you doing here?' she asks, then shakes her head and winces. 'Sorry. That came out wrong.'

'You're good,' I say with a soft laugh. 'I know you weren't expecting to see me.'

Her expression turns sheepish. 'Sorry, I've just been—'

'It's fine,' I say. 'You don't need to explain yourself to me. I get it.'

'Do you?' she asks quietly. She's still not looking at me.

I reach out and press my thumb against her chin, tipping her head gently so she meets my gaze. 'I do. And I'm not here about that.'

'Then why are you here?' she presses.

'I have something for you,' I say, feeling a grin tug at the corner of my lips. 'A gift.'

Imani arches a brow. There's a flicker of curiosity there. 'A gift?' she repeats dryly.

'You still keep a suitcase packed by your door, right?'

She blinks at me. Clearly that wasn't the response she was expecting to her question. 'Yes . . .' she says slowly, dragging the word out until it's at least three syllables too long.

I let her hang in that confusion for a beat longer, then offer a grin I hope is more reassuring than manic. 'Good. You're going to need it.'

*

An hour later and we're pulling up at the private airfield on the edge of the city. Imani's spent the entirety of the car journey here trying to wheedle the location for our final destination out of me, but I've managed to keep it a secret.

Barely.

'Just give me a hint,' she faux-whines as our car pulls into the airfield. 'Just one hint and then I won't ask again.'

I laugh because she's said that at least four times already, each one more dramatic than the last. I briefly consider giving in. Just a little. But the anticipation in her eyes is too good. She looks like she wants to actually wrestle the answers out of my brain. I want to drag this out for as long as I possibly can.

'No hints,' I tell her. 'I want to see your face when you figure it out.'

She opens her mouth, prepared to argue, but the car crests around a bend in the drive and the airfield suddenly comes into clear view. There, glittering in the afternoon sun, sits a dark, sleek jet on its own stretch of runway. The staircase is rolled out and the crew are standing to attention, waiting for us.

Imani's mouth actually falls slack open. She stares at the jet, then at me. Back at the jet. Back at me.

For one perfect, stunned second, she's completely speechless.

'Is that—That's not—Are we taking *that*?' she finally manages.

I nod and she lets out an excited squeak. The car barely

rolls to a stop before she's unbuckling herself and shoving the door open to get a closer look.

I follow her out, and the look on her face is one I want to burn into my memory. She's standing on the tarmac with her eyes wide, jaw slack like a kid seeing Disneyland for the first time.

She turns slowly, taking in every polished inch of the jet. The matte-black exterior gleams under the sunlight, the chrome accents throwing off flashes of gold. She spins back to me, disbelief stamped across her face. 'You've got to be kidding. We're not actually taking this are we?'

I grin. 'We are.'

Her gaze flits between the jet and me again, like she's trying to catch the trick. 'No, you're joking. Tell me you're joking.'

'I'm really not,' I say, enjoying the show far more than I should.

She lets out a small, incredulous laugh and shakes her head. 'You know what's crazy? I've never actually been on a private jet before. Not even once!'

Now *that* surprises me. 'What?'

She shrugs, a faint blush rising to her cheeks. 'My father's rule. He says it's bad optics for us to ask people to spend thousands on Peregrine Airways' first-class seats if we don't fly it ourselves. It always been commercial for us – first class, and obviously Peregrine first class is on a whole different level than most airlines, but still.'

'Well,' I say, gesturing towards the plane, 'consider this an upgrade.'

Her excitement is infectious as we board. She's practically vibrating as we're greeted by the flight crew, and I can't blame her. This jet is one of my father's favourites and insane even by the standards of our social circle. The cabin itself is like something from out of a dream with cream leather seats that look too soft to be real, each one angled towards wide oval windows where the afternoon sun spills in like honey. There's a bar gleaming at the far end of the cabin, glass shelves lined with bottles of champagne, whisky, and other spirits I can't pronounce but know cost more than any rational person should ever spend on a drink. Between the seats, there's a low walnut table topped with a vase of pale roses, and a spread that would make a Michelin chef weep.

Tiny porcelain plates are packed with smoked salmon blinis, truffle arancini, and neat little sandwiches with gold-tipped toothpicks. There's a bowl of fat, glossy green grapes, slices of ripe mango, and an array of miniature pastries that smell faintly of butter and vanilla. A bottle of champagne is resting in an ice bucket beside two crystal flutes that glitter as the light catches them.

Imani's eyes are wide. 'This is ridiculous,' she breathes, running a hand along the back of one of the seats. 'Who even needs this much legroom?'

'You say that now,' I laugh, 'but give it ten minutes and you'll be ruined for commercial flights forever.'

She hums. 'I think I might already be. Don't tell my father, he'd be heartbroken.' She grimaces as she mentions her father's name. It's only for a brief second, but I'm watching her so intently, I don't miss it. Before I have the chance to question it, she's pasted a smile back onto her face like the little blip never happened.

She runs her fingers over the seats, still a little awestruck, and then turns on me, all narrowed eyes and barely restrained curiosity. 'Okay, serious question,' she says. 'How did you even pull this off? You can't just walk up to a private airfield and rent a jet like it's a Lime bike. Who did you blackmail?'

I force myself to laugh and lift my shoulders in a nonchalant shrug. 'I called in a favour.'

I don't mention the part where the 'favour' involved swallowing my pride and asking my father to approve the use of one of the family jets. Or how I made up a whole story about luring Imani into matrimony with a grand gesture, just to grease the wheels and get him to agree.

We're barely buckled in before the crew are gliding through the safety demo and prepping for take-off. Imani slips into the window seat, hands pressed to the armrests, nose practically squashed against the glass. I take the seat beside her.

'Okay,' she says, glancing over towards me with a side-eye that's probably meant to be intimidating, except the effect is blown by how excited she still is. 'Are you going to tell me where we're going, or is this an ongoing hostage situation?'

I stretch out, crossing one ankle over my knee, and give her my best, most infuriating grin. 'Nope.'

She groans, tossing her head back in a way that's absurdly dramatic. 'You're the worst.'

The jet lurches forward and we're off. For a split-second, there's the familiar pressure in my chest – the one that always hits during take-off, right at the moment of leaving the ground, and then we're airborne. I glance over at Imani. She's angled her body towards the window and she's staring out of it with wide, bright eyes.

She's transfixed. She tips her head forward, lips parted in wonder as she watches the buildings shrink beneath us. It's nothing like the Imani I found in the lobby, shoulders caved in on herself, eyes red and haunted. Right now, she looks . . . peaceful. Like maybe for a minute, the world and all its bullshit can't reach her up here.

I want to stay up here forever, suspended with her between everything that's gone wrong and anything that could possibly go right. I want to give her this: a pocket of peace, a slice of freedom, however long it lasts before our lives snap back into place and someone else decides what comes next.

The urge to reach for her hand, or pull her into my side, is overwhelming but I force myself to just sit and let her have this. This is for her, not for me. Our fathers, the merger, the relentless countdown to whenever they announce our impending engagement. It all feels a million miles away, the kind of thing that can't touch us if we just keep flying.

If she's happy, even just for a few hours, then nothing else matters.

CHAPTER TWENTY-EIGHT

Imani

Flying has always been my favourite kind of escape. There's something about being suspended between earth and sky that makes everything else feel smaller. Up here, the noise of the world fades, the pressure in my chest loosens, and I can breathe again.

I sink a little deeper into the plush seat, champagne glass balanced between my fingers, and glance out the window. The clouds are soft and endless, painted gold at the edges by the afternoon light. For the first time since France, I feel like myself again. Like the version of me that existed before overhearing my parents, finding out that the future I thought I had was quietly dissolving beneath me.

None of that matters now. Asher has managed to pull me out of my head, out of the ache that's been burrowing deep in my chest. He's done that for me without even realising it.

He's sitting across from me, jacket discarded, sleeves rolled up showing off toned, veiny arms. Every now and then, our eyes meet and I feel butterflies in my stomach. He catches the look on my face and his mouth tips up at the corner. He leans in, bracing his forearms on his knees, and gives me a once-over that's way too soft to be fair. 'You don't need to get into the specifics, but are you feeling better now?'

'Yes,' I say immediately, and there's no point trying to downplay it because it's the truth. 'I always feel better when I'm around you, actually.'

Asher blinks, clearly caught off guard, and then his smile splits his face in two. It's wide and warm and so stupidly pretty I want to press pause on life and live in this moment forever.

'Really?' he asks, and the softness in his voice does something funny to my breathing. 'Because I was just thinking the exact same thing.'

For a split second, neither of us says anything. There's just the hum of the engines and golden light spilling through the windows.

I shake my head. This is stupid. We've literally got the whole jet to ourselves, and here I am, two metres of distance away from the one person who actually makes me feel like I'm a real person and not just a means to an end. Completely ridiculous.

I can't stand it.

Before I really process what I'm doing, I unbuckle myself and cross the aisle to where he's sitting. His eyes widen briefly but then I swing a leg over his lap and settle myself there, arms draped around his neck like it's the most natural thing in the world.

It feels like it is.

The effect is instant. He lets out an exhale so deep it feels like he's been holding it in for an eternity, and his hands find my waist. He holds me in place like maybe he's worried I'll disappear if he lets go.

And then we're kissing, desperate but soft, making up for every second we've wasted being apart from each other these last two weeks.

His mouth is hot against mine and suddenly I'm aware of nothing except the fact that I am straddling Asher Vouvalis in a private jet at thirty thousand feet in the air. I angle my hips forward and he lets out a deep groan that vibrates against my lips.Maybe it's the altitude or maybe it's just Asher, but I feel lightheaded in the best kind of way.

'*Imani*,' he groans. He says my name like it's the only word he knows. His tongue traces the seam of my lips and my composure goes out the window.

I roll my hips again, slower this time, and he snaps his head back, eyes squeezed shut. 'You're killing me,' he manages, voice strangled.

'Good,' I whisper, and do it again.

If the cabin crew walked in right now, I wouldn't even care.

His tongue slides against mine and my whole body arches into him. I let out a low moan and he tilts his hips up until I feel the hard outline of his dick brushing against me. I tug at his hair and that seems to do something devastating to him. I feel it in the way he shudders, the way his grip tightens, the way his mouth trails from my lips down to my jaw and then back again, like he's starved and desperate to taste every single part of me.

I suddenly hate myself for wearing my tried and tested travelling outfit, consisting of a comfy pair of sweats and matching hoodie. If I'd worn a dress or a skirt, he'd definitely have pulled it up by now.

I whimper softly as his hands settle on my hips, thumbs dragging along the waistband of my sweats like he's physically restraining himself from just tearing them off. I shiver, and it has less to do with the air conditioning blowing and more to do with the way his mouth finds the spot just below my ear. He dips one of his hands under my hoodie and splays his palm, warm and soft, over my stomach. There's a kind of reverence in the way he touches me. I don't think I've ever felt so worshipped in my entire life.

I tip my head back, eyes rolling shut, and lose myself in the sensation of Asher.

He presses kisses along my cheekbone, then drags his mouth lower until he finds the spot just beneath my jaw. He sets his teeth there and bites down. It's the tiniest of scrapes, but I swear I see stars behind my eyes.

His hands slide up, big palms cupping my breasts through my hoodie and bra, and it's so much but somehow not even close to enough. I moan, all dignity utterly gone, and he groans in return like he's the one about to unravel. He squeezes me gently, then a little rougher. His thumbs trace lazy circles over my nipples through the fabric of my bra and I want to sob at how good it feels.

I don't even realise I'm grinding down on him until he's pinching both my nipples through my bra, rolling and tugging until I can't actually think, let alone remember how to breathe. My entire body lights up like a power grid. He's still working his mouth over the spot on my neck where my pulse is hammering and then he sucks, hard, and I nearly scream. His fingers run over my nipples, not gentle, not rough, somehow just excruciatingly perfect. His thumbs coax tight little spirals of pleasure out of me until I'm grinding down on him helplessly, the cabin blurring at the edges of my vision. I feel like I'm short-circuiting. I want to say something witty or devastatingly filthy, but all that comes out is another whimper.

I can feel the heat blooming down my neck, my chest, everywhere, and it hits me that I'm half a second away from coming in my sweatpants, in the lap of Asher Vouvalis, on a private jet.

The thin fabric of my bra isn't any kind of barrier at all; it's like he knows exactly how to touch me to turn my brain to static. He circles my nipples with his thumbs, over and over, sometimes gentle, sometimes hard enough to drag a gasp out of me.

I can't stop grinding down on him and he's matching me, hips surging up, like he needs this as badly as I do. His hands are relentless. He finally slips one under the cup of my bra, finds my bare nipple, gives it a perfect, quick pinch—

Oh my *God*.

I shatter. Right there. Lights out. Brain off.

My body feels like a livewire as pleasure rips through me. I ride the wave, choking out his name, and he just holds me. All the chaos that's been knotted up inside me unravels. I'm boneless, weightless, trembling in his lap, my forehead pressed to his shoulder and my breath coming in wild little gasps. I can feel his heart hammering right through his sweatshirt.

'*Imani*,' he says, his voice hoarse. The way he says my name nearly finishes me off for a second time.

I keep my face hidden in his chest, trying to slow my pulse and failing completely. The hoodie I'm wearing suddenly feels too hot and too tight, and it feels like my skin is buzzing under his hands. He doesn't say anything, just rubs slow, soothing circles over my back until the aftershocks have faded and I'm just left in an absurd, delirious sort of bliss.

Eventually, I tilt my face up. There's a flush climbing all the way up his neck and into his cheeks. His hair is a mess, thanks to me, and his lips are kiss swollen and red. The look he gives me is so nakedly hungry and adoring that it sends another spasm of pleasure shooting through me.

I groan and rock against him. He's hard under me, thick and insistent, and the press of him through his trousers is borderline obscene. I flatten my palm over him and the action sends a jolt of *something* shooting through his body.

His head tips back, his teeth digging into his lower lip so hard it looks like it might bruise. He bucks up into my touch, and I squeeze just a little harder, the tips of my fingers brushing the shape of him, and—

A clatter from the galley snaps me back long enough to remember that, yes, we're technically in public and, yes, the cabin door could open at any second.

I don't move. Asher doesn't move. We're statues. Very horny, very obvious statues.

When, after a few seconds, nobody bursts through the door and catches us, I let out a breath and collapse, giggling, against Asher's chest.

Asher looks dazed. His curls are shoved in every direction, lips still wet and swollen, cheeks burning red.

I grind down on him one last time just for the hell of it to see him shudder.

Worth it.

I go to slide off him, but Asher won't let me. His arms lock around my waist and he pulls me in tighter, his lips pressed to my temple. I squirm and an embarrassingly pleased little whimper escapes me. He laughs and then reclines our seat until I'm basically on top of him, right where he wants me.

I open my mouth, but he hushes me and tucks me against his chest. I can still hear his heart racing.

'Stay,' he murmurs.

I don't need to be told twice. I burrow closer, my head pillowed on his shoulder as his fingers trace soft lines against my back.

I must fall asleep against his shoulder because when I come

back to myself, the cabin lights are dimmed, and Asher's hand is still tracing lazy, gentle shapes on that bare strip of skin above my waistband. My whole body feels warm and boneless in a way I don't think I've ever felt in my entire life. I want to freeze this moment and live in it forever, this perfectly preserved pocket of peace.

A gentle chime cuts through the haze. Then the soft, professional voice of the lead attendant: 'Mr Vouvalis, Ms Davies, we'll be arriving in the Seychelles in approximately one hour. If there's anything you'd like before our descent, please let us know.'

I jerk upright so fast I nearly clock heads with Asher. 'Did she just say the Seychelles?'

Asher cracks a slow smile. 'Surprise.'

For a second, I can't even say anything.

The Seychelles.

It's a single word, but it hits like a punch to the chest. Not just because it's beautiful or far away or the kind of destination you only ever see on a desktop background, but because I know exactly why it matters so much to me and, apparently, so does he.

I look at Asher and my heart starts to race. He's quietly checking my face like he's worried he might've got it wrong, that I wouldn't want this, that maybe it wouldn't mean anything to me.

He couldn't be more wrong.

My throat goes tight. Like dangerously, embarrassingly tight. I can feel my eyes stinging in that way that means I'm exactly two seconds away from either kissing him senseless or bursting into tears. Possibly both.

Asher reaches for my hand, thumb brushing slow across my knuckles, and I can feel the question vibrating between us before he even says it.

'Are you okay?' he asks carefully, as if he's afraid he might shatter me just by asking.

For reasons I cannot begin to understand, this is what does me in. Not the surprise trip or the jet or the fact that my entire future is crumbling and the only thing I actually want is right here in front of me. No, it's just Asher, looking at me like I'm the only thing in the world he cares about.

I nod, and my voice comes out so raw I almost don't recognise it. 'Yeah. I'm . . . yeah. Thank you.' I laugh, a watery, breathless mess. 'I just can't believe you remembered. Or that you'd even want to do this for me.'

He squeezes my hand, eyes crinkling at the corners. 'Of course I wanted to. You deserve everything.'

The kiss, when it comes, is slow and impossibly gentle. He leans in, and my heart skips and I don't know why I'm suddenly nervous. I've kissed Asher before. I know what his mouth tastes like. But this isn't like any of the other kisses we've shared. This is the kind of kiss you dream about and then wake up convinced it can't possibly exist in real life because nothing could ever be this good or right or *devastatingly perfect*.

My heart trips over itself, then starts up again, double-time and wild in my chest. His lips are so soft it almost hurts. And just like that, something unspools inside me. Something huge and bright and terrifying. He pulls back just enough to look at me, eyes dark and soft, and it suddenly hits me all at once.

Oh.

Oh no.

Oh God.

I'm think I'm in love with him.

Deep, can't-breathe-without-you, stupid, messy love with Asher Vouvalis. The realisation consumes me so entirely, it's like I'm drunk with it.

He's kissing me like I'm both his joy and his undoing and all I can think is – this is it. This is what I've been trying not to feel and now I can't imagine ever feeling any other way. There's no going back. My hands are in his curls, my chest is caving in, and every part of me is humming with him and there's absolutely no denying it now.

This is *love.*

CHAPTER TWENTY-NINE

Imani

If heaven had an ocean view, I'm pretty certain that it would look like this.

From our floating bungalow, the water stretches out in a hundred shades of blue, pale as glass near the shore, darkening into something so deep and rich the further it goes out, that it looks almost unreal. Even the waves move slower here, curling lazily beneath the deck as though time itself has decided to take a break and enjoy the beauty that is the Seychelles.

I step outside and the warm, salty, tropical air hits me. Our private deck floats right above the water, complete with an infinity pool that looks like it's melting into the ocean. The other bungalows are spaced far apart, so it's genuinely quiet except for the lazy lap of the waves and the occasional cackle of some island bird off in the distance.

We've been here for three days already, and we've

been making the most of it like we're on borrowed time. Technically, I guess we are.

In the mornings, we have breakfast on the deck: fresh papaya, pineapple slices dripping with juice, croissants still warm from the oven. By afternoon, we're out exploring one of the local villages and the surrounding areas. I take Asher on hikes along trails framed by wild hibiscus and palm trees that look older than time. No maps for us, we just follow the scent of sea salt and frangipani until we find hidden beaches no one else seems to know about except a handful of locals fishing or barbecuing on the golden sand.

We've visited a spice garden, where the air smells like cinnamon and vanilla, and the scent sticks to our clothes long after we leave. We've taken a boat ride to the tiny island of La Digue, rented bikes and spent the afternoon exploring, riding past pastel-coloured houses and children playing barefoot in the street. We get caught in a flash tropical storm and we spend an hour camping out under a palm tree, soaked, laughing, and stealing kisses with the rain drumming overhead like a heartbeat.

We have dinner with Marie to discuss her eco-lodge and Asher doesn't mind in the slightest when Marie and I spend the entire evening chatting about plans for potential tourism packages. He just sits back and lets us brainstorm, a soft smile plastered across his face whenever I glance up in his direction. For the first time in a very long time, my dream feels tangible and it's because of him.

If I think too hard about the fact that soon we'll have to fly back home to London and to the mess waiting for us there, my chest goes tight. So instead, I just lean against the railing and watch the sunlight scatter across the water, pretending for one more moment that this is my everyday life.

'Asher?' I call over my shoulder.

He's inside the bungalow, humming off-key to a song I can't quite catch. A moment later, he appears in the doorway, barefoot, shirtless, holding two glasses of freshly squeezed mango juice. His hair's still damp from the shower, curling against his temple, and just the sight of him makes my stomach flip. I wonder if I'll ever stop reacting to him like this. Aside from sightseeing and exploring, we've spent a, quite frankly, ridiculous amount of time in bed together.

It's strange to think about how intimately I know him now, compared to that first meeting months ago. Back then, I only knew his name, but now I know every low, rough noise he makes when I touch him just right. The way his breath catches when I claw my nails gently down his back. The needy, broken sounds he tries, and fails, to stifle in my neck when he's losing control. I've mapped every inch of his body with my hands and mouth. I know the constellation of freckles under his jaw, the exact spot on his hip that makes him tense and gasp (and where he has a poorly done stick and poke tattoo of a cactus), the way his eyes go slightly unfocused when he's trying not to come too soon. The way he looks at me, afterwards, like I've remade the world just for him.

It's a miracle I'm even vertical right now. If I'm being honest, the effort of putting on actual clothes and stepping outside instead of crawling straight back into his arms might just be the most willpower I've ever demonstrated in my entire life. And from the way Asher's looking at me right now, head tilted, eyes lazily roving over my body like he's imagining peeling me out of my sundress and dragging me back to bed? I'm not sure my willpower is going to last much longer.

No, I tell myself. It's our last day and we need to make the most of it.

A traitorous voice in the back of my mind slyly says that spending the day in bed with Asher, his head between my legs, his tongue giving me an encore from this morning's performance, might just be the best way to spend our last few hours here, but I ignore it. Just about.

'I'm thinking Curieuse Island this afternoon?' I say as he approaches and hands me a glass.

He hums in agreement, the sound rumbling low in his chest as he takes a sip from his own glass. 'That's the one with the giant tortoises, right?'

'Mhmm,' I say, leaning against the railing. 'They live forever practically. Over a hundred years old. They've seen everything – storms, tourists, probably a few bad love stories – and they're still just there. Living peacefully and completely unbothered.' I let out a wistful sigh.

He grins. 'You're jealous of a tortoise.'

'Maybe a little,' I admit. 'They've got it figured out.'

He laughs quietly, and the sound rolls through the warm air, easy and familiar. It's impossible not to smile with him. Then my phone buzzes suddenly on the nearby table, pulling me out of the moment. I glance at it and instantly feel my stomach sink.

DAD.

My good mood dissolves in an instant.

I stare at the call then, without hesitation, I hit *ignore*. The sound cuts off. Silence fills the air again.

Asher looks at me sideways. 'You're not going to answer?'

'No.' The word comes out colder than I intend. I exhale and try again. 'I know what he wants.'

'What's that?'

'He's going to tell me it's time,' I say, staring out at the horizon. 'That the merger's moving ahead, that I need to stop stalling and agree to marry you.'

Asher glances away. After a moment, he says quietly, 'Do you ever want to get married?'

I freeze. Of all the questions I thought he might ask to follow up, I wasn't expecting that. The question lingers in the air. I take a breath and let the sound of the waves fill the silence before I answer. 'I do,' I say finally. 'But I want it to be my choice. My terms. If we start like this, with them forcing it on us like this, it'll always feel tainted.'

Asher hums in agreement, his lips twitching upwards into a wry smile. 'Do you know what's funny?'

I shake my head.

Asher takes a step closer towards me and braces his palms

on either side of me against the railing, caging me in. I reflexively lean against him and let out a soft sigh. 'If our fathers hadn't forced this on us, I kind of think we might've got here on our own.'

'You think so?'

Asher grins, then spins me round so we're standing chest to chest. He tips my chin upwards so I can meet his gaze, and I can't help but lean into his touch. 'I do. There's clearly something here. Something between us.'

I pretend to look confused. 'Is there? Hadn't noticed.'

He rolls his eyes. 'I'd be happy to give you a repeat of this morning if you need something to jog your memory.'

My cheeks burn at the memory of Asher's mouth on me, the slow, ruthless way he fucked me against the tangled sheets just hours ago. I can still feel the echo of him right where I'm aching for more. I lick my lips, and his eyes track the movement like a predator, lazy smile gone razor-sharp.

He moves in, crowding my space until I'm hemmed in by nothing but him and the ocean and the possibility that I might let him wreck me a dozen more times before this day is over. But then, all at once, his expression changes. The hunger is still there, but something else muscles its way to the surface. He looks almost . . . shy?

'I have something to tell you,' he says.

'Something bad?'

He laughs softly. 'No. Never. Something a little embarrassing.'

I tilt my head and wait.

Asher's smile turns bashful. 'We've met before. I don't know if you remember.'

I frown, not quite understanding what he's getting at, and then—'Oh, yeah. At university, right? Like once at a party?'

He nods. 'It was just the one time, but I guess you could say I had a thing for you.'

I blink at him. 'Are you—Are you saying you had a *crush on me*?'

'A little one,' Asher laughs. 'You were nice to me and even though I didn't know you at all back then, there was something about you that I . . .' He cuts himself off and shakes his head almost ruefully. When he speaks again, his voice is low and quiet in a way that feels private, even out here with nothing but sun and ocean and maybe a few eavesdropping tortoises in a five-mile radius. 'I've never felt about anyone the way I feel about you. I know circumstances aren't ideal, but I really think we could make something incredible out of this. Even if it started out wrong. We could make it right. We could make it ours.'

'I—' I croak out. 'What are you saying?'

He takes a breath, like he's bracing for impact. 'I'm saying we don't let them define this for us. If we have to play along and get engaged for the sake of their deal, fine – we do it. But that doesn't have to be the real thing. Not for us. We'll treat it like what it is: an arrangement. And then, someday, when you're ready, when it feels right for you, I'll ask you again. Just us. I'll propose for real, and that can be the one we actually care about.'

He's so close I can see the flecks of gold in his irises and the stubborn set of his jaw that says he's not just saying this to make me feel better. He means it. Every word.

He gives me a soft, slightly sheepish smile. 'I'd wait forever if that's what you wanted. I want you, Imani. Actually want you. Not because of our fathers or because my father told me to, and definitely not because of a deal.' He leans in, his forehead pressed to mine. 'I want a life with you. I don't care how long it takes – I'll do it your way.'

I want to say yes. I want to yell it, scream it off the deck and let it echo all the way to London and back.

I press my hand flat over his heart and feel it hammering against my palm.

'Yes,' I hear myself say. My voice is soft and embarrassingly shaky, but I don't care. 'Yes, Asher. That's what I want. I want you.'

The look on his face nearly does me in. He covers my hand with his own and pulls me against him until there's nothing between us but sunshine and the dizzy rush of relief. I tip my chin up a little and he kisses me.

For one perfect moment, the world is just us.

And then, because the universe is apparently allergic to my happiness, my phone starts ringing again. I groan, but this time when I glance down, it's not my father bombarding me with call after call, it's Sloane, lighting up my lockscreen with a flurry of missed calls and messages.

I snatch it up immediately.

Sloane

Um? What the fuck? Are you okay?

Just saw the news . . . what is going on?

HELLO

ANSWER YOUR PHONE

I frown and go to message Sloane back, but then my father calls and I decide it's time to stop delaying the inevitable.

I answer on the second ring, bracing myself. 'Hello?'

He doesn't waste a single breath on pleasantries. 'Imani. Have you seen the news?' He sounds . . . wrong. Panicked in a way I've never heard from my father before. I have no idea what's just hit the news, but I know there can only be one thing that would ever rile him up like this.

'No,' I say. 'I just woke up. Is this about the fact we're broke?'

Asher looks at me like I've suddenly grown two heads, but I can't focus on him right now. My father inhales sharply. 'How did you—'

'I overheard you and Mum at dinner. I know the company's broke. I know that's why you want me to marry Asher. It makes me sick that you'd use me for a bailout. That you and Georgios think that Asher and I are nothing but some kind of asset to be bartered.'

There's a brief moment of silence and then my father belts out a deranged cackle. 'You think Georgios knows about this? Our perceived capital was the only reason Georgios was even interested in the merger! Without that, this whole plan falls apart. Peregrine Airways is over. Over!' He lets out a noise that sounds like a sob, but I can't bring myself to feel any sympathy for him.

And that's probably a good thing, because the next words that come out of his mouth come out in a snarl. 'You need to come home. Today. I don't care where you are. The press have got wind of the collapse, the investors are in a tailspin, and unless you want to watch everything I've ever built burn to the ground, you need to come home and present a united front with your mother and I.'

I stare at the horizon, at the blinding blue, and try not to let the familiar nausea crawl up my throat. 'This isn't my fault,' I say. 'It's not my problem to fix. You did this.'

'Don't you dare,' he hisses. I can picture it: the vein above his eyebrow pulsing furiously, his knuckles going pale as he grips his phone so tightly, it might just shatter. 'Everything I've done has been to protect this family. And now you've gone and destroyed it because you couldn't just do one thing I asked of you.'

I could argue. I could remind him that I've spent my entire life jumping through hoops, contorting myself into whatever version of 'daughter' would be most useful to him at the time. But I'm tired of appeasing my father.

'Goodbye, Daddy,' I say.

'Imani, don't you—'

I drop the call. The silence that follows is thick and almost suffocating. I stare down at my phone, still glowing in my hand, until the screen finally goes black. The waves crash lazily against the stilts below our deck, the world moving on as if my life hasn't just fractured in real time.

My lungs feel tight. My heart's still hammering from the adrenaline, from the echo of his voice in my head. The ocean's too blue, the sun too bright, and I can't tell if I want to scream or cry or both.

'Imani?'

Asher's voice is softer than I deserve right now. He's been quiet this whole time, giving me space but not stepping away, and when I finally look up at him, I know he sees it. The exhaustion. The anger. The way my world has tilted on its axis, and I don't know how to stand straight anymore.

He takes a tentative step towards me. 'Are you okay?'

I inhale a shaky breath that doesn't quite make it all the way out. 'Honestly?' My voice wavers. 'No.'

Asher's arms are around me before I can say anything else. I fold into him without hesitation. He holds me like he's afraid I might come apart if he lets go.

I squeeze my eyes shut and whisper into his chest. 'But I will be.'

CHAPTER THIRTY

Asher

My father won't stop pacing. He's storming up and down the length of his office like a caged animal. I can practically see the vein in his neck pulsing under the collar of his shirt.

He's been at it for at least ten minutes now, moving like a tornado back and forth behind his desk with a scowl so deep I'm half convinced it might actually be permanent. He's yelling, of course. Words ricochet around the room, half in Greek, half in English, and all of it venom.

I keep my expression blank and wait for him to finish. If there's one thing Georgios Vouvalis hates more than failure, it's being interrupted while he's in the middle of assigning blame for it.

'Unbelievable,' he mutters, still furiously pacing. 'Completely unbelievable. A hundred different ways I was certain *you'd* be the one to ruin this, but *Davies*?' He stops short, spinning towards me with a snarl I'm not sure I deserve. 'I never imagined I'd have to worry about *him*.'

He's talking, of course, about the fact that Peregrine Airways is broke and that Malcolm Davies has been stringing my father along, hoping for an injection of capital, for months now. The story has been dominating the financial broadsheets *and* @TrustFundTea for the last week. I'm surprised it's taken my father this long to bring me in. Not that I'm complaining; the more time I spend away from him, the better.

He finally stops in front of me, breath heaving, eyes wild and bloodshot like he hasn't had a solid night's sleep in days. 'We'll need to move quickly,' he says.

I frown. 'To do what?'

My father looks at me like he'd very much like to throw me out of the nearest window. 'To do what?' he parrots, scoffing with unrestrained distain. 'Don't play dumb with me. The entire deal has gone to hell. We'll need to find another partner. Maybe the Cavendish Group? Or Farrow Capital? Do any of the CEOs there have daughters? I suppose there's that Italian heiress – what's her name? The one with the shipping dynasty. That could work. That might—'

I stare at him. For a second, I actually can't process what he's just said. I was braced for a lot of things walking into this room, but the idea that my father would pivot to shopping me around like a piece of luxury real estate before the ashes of the last plan had even gone cold? That's impressive, even for him.

He rattles off another name, this time a socialite from Monaco, and then starts muttering about her family's yacht business. I honestly can't tell if he's talking to me or just to himself at this point.

'So that's it?' I hear myself say finally, voice flat even to my own ears. 'We're just pretending none of the last six months happened?'

He waves a dismissive hand in my direction. 'That's how it works, Asher. You cut your losses and move on. I'm not going to waste another second on people who can't keep up.'

I couldn't care less about Malcolm Davies and the fate of Peregrine Airways, but—'What about Imani?'

Georgios blinks at me. 'What about her?'

The surge of irritation shooting through me is instant. 'What about her?' I repeat. 'Because of your stupid plan with Davies, her name has been dragged through the mud for months.'

He shrugs. 'That was your fault, not mine.'

'We wouldn't have had to go to those lengths if it wasn't for—'

'Why do you even care?' he asks, sounding bored. 'I thought you'd be happy you no longer have to be tied to her. You barely even know the girl, your—' He cuts himself off and smirks at me. Your little *evening* together notwithstanding. I'm sure you'll get over her quickly enough.'

I open my mouth to argue. To tell him he's wrong and that I know Imani better than I've ever known anyone. I know the rhythm of her laugh, the way her eyes soften right before she smiles, the quiet strength in her silences. I know her the way I know my own heartbeat: steady, constant, and impossible to live without.

I love her.

God, I love her.

But I stop myself because he doesn't deserve to know what that feels like, the warmth she brings into every corner of my life, the way she makes even the darkest parts of me feel bright.

My father narrows his eyes, waiting for me to break first, but I don't. I just sit there in silence, and the truth that settles in my chest is a secret I'll never give him the satisfaction of hearing.

He sighs and then shakes his head, like I'm not worth the effort. 'Back to business. Since Davies has practically torched what was left of Peregrine, we'll have to change tack. The Cavendish Group could still be a possibility. Or maybe the Watanabe Conglomerate – if their daughter's still single.'

He says it like he's browsing a menu.

My last bit of tolerance I have towards my father snaps.

'Are you even listening to yourself?' I ask. 'You're just going to line up the next heiress and hope that this one sticks? Is that really the plan?'

He looks at me like he's seeing me for the first time – which, to be fair, maybe he is. I've spent the better part of two decades trying to make myself as unnoticeable as possible to avoid his ire. But everything's changed now. Maybe it's the months I've spent with Imani and the realisation that there's a version of life that doesn't involve being bulldozed and bullied by this man. Or maybe I'm just tired.

I push back from the chair so suddenly it scrapes loudly against the floor. My father's head snaps up, startled, and I savour the rare moment I've actually managed to throw him off balance.

'I'm done,' I say. 'I can't do this anymore.'

My father blinks at me in silence for several long seconds.

'I quit,' I say when the silence stretches on. 'The company. The family. I don't want anything to do with any of it.'

When he finally finds his voice, the words come out as a sneer. 'If you walk out now, don't even think about coming back. You're finished. You won't have a penny to your name, not a single asset, not a single share. Nothing. Do you understand what that means?'

I shrug, because, honestly, what else is left to take? 'I'd rather have nothing than sell out for you again.'

His face goes red, then white, then a weird shade of purple I don't even have a name for. But I don't wait for his next threat. I turn, spine straight and pulse hammering, and walk out without looking back.

CHAPTER THIRTY-ONE

Imani

It feels like the world has imploded around me.

Every channel, every notification, every news alert – it's all Peregrine Airways. The headlines are screaming about fraud investigations, shareholder outrage, potential criminal charges. Photos of my father looking like he's aged twenty years overnight, paired with grainy shots of me from some event months ago, are slapped under dramatic headlines like THE FALL OF AN EMPIRE.

My phone hasn't stopped vibrating since the news broke. Everyone wants to know what the hell is going on and what's going to happen to the company, and I don't know how to tell them that I don't know. I haven't spoken to my father since hanging up on his call in the Seychelles, and I have no plans on doing so any time soon. I meant what I said when I told him that this wasn't my fault and it wasn't my problem to fix.

Still, the guilt settles in anyway.

Peregrine Airways has been looming over me since the day I was born and now I'm just . . . what? Walking away from it? Turning my back on it while it crashes and burns around me?

The thought unsettles me more than I want to admit. Peregrine Airways has always been the constant force in my life. It's been my family's legacy, my safety net, *and* my cage. Without it, I don't really know who I am. But even beneath the flash of panic that's started to spark up inside me, I can't pretend that I don't feel a flicker of relief.

I've always had money, connections and comfort, but I've never really had a choice. Every decision I've made has come with strings attached. Now, for once, there's nothing tying me down.

I have no idea what I'm going to do with this new-found freedom, but I do know that I'm not going to waste it.

My phone vibrates again. I glance down and the notification that pops up on the screen brings an automatic smile to my face.

Asher
I'm downstairs. Can you buzz me up?

I immediately run to the door and hit the button to let him in. By the time he reaches my floor, my heart's already doing its best impression of a drumline. I pull open the door before he even has a chance to knock.

He looks tired. Exhausted, even. For a split second I wonder if he's changed his mind. About me. About all of this. Maybe the news cycle finally caught up with him and he's realised hitching himself to a sinking legacy isn't as appealing when you're not contractually obligated to do it. But then his eyes find mine and suddenly some of the tension drains out of him. His jaw unclenches, his shoulders drop, and there's this tiny, barely-there smile that tugs at the corner of his mouth. Like just seeing me is enough to convince him that none of the rest of the bullshit matters for a little while.

I step back, and he steps in.

He takes one look at the little cocoon of blankets I've made on the sofa, my laptop open on the coffee table with about a million tabs open, and raises a brow. 'You okay?'

'As good as I can be, given the circumstances,' I say with a shrug. 'Are you?'

He matches my shrug with one of his own. 'I think so.' Then he nods assuredly. 'Yeah, actually. I am. I just left my father's office for the last time.'

I frown. 'What do you mean?'

'After twenty minutes straight of him ranting and raving, I suddenly realised that I just don't care anymore. So, I'm done. With him. With Vouvalis Resorts. With all of it.'

I blink, stunned. 'You're *done*?'

'Done,' he says again, firmer this time. 'I told him I'm walking away.'

I stare at him like he's speaking another language. 'Asher, that's . . . that's your entire life. Your family's company.

You're really willing to throw all of that away?' And maybe I'm being presumptuous, but the way he's looking at me makes me think I'm not, so I add, 'For me?'

Asher doesn't hesitate. 'I've never been more sure of anything in my life.'

My chest tightens, somehow painfully and beautifully all at once. I take a small step closer to him. 'So, what happens now? You go live your life, and I figure out what's left of mine?'

He tilts his head, brows furrowing ever so slightly. 'Do you want me to leave?'

I swallow hard and shake my head. 'No.'

'Good,' he says with a soft smile. He reaches out and pulls me into him. 'Because I'm not going anywhere.'

Before I can respond, he closes the distance between us. His hand finds mine and he threads our fingers together. We fit, perfectly. 'I meant what I said, Imani,' he murmurs. 'About proposing to you one day. On our terms. When we're ready. Being with you these last few months has been amazing – and if it's only a snapshot of what getting to love you is like, I can't imagine what being able to love you out loud is going to be like. And I can't wait.'

My eyes burn with the threat of tears. 'You know this is going to be a mess, right? The company's collapsing. My dad's probably going to be indicted—'

'Mine too,' Asher says, sounding almost pleased.

'*What*?' I ask. 'What the hell?'

He shrugs. 'I don't know any of the details, but apparently

he's on the NCA's radar. It's only a matter of time. He's going to get what he deserves.'

'Wow,' I say. Asher doesn't look at all bothered by the fact that his father might soon be behind bars, and I can't say that I blame him. But still . . .'You know there's a very real chance that I might actually be broke once this has all settled.'

Asher smiles faintly. 'Then we'll be broke together.'

The laugh that bursts out of me is loud and helpless and a little hysterical. When I finally catch my breath, I look at him and the warmth in his eyes feels like sunlight after weeks of rain.

It's too much. The way he looks at me is just *too much.*

'I love you,' I blurt out, almost choking on the words. My heart is beating so loud and fast, it's got to be audible from the next building over. 'I love you, Asher.'

He goes still for half a second, and then the smile that breaks over his face is so beautiful it almost hurts to look at. 'I love you, too.'

And then he's kissing me.

My heart stutters in my chest. My knees threaten to buckle. I cling to him and let myself fall, because I know he's not going to let go.

It's strange how the whole world can be falling apart around me and still somehow feel like everything is finally slotting into place.

Outside, everything's chaos. Headlines, outrage, the slow-motion collapse of an empire. But here, in my apartment, the only thing that matters is Asher.

When he finally pulls back, he rests his forehead against mine. 'We'll figure it out,' he murmurs. 'All of it. The mess, the future, and whatever comes next, we'll do it together.'

Somehow, that's the first thing I've heard all day that makes sense. Maybe Peregrine Airways has gone. Maybe everything safe and certain in my life has essentially been burned to the ground. But as he wraps me up in his arms, I realise it doesn't feel like an ending. Not really.

It feels like a beginning.

@TrustFundTea

Looks like love really *does* rise from the ashes … or should we say, from the wreckage of an airline empire? 👀

Spotted last night in Mayfair: none other than **Imani Davies**, former Peregrine Airways princess turned headline fixture, and **Asher Vouvalis**.

But here's the twist – there was no cold shoulder and no fighting this time. Nope. These two were **holding hands**, laughing, and, wait for it … *kissing*. In public. It's a far cry from their drama-filled antics just a few months ago.

Weeks after the collapse that tanked her family's company, Davies looks positively glowing. New chapter? New love?

You know the drill. If anyone's got pics or tea from last night, you know where to find me 😉

xoxo,

TFT

✈️💋

EPILOGUE

Imani

It's 5am, the sun is steadily rising over the horizon, the air smells like fish and salt, and I have sand between my toes. I don't think I've ever been happier.

Grand Anse beach in Saint George, Grenada, is quiet at this hour, save for the soft slap of the water against the hulls of the fishing boats bobbing just a little past the shoreline. I'm standing under a tree, a cup of coffee in my hand, waiting for a group of people I only met two days ago to come back from a fishing trip. Behind me, Asher is sitting at the small wooden table we dragged down here yesterday afternoon, one leg crossed over the other, his laptop open and a heavily scribbled-on notebook beside it. He's barefoot, already sun-kissed despite the early hour, hair rumpled in that way that still makes my heart flutter something stupid in my chest. Every now and then he glances up at the horizon, then back down again at his notebook and laptop, cross-checking times and messages.

A year ago, if you'd told me that this would be my life, I would've laughed in your face. And yet here we are.

It doesn't feel real. The last year and a half, our lives have been something of a blur. Peregrine Airways is in administration and my father is a shell of his former self. He's managed to avoid any criminal charges, but a new civil lawsuit from investors who feel cheated seems to land in his mailbox every other day. Sometimes I wonder if it makes me a bad person that I can't bring myself to feel even an ounce of sympathy for him, and then I remember how he treated me, as nothing more than a pawn, and I decide that I don't care, even if I am.

Asher's father hasn't fared much better. The NCA descended on him soon after everything exploded with Peregrine, and his trial is currently ongoing. His brother, Andreas, has taken over the helm of the company and is in the middle of trying to do a rebrand. Asher and Andreas' relationship hasn't quite recovered, but they're on speaking terms at least. He's trying to get Asher to come back and help him and Teddy rebuild Vouvalis Resorts, but he always declines. Says he's good where he is.

'The boats should be back in about fifteen minutes,' Asher says suddenly. 'Marcel radioed in – said they had a good haul. Plenty of yellowtail.'

I can't help the grin that spreads over my face. This trip was my favourite idea when I put the itinerary together. An early morning fishing trip with Grenadian locals who've been working these waters their whole lives, followed by a cooking course later in the day at a small family-run restaurant up the hill. Nothing flashy, just people learning where their food comes from, who catches it, and how to prepare it properly.

Given the circumstances surrounding my father and Peregrine Airways, I was able to petition a judge to adjust the terms of my trust fund, giving me full access to it. Between that and the various investments I'd made over the years – my father did teach me well in that regard – I had more than enough money to keep me afloat whilst I started up the agency. Don't get me wrong, it was an adjustment, I had to sell my penthouse apartment for one, but I made it work. *We* made it work. Andreas is still paying Asher, rationalising it as he's a consultant for the business, but we're both fairly certain it's out of guilt and we're not going to complain.

When we first went live with the agency, I was sick with nerves. I wasn't sure anyone would care. I just knew that I needed to make something for myself and that I couldn't keep doing travel that took without giving anything back. Turns out, people do care. Enough to fly across the world for it.

I turn to Asher and he grins at me in that easy, familiar way that still manages to catch me off guard sometimes. Somewhere along the line, he slipped seamlessly into handling the logistical side of the business: scheduling, permits, transportation, back-up plans for when something inevitably goes wrong, just about everything. He's calm where I get restless, practical where I get idealistic, and our business partnership works in a way I don't think either of us expected, though I'm not sure why we were surprised.

The sound of an engine hums in the distance. I shade my eyes and spot the first boat cutting through the water towards shore. A familiar swell of emotion rises in my chest: it's gratitude, pride, and joy, all tangled together.

'They're back,' I say.

Asher stands, comes to me, and slips his arm around my waist, a move he's done countless times by now. It still makes my heart flutter like it's the first time, though. 'You did good,' he murmurs.

'*We* did,' I correct, leaning into him.

The boats pull in, laughter carrying across the water. One of the guests waves enthusiastically, holding up a fish like a trophy. I laugh and wave back, feeling something settle deep inside me.

There was a time when I thought my life had already been decided for me, when safety meant legacy and money and a name that carried weight in important rooms. Losing all of that would have felt like the end of the world back then. Now, standing here with sand on my feet and the sun fully breaking over the water, it barely feels like a loss at all.

Asher presses a quick kiss to my temple before heading over to help everyone off the boat and guide them towards the transport that will take them to the restaurant. He's already in his element. I take a breath, square my shoulders, and walk towards the group, ready to start the day.

I wouldn't have my life any other way.

ACKNOWLEDGEMENTS

Large chunks of this book were initially written in the notes app on my phone, mostly in the early hours of the morning, freshly postpartum, with a newborn sleeping (or, more often than not, not sleeping) in my arms. It was, without question, the most challenging book I've ever written, but it was also the most freeing. In the throes of new motherhood, it became a much needed creative outlet that was entirely mine and a place to put thoughts and feelings when everything else felt brand new and overwhelming. I'll always hold this book close to my heart for that reason alone.

I've got to be very blunt here: this book simply would not exist without my husband. Equally sleep-deprived thanks to our newborn, he somehow still made sure I had time, outside of my 3am phone-writing sessions, to write and type up my notes. Thank you for holding our home and family together so I could create something just for myself.

To my agent, Emma, who is always in my corner, but was especially so during a time in my life when I wasn't as responsive as I normally am. You advocated for me, supported me, and never once made me feel like I was falling short. I'm endlessly grateful to have you on this journey with me.

To my wonderful editor, Molly, who heard "fake exes and chaos enough to rival a K-drama" and immediately jumped on board, thank you for your insight and for trusting the vision and making this book even better than I imagined.

To the equally amazing Misha, who is not only a delight to email with but also somehow manages to keep me on track and everything running smoothly at all times, thank you for all your help.

To Sarah Madden for producing yet another absolute banger of a cover, and to Clare Wallis, Gillian Hamnett, Kate Kaur, Laurie McShea, and everyone else at S&S who had a hand in making this book happen, you're such a wonderful team, and I'm so grateful for all of you.

To Nyla, Shannai, Kacey, Shaima, Tamara, Tyler, Janelle, Andriana, Stephanie, Chevonne, Lilian, Monica, Janet, Brooke, Sera, Camryn, Chelsea, Sky, Ashley and SO many more. Thank you so much for being such amazing champions and supporters of my work from the very beginning.

To all the readers who have picked up my books and fallen in love with my characters, thank you, thank you, thank you! Every message, every email, every comment on social media truly touches my heart and I would not be here without each and every one of you. I hope I can keep bringing you the stories you love for years to come.

Do you want to keep in touch?

Scan the QR code to sign up to Anise's newsletter and stay in the loop!

DISCOVER MORE FROM ANISE STARRE

AVAILABLE NOW